Aiko's Choice

Aiko's Choice

Chase Gamwell

PRESS

Published by Vulpine Press in the United Kingdom in 2026

ISBN: 978-1-83919-713-0

www.vulpine-press.com

For everyone who has walked with me on this journey. You made sure I never had to do it alone.

1

I trace the cool, smooth edge of Fallah's amulet with my thumb as I stare out at another new world.

Slate gray clouds hunker over a packed dirt road stretching between two rows of wooden buildings. Each structure is cobbled together from a random assortment of planks, bleached a faded gray and warped by the sun.

But my destination—the source of the tiny voice whispering at the periphery of my mind—lies amidst the towering trees of the forest beyond.

"Are you sure this is the place?" Captain Su'mik warbles at me. The Rhandannan is about a head shorter than I, feathers as black as my hair with white tips.

In the six months since I left home to follow this new path, Su'mik has asked that same question whenever we make landfall. Every time, I give him the same answer.

"This is it."

"I can't fathom what you could want with such tiny trees," he quips, ochre beak clacking in the Rhandannan version of laughter.

I offer a thin smile and start down the ship's ramp. "It isn't the trees I'm here for."

"How long?" Su'mik calls after me.

I pause and probe at the whisper in my mind. "A day at the most."

He bobs his head in acknowledgment. "We shall wait."

I smile again, broadly this time, and return his nod. "Thank you."

The exchange has become a welcome ritual, a small semblance of consistency in my life since leaving Fletcher, Gohk, and Rhuk behind. I miss them, but the path I've chosen doesn't leave any room for attachment. Or respite. How can I rest knowing Darkness lurks out there? Knowing I'm the only one with the power to halt its inexorable, creeping progress across the galaxy?

That reality speeds my steps the rest of the way down the ramp, onto packed dirt as hard as the metal my feet just left. Yet, I welcome the incremental springiness of the natural surface. And I appreciate the uniqueness of my surroundings: fresh air heavy with the scent of pollen and moist soil; deep browns and vibrant greens, which are a welcome respite from the matte sheen of metal; and the wide open space and limitless sky of an actual planet.

A wooden wall, slanted outward, rings the perimeter of the landing pad, hiding the settlement from view, but not the pointed tips of the trees spearing toward the gray sky. It's most likely meant to redirect dust, dirt, or pebbles kicked up by a ship's exhaust. A narrow opening allows passage through the wall, to the packed dirt road I spotted before.

It's a few dozen steps to the first building, but before I even make it halfway, a board falls free. Instead of clattering on the ground, two pairs of legs unfold, catching its fall. The central 'board' remains stiff, but two stalks uncoil from the leading edge, bulbous, multifaceted eyes appearing at their tips.

Beneath where the stalks connect to the board, a third stalk uncoils, ending in a round opening. Its mouth, maybe? I'm proven right when it chitters at me in sounds I can't decipher. The computer Rhuk built into the powered sleeve he gifted me spits out a translation.

"Hello! Welcome to Aessup."

I freeze in place, staring up at the living board towering over me. "Uh…Hi."

Its eyestalks point down at me. *"What brings you our way?"*

"I'm just passing through," I say, and wave to the forest at the far end of town.

It pivots to look down the street, to where the packed dirt disappears into the trees. Then, it swivels back, and its bark-like skin lightens from an ashen gray to off-white.

"The forest is dangerous."

"I have business there."

The living board considers me with its unnervingly mobile eyeballs for a very long time.

I stare back, wondering what it's thinking. Does it find me as strange as I find it? Of course, *I'm* the alien here. In fact, I've been the alien on every single planet and space station I've visited over the last six months. Across a dozen worlds, and as many species, I'm the only one of my kind. Unless I count all the Kaisin I've saved. Which I don't.

Finally, the living board stirs.

"Take care. Do not stray far and do not linger past dark."

"Why not?" I ask. In my experience, it's better to know what dangers I may run into rather than stumbling upon them unaware.

"There are white monsters deep in the forest," it replies. *"They steal our nectar and kill us."*

"I'll be careful," I say, anger blooming in my chest over what the Kaisin have done to these tranquil beings.

Without another word, it turns and walks back to the building it fell from.

As I continue between what I thought were buildings, more planks begin to stir. Some fall like the first, fully transformed from their inert state before hitting the ground. Others stay put, but lean away from their respective wooden structures, eye stalks straining to get a view of their strange visitor.

Between the shifting planks, I glimpse stacks of clear spherical globules filled with an amber substance—presumably the nectar the first living board mentioned. Each structure is packed with spheres. Likely the reason the Kaisin are here in the first place. What could this nectar be for that they'd set up shop here and kill the indigenous population for it? Whatever the answer, I'm not surprised by the Kaisin's foul behavior; I've witnessed far too much of it over the years. It's something I can't save them from.

I turn my attention back to the packed dirt road and follow it into the trees.

The dull light of the overcast sky is muffled by canopies so thick I can't even glimpse the sky. A few steps into the ghostly twilight, I reach for the visor clipped to my right shoulder, slip it over my eyes, then tap a button on my wrist. The scene before me brightens, but shifts to sepia. Still, a little loss of color is far superior to stumbling my way around in the dark.

I thank Rhuk, for the thousandth time, for the gift he gave me. I wear it like a second skin, and it has turned out to be as useful in my crusade against the whispers crowding the back of my mind.

A little deeper into the forest, the path narrows and begins to snake around the trees. Not too long after that, it disappears altogether. But even without a road to guide me, I know where I'm going.

I clamber over a fallen tree, detour around a cluster of boulders, then pick my way up a steep slope. The tree trunks serve as handholds as I haul myself from one protruding root to the next. At the top, I follow a winding ridgeline toward the whispering in my mind.

The darkness hiding inside every Kaisin.

I called my own little sliver of darkness Iali, which is the Quiloh word for darkness. And I gave it a name because it exhibited an inkling of individuality. A trait I believed the collective entity as a whole didn't possess. However, hunting *It* across the sector has proven me wrong. *It* very much possesses flickers of individuality. Shadows of self.

So, that's what I've named *It:* Yuul. The Quiloh word for 'shadow'.

I fidget with the smooth wooden pendant tucked into my left pocket. In times like these, the reality of being all alone hits full force. Of course, being alone isn't my preference. While Fallah is always with me in spirit, the fact she never got to share the freedom I've gained stings. Every single day. And believe it or not, I even miss Iali's warm pressure at the back of my mind.

Beyond those two, I can't imagine anyone else as a companion on my journey. Not Fletcher. Not Gohk. Not even Rhuk, despite how supportive he'd been of my decision to strike out on my own. Because as much as I want a companion, I can't trust anyone enough to tell them the truth about the Yuul hiding in every Kaisin. Nor can I allow them to share in the danger of my task.

So, all alone, I continue into the wilderness.

The ridge eventually descends into a valley, where the forest thins out enough for the overcast light to reach me. I move faster without my visor, and the whispering at the edge of my mind grows to a crescendo.

I hurry up a gentle rise and crouch next to a tree at the top. Below, in a clearing, is a collection of square wattle and daub huts grouped around a circular fire pit maybe a dozen feet across, judging by the three Kaisin crouching beside it. Next to the settlement is a packed circle of dirt ringed by a wooden wall. A landing pad, it looks like. Probably how they're shipping all the stolen nectar off world.

Movement at the treeline draws my attention to the far side of the settlement. A few more Kaisin walk into view, carrying spears and dragging what looks like one of the living boards between them. The dark stain smeared on the dirt in their wake suggests why the living boards call these Kaisin monsters.

Settling down next to the tree, I spend the next few hours watching the Kaisin. From their comings and goings, I'd guess about ten live in the small community. And by the strength of the whispering at the back of my mind, there's a greater than usual concentration of Yuul shared between them. That shouldn't be a problem. If things go off without a hitch, they won't even know I was here.

I place my back against the tree, out of sight of the circle of huts, intending to wait until nightfall. Hours pass, yet the overcast sky remains the same shade of gloomy gray, as still and eerily silent as the forest pressing in around me. I almost breathe a sigh of relief at a peal of distant thunder.

But it isn't thunder.

The rumble grows in intensity, joined by the characteristic high-pitched whine of engines. I poke my head out from behind the tree just in time to watch a ship dip beneath the clouds and descend toward the settlement. A cloud of kicked-up dust obscures the craft for a moment. When it clears, the silvery oval is sitting in the middle of the landing pad, balanced on four thin struts.

A ramp extends from the craft's side, and a Kaisin wearing a bright red jumpsuit strolls out. The residents of this settlement meet the visitor—obviously a stranger—with drawn spears.

Their conversation is unintelligible at this distance, but whatever words are exchanged shift the mood from tense, to wary, to cordial. And eventually, the visitor is ushered into the settlement and offered a seat by the fire. Food is cooked, drinks are served, and raucous conversation drives back the forest's eerie silence.

Settling back into my hiding place, I stare into the trees. Night falls more slowly than I'd like, creeping closer like a specter. Shortening my vision, until the nearest trunks are shadowy pillars in the flickering light of the roaring bonfire at the center of the Kaisin settlement below.

My hand twitches toward the visor clipped to my shoulder, but I stop myself from slipping it on. Saving the charge left in my powered arm's batteries is more important than glimpsing a bit farther into the trees. While staring into the darkness, however, I hear a low drone carrying through the forest. The noise grates on my nerves and sets my teeth on edge as it fills the silence.

Finally.

Leaving my hiding place, I peer down into the circle of huts. It's quiet and still, except for the flickering of flames in the fire pit.

Something is off.

I reach toward the edge of my mind for the whispering of the Yuul, but it's gone.

That doesn't make any sense. The Kaisin were just here.

In a low crouch, I hurry down the slope, toward the circle of huts while listening for the sound of footsteps. Or voices. Or any other sign of the Kaisin I've been watching all day. Only the persistent drone carries through the forest. As does the crackling of the bonfire.

I pause at the corner of the first hut and peer around the circle for Kaisin. When none appear, I slip into the hut. Donning my visor, I thumb the button on my wrist that activates dark vision. The tiny room is bare, except for a narrow cot against the far wall with a rough wooden chest beside it. A single Kaisin is lying on the cot. Asleep. Just as I intended.

Creeping toward it, I reach out my right hand and lay my fingers on the Kaisin's bare arm. When I probe inside, I find nothing.

I frown and try again, reaching deep for the remnant of the Yuul that should be lurking inside. Again, I find nothing. This Kaisin is somehow free of the Yuul.

Puzzled, I retreat to the door and make my way to the next hut. Another Kaisin is sleeping inside. When I lay a hand on their bare skin, I detect no sign of the darkness I expect to find lurking deep inside. Just like there's no longer any whisper at the back of my mind.

My heart begins to race as I slip to the next hut.

In my haste, I stumble into something by the door as I enter. The makeshift spear clatters to the ground, bouncing on the soft dirt floor. I clench my teeth and freeze, glancing down at the spear then at the Kaisin on the cot across from the door.

They don't stir.

Pulse thundering in my ears, I cross the hut and bend down to lay a hand on the Kaisin's exposed shoulder. Its skin is icy. And for the first time, I notice the Kaisin isn't breathing.

Something shuffles at the door.

I spin and raise my arm in time to block a powerful blow. The servos in the arm Rhuk built for me whine under the strain of holding back a fist coated in undulating darkness. More of the black ichor coats half of the Kaisin's face, leaving the other half exposed, its jittery blue eye struggling to focus on me.

This isn't good.

I scramble backwards in an attempt to create some space between us. The Kaisin leaps after me, tackling me over the lifeless body occupying the cot. My head slams into the wall, knocking the visor free of my face and sending a burst of stars across my vision.

Hands knot in the fabric of my shirt, and I lash out. My fist hits something hard, and the Kaisin recoils.

Leaping to my feet, I dart past the reeling Kaisin and into the flickering firelight. A moment later, it stumbles into view. Lunges at me. I catch its outstretched ichor-coated fist and twist to avoid the sluggish follow-up swing from the other.

I slam my palm up under its chin and grab hold of its jaw, fingers sinking into the wriggling darkness. Then, I reach inside and draw the Yuul out of the Kaisin. It struggles and fights, but there's no escape as I crush the darkness out of existence. When I'm finished, the Kaisin goes limp and the whispering ceases.

Easing the now-lifeless body to the ground, I sag to my knees beside it. The warmth of the crackling fire nearby soothes the aching in my head and the tender spots popping up across my body that'll be bruises by tomorrow.

I let out a sigh and glance down at the dead Kaisin, for the first time noticing his red jumpsuit. This was the strange Kaisin that the others greeted with so much hostility.

Why is this Kaisin here? If it isn't for the nectar, then is it here for me? But why? Could the Yuul be responding to my actions these last six months? Maybe so. But *why* did it take so long for the Yuul to respond?

I frown when no answer springs to mind, which leaves me with a sinking feeling I can't shake.

Like whatever happened here is the start of something bigger.

I look at the dead Kaisin again, its blue eyes glassy and lifeless as they stare up into the starlit sky.

All I can do is hope this was just a fluke. A one-off occurrence that won't repeat itself. Because I really can't stand things becoming any more complicated than they already are.

2

I rest beside the fire until morning—better here than out in the dark with whatever is creating that grating drone. By the time the sun is high enough in the sky to pierce the veil of clouds, it's as dead as the Kaisin who lived here.

Heaving to my feet, I leave the small circle of wattle and daub huts behind, glad to be rid of them. Glad to have one less voice scratching at the edge of my mind. Yet, the sinking feeling from the night before lingers, accompanied by a twisting in my stomach that isn't hunger.

As if sensing my trepidation, the clouds open up.

Were it not for the trees, I'd have been soaked within seconds. Yet, the protracted drip of water through the canopies allows me ample time to experience the process of getting wet in slow motion. The water is frigid, sapping the fire's leftover warmth with each drop. And before long, I'm shivering as I make my way back up the narrow ridge I descended the previous evening.

Instead of wallowing in the misery of being soaked from head to toe, I focus on the sizzle of rain on the canopies above and the tranquil patter of raindrops around me. I even strain to detect the grating drone from yesterday, but it's gone. Washed away by the rain.

Good riddance.

For a brief moment, I turn my attention inward once more, to the whispers at the edge of my mind. Double checking that the darkness I'd come to destroy is gone. I detect no trace of it or any other voices nearby. As if it, too, had been washed away. With the confirmation comes a sliver of the triumph I missed out on the night before. I grab onto it like an ember of the fire I left behind, allowing it to warm me and buoy me the rest of the way back.

The packed dirt street is now a runny mess of mud and puddled water. It sucks at my boots as I trudge toward Captain Su'mik's ship—the *Ku'lu*—still waiting on the landing pad. Like he promised.

The living boards stir once more as I pass between the structures I once believed to be buildings. Eye stalks swivel to track my movement, and a chorus of chittering reaches me over the hiss of rain. I don't need a translator to recognize surprise. After all, I survived a night in the forest with the monsters who had been terrorizing them for who knew how long.

But no longer.

At the last building, I approach one of the creatures. I have no idea if it's the same individual as before, but it's just as imposing as it towers over me. Moreso, since it's little more than a looming shadowy shape through the water dripping into my eyes.

"The white monsters won't bother you anymore," I shout over the rain.

It chitters back, *"Truly?"*

"Truly," I reply, wishing I had some kind of proof.

The living board rears up on its hind legs and lets out a deafening bellow.

I slap my hands over my ears to muffle the sound and realize it's the same as the drone echoing through the forest the night before.

After a moment, an accompanying drone crops up in the distance, joined by another. And another even farther away. Until the entire forest is filled with a grating chorus.

The living board in front of me suddenly stops and considers me quietly. Then, it turns and ambles back to the nearby structure and reaches inside with one of its front legs, drawing out an amber sphere. Turning back, it presents the sphere to me. *"A gift for a gift."*

I accept the sphere with both hands. "Thank you."

The living board responds with a chitter the translator doesn't translate, then returns to its kin.

Hugging the small sphere to my chest, I jog through the soupy muck and past the canted wall. The *Ku'lu* sits in the middle of the landing pad, balanced on two thick struts. Massive, forward-swept wings sprout from its cylindrical fuselage, which narrows to an angular cockpit. Details in the paint and metalwork make the ship look like an oversized bird of prey. Intentional, since the *Ku'lu's* captain and crew are all Rhandannan.

I sprint for the ship, happy to gain the shelter of its wings. Setting the amber sphere in the damp dirt between my feet, I tap the comm button on my wrist and input the *Ku'lu's* frequency. "You there, Su'mik?"

Static mingles with the rain. Then, the familiar, high-pitched warble of Al'nor, Su'mik's second in command, answers: "You're back. A moment, if you please."

As soon as the line goes dead, a ramp drops from the *Ku'lu's* belly. Grabbing my globule of nectar, I hop onto it as it settles into the dirt.

Su'mik is at the top, beak hanging open in the Rhandannan version of a smile. "Hello! Welcome back! Get your fill of tiny trees?"

"Yes, I—"

A deafening roar drowns out the rest of my answer. The rain. Everything. It grows in volume and pitch until it's a screeching wail. I drop the sphere and collapse to my hands and knees, unable to catch my breath from the sheer agony of the cacophony scraping against my consciousness. It doesn't stop. Not even when I drop my head to the ramp, press my hands over my ears, and squeeze my eyes closed.

An unintelligible voice booms behind me.

I bolt upright and spin toward the fading echo of meaningless words. Hovering above the soggy dirt, is a yawning abyss. At the center of the darkness is a blue orb, like a solitary eye. Its gaze is as heavy as the weight of a planet. And it doesn't waver or blink as it advances toward me.

I try to stand, but my legs won't move.

The voice booms again, shaking the very foundation of my being as darkness curls around me. Only the light from the blue orb remains, glaring down at me. I shrink under its gaze, bowing my head and squeezing my eyes shut. And I press my hands back against my ears as if doing so will hide me from it.

"Aiko."

If I just ignore it, I'll be fine.

"Aiko!"

I'm yanked upright.

"Are you alright? What's wrong?" The voice is familiar. And gentle.

When I open my eyes, Su'mik is bent over me, head turned, one of his large black eyes staring down at me. His wingtips are on my shoulders, and his feathers are bristled with concern.

"I'm fine," I say. Which is an absolute lie. My heart is still racing, and my hands are shaking.

"You're sure?" Su'mik presses.

No. "Yes."

"Still, you should let Na'min examine you," he says, tapping me on the shoulder with his wingtip. "She will confirm you are okay."

I nod and climb to my feet; my legs are shaky, too.

Su'mik disappears inside the *Ku'lu.*

I hesitate for a moment and probe the edges of my mind for any lingering evidence of what just happened. Only the memory of that single blue eye glaring at me remains. I don't even detect a whisper of the Yuul anywhere nearby. What else could it have been?

With a deep breath, I start up the ramp, then remember: the amber sphere! I'd dropped it to slap my hands over my ears! Did it break? Spinning, I search for its shattered remains on the ramp. I spot it nestled in the moist dirt at the bottom of the ramp, intact.

I sigh and retrieve the sphere of nectar before hurrying inside.

The *Ku'lu* is very different from the *Undertow.* While Fletcher's ship prioritized form over function, the Rhandannan vessel skews toward comfort. At the top of the ramp is a small room with textured metal floors and gray polymer-paneled walls—a marked step up from the industrial metal finish of the *Undertow's* interior. A staircase leads up to the ship's main deck. Tucked to either side of the staircase are doors leading into a cargo bay about the same size as the *Undertow's* dive room, with a similar door in the center of the floor through which cargo can be loaded. Su'mik showed me the room once, but I haven't been inside since.

At the top of the stairs is a small landing with double doors leading into the engine room. I head the other direction, down the ship's central hallway that continues all the way to the bridge. Here, the metal floor is both textured and tiled, and the wall panels are a deep green the same shade as the tree tops outside. Illumination strips border where the panels meet the arched roof, bathing the space in warm, comforting light.

Halfway down the hall is a small offshoot to the left, leading to another, narrower parallel corridor where all the crew quarters are located. Mine is to the right, at the very end. The room is about the same size as the one I had on the *Undertow*, with a small personal bathroom across from the door and the added benefit of three porthole windows over the bed to my left.

I never made it a priority to accumulate any belongings over the last six months. So, beside a few changes of clothes, I don't own anything that won't fit in my pack. It sits on the floor next to the bed, unzipped and open, just how I left it. I nestle the sphere of nectar inside, then shuck off the powered arm Rhuk gave me. It's soggy and stinky from a mix of sweat and a little bit of rain that managed to seep inside during my trek back to the ship. I'll clean it later, after my mandatory trip to the infirmary.

As much as I'd prefer to avoid getting poked and prodded by Na'min, the ship's medic, I don't have much of a choice. Su'mik insisted, which means he'll bug me about it until I do what he says. If I don't, he'll send Na'min to visit me in my cabin, which he's done before. So when he orders me to the infirmary, I obey.

Much to my chagrin.

The infirmary is a short walk from the crew quarters, on the same side of the main corridor but closer to the back of the ship. Na'min is perched behind a desk across from the door, waiting, probably because Su'mik told her to expect me. Her magenta feathers ruffle when I appear, and she clacks her beak at me in a gesture I've come to learn signifies impatience.

She turns her head to stare at me with a single turquoise eye. "Su'mik says you are ill."

"I don't think—"

"Sit," she commands, pointing with a wingtip. The feathers on the underside of her wing are a beautiful royal purple, contrasting with the pale green floor, walls, and ceiling of the infirmary.

I shuffle to the one, low treatment bed on the left side of the room and sit, feeling very much like a child as she begins to poke and prod.

She starts at my head, probing my scalp with the prehensile fingers all Rhandannan have at their wingtips. Singular—one finger on each wing. Curled with a claw tip to make up for the lack of a thumb. Even after six months, it's still strange. And even stranger to think that throughout all the years I lived in close proximity to Ki'leh, I never noticed him using his fingers for anything. Then again, he didn't have a need to use them in the cramped common area where the Headmistress kept us.

Na'min's finger passes over the tender spot where I knocked my head fighting the Kaisin, and I wince. She circles around me and leans in to study the wound.

"You're bleeding," she says. "And I bet you have a fair few bruises to go along with this gash. Like usual."

I don't give her the satisfaction of an answer. She'd probably be prickly about it, anyway. She's prickly about *everything*. Which reminds me of Gohk. I guess every crew has their own Gohk.

"What do you do to get banged up like this?" Na'min asks, walking to a locker inset in the far wall and gathering some supplies.

This time, when I don't answer, she gives a wordless squawk.

"It's complicated," I offer.

Na'min looks back at me and opens her black beak wide—a gesture the Rhandannan use for a range of negative emotions. Though, in this case, it's most likely a frown. Or a scowl. "Fine. Want to tell me about what happened outside?"

I hesitate to answer as she returns to me and starts dressing the wound on my head, not quite sure how much I should tell her.

"If it makes you feel better, I'll keep it between us." Her tone is harsh, yet there's a tender, sympathetic undercurrent that makes me want to trust her with at least some of what I experienced.

I clear my throat. "I heard a deafening roar. And when I closed my eyes, I saw darkness rushing toward me."

"Hmmm." Na'min spins away from me again and returns to the locker. This time, she comes back with a medical scanner and a pneumatic syringe. She passes the scanner around my head with one finger and taps the syringe into my forearm with the other to draw some blood. Then, she waddles to her desk. After a few minutes of analysis, she looks up at me. "Your brain is fine. Though, the bump on your head gave you a mild concussion. And your blood is free from any toxins you may have encountered during your time out in the forest."

"That's good to hear."

"But your cortisol levels are remarkably high," she continues without missing a beat.

I blink at her. "What does that mean?"

"You are *very* stressed." Na'min crosses the infirmary and opens up a different locker next to the first. While rummaging inside, she says, "I'm not surprised. You never rest."

"I get plenty of rest between stops."

"Inaction is not the same as rest," she replies. "You need to take a break. Because whatever you're doing is starting to catch up with you."

I shrug. "Sure."

Na'min lets out a heavy sigh. Which, from a Rhandannan, comes out as a hiss. "If you will not heed my warning as the ship's doctor, then perhaps consider a few friendly words of advice: stress kills if you let it catch up to you. Don't. Slow down. Take a break from whatever it is you're doing."

Her tone is uncommonly gentle. And her feathers are pressed flat, which can be interpreted as sincerity. It's touching to realize she cares about what happens to me. A little jarring, too, since I'd been keeping my distance from Su'mik and the rest of the crew.

But I guess I'd inadvertently grown on some of them more than I thought.

I offer a halting nod. "O-okay."

She paces to me and holds out a small cup with a collection of pills inside. "Take these."

"What are they?"

"Something for the ache in your head. And for the concussion. And a mild tranquilizer." She points a wingtip at me. "Take all of them."

I nod again.

"And seriously consider taking a break. Alright?"

"I will," I say for her benefit. Because I can't stop what I'm doing. It's more important than she—or anyone else in the galaxy besides Rhuk—knows.

Na'min returns to her desk and waves me away without another word.

Clutching the cup of pills to my chest, I hurry out of the infirmary, happy to be free of the confusing blend of stern bedside manner and kind words. It's enough to make me miss the cold, impassiveness of the Thalijh.

I walk back to my room and take the pills with a swig of water from my bathroom sink. They go down hard, and a lump lingers in my chest.

Na'min's warning echoes in my mind, but so does the thunderous voice. I'd love to believe it was a symptom of stress and overexertion, but—

My door chimes.

Tamping down my runaway thoughts, I cross my room and open the door. Al'nor is standing on the other side.

"Welcome back!" she says, parting her onyx beak in a smile and stepping forward to wrap deep crimson wings around me in a warm, ticklish hug. "How many bumps and bruises did you come back with this time?"

Stepping back, I tilt my head down so she can examine the spot Na'min dressed a few minutes before.

Al'nor gives me a disappointed squawk.

"I'll be fine," I say, not even managing to convince myself. She gives a skeptical coo. I ignore it and change the subject: "What's up?"

"Su'mik wants to know where we're headed next."

"Haven't given it any thought. Mind if I take a look at the sector chart?"

Al'nor bobs her head and turns away from my door. I follow her all the way to the bridge.

Unlike the *Undertow*, the *Ku'lu's* bridge is much more spacious. Double doors lead into an oval room. Two independent stations jut from the floor near the front, each paired with a bar for the Rhandannan stationed there to perch on. In the very center of the room is a single chair. Well 'chair', since the Rhandannan don't sit the same way I do. It's more of a U-shaped cradle with a bar at the bottom for their feet to grab hold of and padded rests at the top of the U for them to rest their wings on.

Accentuating the space is a huge, wide viewscreen dominating the front half of the bridge, granting a stunning view of the settlement, the trees pressing in around it, the thick span of forest blanketing a hill rising into the distance, and the overcast sky above. The rain is now a fine mist, which gives the forest an ethereal ambiance, almost like the Kaisin decided to haunt the living boards in an entirely different way.

Su'mik turns as soon as the bridge door hisses open and smiles. "Ah, hello. Where are we headed next?"

Right to business, which means Na'min must have told him I was fine. Which also means she kept her promise.

"Let me see." I turn to the large sector chart along one side of the bridge's curved back wall. A red dot indicates our current location, with a dense scattering of white dots around us, each representing a different star.

I start to reach for the nearest whisper, but hesitate as fear causes bile to rise in the back of my throat. The whispers at the edge of my mind aren't the same as what I experienced on the *Ku'lu's* ramp. Decidedly not Yuul. If it was, I'd be able to detect it even now, without having to reach out. So, steeling my nerves, I close my eyes and pinpoint the closest whisper to where I am. It's quite far away, in part due to how many other whispers I've silenced over the last six months. Opening my eyes, I tap the sector map, calling up a star system two week's distance from our current location.

"Here," I say.

"So far." Su'mik's comment is almost a grumble.

I stifle the urge to apologize. After all, I've been paying him a decent fee to ferry me around. Another thing I'll have to thank Rhuk for when we reunite. For now, I have to stay focused and move forward, one whisper at a time. The sooner I can get rid of them all, the sooner I can take that break Na'min suggested. Hopefully, before whatever it is I experienced gets any worse.

3

Despite my room having its own windows, I prefer the more spacious lounge across from the crew quarters; the windows are bigger, and there's a cozy little spot for me in the corner where the only 'normal' chair on the ship is placed. I can sit and split time between looking out at the star-speckled darkness and watching the crew.

Tonight, the mood in the lounge is especially vibrant. Al'nor is perched at a table with Xi'nom and Bi'nom, the ship's engineers. They're brothers hatched from the same egg, both pale gray with aquamarine eyes and burnt orange beaks. I have no clue how to tell them apart, even though everyone else on the ship has no trouble at all.

Na'min is at a table by herself, pecking at a meal of rehydrated cowl worms—a delicacy from the Rhandannan homeworld—while reading something exciting enough to bristle her feathers.

On the other side of the lounge are Da'fil, the ship's cook and requisitions officer, and Cu'lin, the navigation and communication specialist. They're sitting with Su'mik. Ironically, Da'fil is the pudgiest Rhandannan on board, with enough extra meat around his midsection to poke his wings out from his sides. He's ruddy brown with a white fringe at the top of his head, black eyes, and a bright yellow beak. Cu'lin is as colorful as the rest of the female Rhandannan on board, her golden feathers and beak almost glowing under the lounge's bright lights, a distinct counterpoint to her blood-red eyes.

Usually, only one or two of the crew are in the lounge at the same time, but the deep darkness between suns requires a bit more levity. Because, after a while, the darkness starts to creep in. I'd know, since I carried around real, live darkness for a while.

All that said, as much as I *need* to be alone, I don't like being lonely. I never have been. Once I lost Fallah, I wound up with Fletcher. Then, Iali.

Even now, I'm a little bit sad about losing Iali. Having its presence nestled against the edge of my mind was comforting. Always there to share my thoughts. At the time, its proximity felt like an intrusion. Now I can't say I wouldn't welcome Iali at the edge of my mind instead of the myriad incessant whispering of the Yuul.

So, to drown out the whispers, and suppress the loneliness, I spend time near the crew. Which is pleasant enough. Especially on nights like tonight.

"Why don't you ask Aiko?" Al'nor blurts out.

Xi'nom and Bi'nom turn toward me in unison, and the quiet conversation between Su'mik, Da'fil, and Cu'lin stops as they look at Al'nor, then at me. Even Na'min glances up from whatever she's reading.

My face warms under the sudden weight of their combined stares. "Uh…ask me what?"

"Where are we going this time?' Al'nor hops up from her perch and waddles across the lounge. She plops herself down on the other side of the table from me and turns her head to regard me with a single black eye.

The pungent scent of fermented seilon-seed wine stings my nose. "I have business there."

"What business could be so important it warrants a two-week cruise?" Xi'nom—or Bi'nom?—asks with a hint of frustration.

For the hundredth time, I consider telling them everything. It would be *so much easier* if they knew why I was hopping from planet to planet. But if they knew the terrible truth about the darkness lurking inside each and every Kaisin, I doubt they'd be willing to continue ferrying me around. Besides, the funds Rhuk gave me at the start of my journey have depleted to the point where I won't be able to hire another ship. So, better to keep the truth to myself.

"It's personal."

My answer garners squawked grumbles and ruffled feathers from the twin engineers.

Al'nor squints her eye at me and leans closer. Before she can press for an answer, the ship bucks hard enough to toss me forward against the edge of the table.

Without hesitation, Su'mik leaps to his feet and begins squawking orders in his native tongue. The crew respond as one, jumping up and rushing into the hall. Not sure what else to do, I follow, but freeze at the lounge door. Su'mik, Al'nor, and Cu'lin are racing to the bridge on my left, while Xi'nom, Bi'nom, and Da'fil are hurrying toward engineering and the cargo hold on my right.

What should I do? Can I help?

The ship bucks a second time, harder than before, and I crumple to my hands and knees. I clutch at the textured metal deck tiles as the ship continues to shudder. Then, the tortured screech of metal on metal fills the air.

I crawl toward Su'mik. "Did we hit something?"

"There shouldn't be anything out here for us to hit," Cu'lin replies in his stead, hopping to her feet.

Before I can ask any follow up questions, a terrible tearing noise erupts from the rear of the ship followed by an equally terrible silence.

A moment later, Kaisin bound up the stairs at the end of the *Ku'lu's* main corridor. Four of them. No darkness is visible on their exposed skin, but that doesn't mean it isn't there.

They surge toward Xi'nom, Bi'nom, and Da'fil. The three Rhandannan make an about face and scramble toward us, but Da'fil is too slow. The leading Kaisin tackles him to the deck and starts wailing on him. The rest of the Kaisin rush past, chasing the twins toward *us*.

"Down!" Su'mik shouts behind me.

I'm already on all fours. Ahead of me, the twins dive to the deck.

Laser blasts zip over my head and drill into the leading Kaisin.

It doesn't falter. Or fall. Despite the growing number of holes in its grease-stained jumpsuit. Eventually, a wriggling patch of darkness becomes clear beneath the Kaisin's damaged clothing.

The Yuul.

But why can't I detect it?

The other two Kaisin leap on the twins, while the third continues to stroll toward us.

My breath catches, and icy fingers of fear root me in place. I've gotten so used to taking the Yuul by surprise, the opposite never seemed possible. Now Su'mik and the others have come face to face with Kaisin controlled by it. Which is a battle they can't win. A battle they're fighting because of *me*.

The realization thaws my fear, and I leap into action. Scrambling from all fours to my feet, I sprint for the advancing Kaisin and tackle it full force. As we tumble across the ground, I snuff out the darkness hiding inside.

The three remaining Kaisin freeze, and their attention snaps to me.

I roll off of the unconscious Kaisin as the nearest two lunge at me. The first swipes with talons made of hardened darkness, which I dodge away from. Right into the wall.

The pair loom over me, but a laser blast slams into one of them. The Kaisin cries out and crumples to the side, smoke rising from a new hole in his jumpsuit. Darkness begins beading on his pasty white skin like corrupted sweat, dripping onto the metal floor and coalescing into a wriggling pool.

I slap my hand into the middle of the pool of darkness at the same time as the other Kaisin. He lashes out, catching me on the chin, and stars burst across my vision. At the same time, the slimy ichor slips from beneath my hand.

Curling into a ball, I shield my head with both arms in case of another blow. Instead, more laser blasts zip over me and screeching squawks fill the air. Al'nor yanks me to my feet. Su'mik is beside her, directing sustained laser fire at the Kaisin, driving him back, one step at a time. That won't stop him. *It*.

Only I can.

"Cover me!"

I dive for the Kaisin still on top of Da'fil and destroy the darkness lurking inside. Free of the Yuul's influence, the Kaisin slumps to the side.

One left. One final fragment of darkness.

The Kaisin turns and bolts for the stairs. But I can't allow any of the Yuul to escape.

I rush to the railing and vault over, crashing down on top of the Kaisin as he reaches the landing below. Pain arcs up my calf as we collapse into a heap of tangled limbs. Dazed, and sluggish, I grasp at the Kaisin. Grope for smooth skin instead of rough fabric.

The Kaisin doesn't struggle like I expect. He goes limp when I clamp my hand on his exposed forearm and snuff out the fragment of darkness lurking inside; far less than there should be, considering he absorbed the darkness of his comrade.

A flicker of movement at my periphery draws my eye to one of the doors beside the stairs. I find nothing. Closing my eyes, I do a quick sweep for any nearby whispers. Still nothing. Little comfort, considering I didn't detect these Kaisin in the first place.

I sit up, disappointment coursing through my mind. When I try to stand, pain arcs up my right leg. With a cry, I crumple back to the ground.

Al'nor's head pokes over the railing. "You alright?"

"My leg. How's everyone else?"

"Xi'nom and Bi'nom will be fine," she says, "but Da'fil…"

The way she trails off suggests it isn't good.

I crawl to the stairway railing and haul myself up on my good leg. Gritting my teeth through the pain shooting up my calf, I ascend to join the others.

Da'fil is sprawled on his back a dozen paces past the top of the stairs, surrounded by loose feathers and streaks of blood. Na'min is perched beside him, cooing softly in their native tongue as she tends to the deep slashes visible even through his thick coat of feathers.

The rest of the crew huddle nearby in a tight group, feathers bristled and beaks hanging open.

I remain frozen at the top of the stairs, pulse pounding in my ears as I watch Na'min work. And I hope she's successful, as the reality of the situation crashes over me like an inexorable flood: Da'fil very well may die. And it would be *my* fault.

He lets out a gurgling cough and tries to sit up. Su'mik squats at his side, a wingtip curling under his head. They exchange words in their native tongue, Su'mik's shaky and uneven, Da'fil's hoarse and bubbly. Then, Da'fil slumps back, and his chest heaves with a final, rattling breath.

A unified cry rises from the crew. And I can't help the sudden lump rising in my throat, threatening to choke me. Despite how long I've been on the *Ku'lu*, I didn't know Da'fil very well. Watching him go still prompts a pang of regret. After all, his death is my fault. At least, in part.

As if on cue, one of the nearby Kaisin groans and stirs. He gathers his hands under himself to push off the floor, but Su'mik pounces on him, slamming him back down onto the metal floor tiles with a taloned foot.

"Why are you here?" Su'mik leans down and screeches in the Kaisin's ear.

The Kaisin sputters, cheek smashed into the floor, jittery blue eyes darting around, wide with surprise. Of course. The Kaisin

30

was controlled by the Yuul. He likely has no idea where he is. Or how he got here.

"Answer!" Su'mik snaps, flexing his claws.

The Kaisin cries out, and little red circles bloom on his already stained jumpsuit. "I don't know."

"LIAR!" "Su'mik lifts his foot and drives it back down into the Kaisin's back, prompting another cry of pain. He swivels his head to glare at Al'nor. "Wake the other."

Al'nor flips over the other unconscious Kaisin with her foot and slaps his face with a wingtip. Then again, harder.

The second Kaisin starts awake, surging upright at the sight of a bloody crimson Rhandannan looming over him.

Al'nor kicks him back down and holds him there with a taloned foot.

"Why are you here?" Su'mik asks, his glare piercing enough to rival the laser pistol clutched in his finger.

Just like the other Kaisin, this one splutters and stammers in equal parts fear and confusion. "I don't know."

Su'mik lets out a frustrated screech, tightening his grip on the Kaisin under his foot while pointing his weapon at the one Al'nor woke. "Answer, or you both die."

"I don't know how I got here. I don't even know where 'here' is," the Kaisin insists.

"You lie," Su'mik says. This time, his voice is even. Deadly.

"I swear!" The Kaisin's eyes are wide with terror. "The last thing I remember, we were scouting an uncharted planet. Then, I'm here. I don't know how. You have to believe me!"

Su'mik lets out another frustrated screech, the weapon in his hand trembling.

As much as I hate Kaisin for taking Fallah from me, and so much more, I can't stand by and watch Su'mik murder these two.

So, before he can pull the trigger, or sink his claws any deeper, I step forward.

"They won't know."

Su'mik's burning gaze jumps to me, and his eyes narrow. "Explain."

For a heartbeat, I consider caving and spilling every detail I've held back for the past six months. But I can't fathom the reaction of Su'mik, Al'nor, or the rest of the crew when they find out the truth about why I'm dragging them from planet to planet. Especially *now*.

"I'm sorry. I can't."

He removes his foot from the Kaisin's back and steps toward me. The heat of his breath wafts across my face as his beak pokes into my face, close enough I make out the tiny sawtooth ridges along its inner edges, meant for tearing through flesh. "Why not?"

"I just can't," I say, forcing myself to stare into his beady black eye. "But I *can* tell you they have no idea where they are or how they got here. They won't even remember killing Da'fil."

"And how do you know that?"

"I can't say," I repeat.

Su'mik growls in the back of his throat. I half expect him to channel his anger at me and press for an answer. But he remains silent. Pensive.

"The Kaisin were here for you," Su'mik says.

I nod. There's no point denying it.

"Why?"

"The Kaisin hold a grudge against my kind. And if I stay in one place for too long, they come for me."

The half-truth makes my stomach churn, but it's necessary. I can't tell Su'mik about the nameless darkness lurking inside every Kaisin. For his safety, mine, and everyone else in the galaxy, that terrible truth must remain hidden. At all costs.

Su'mik stares at me for a long time. Finally, his feathers bristle. "So, the Kaisin will come again."

"Not if we keep moving as we have been."

"That didn't stop them from finding us," he replies, indicating the two Kaisin on the floor nearby, one of them still under Al'nor's foot. "Which means it's only a matter of time before they catch up with us again. And when they do, I have no desire to lose another crewmember."

"I'm sorry," I mumble, looking past him, to Da'fil's lifeless body.

Su'mik gives a slow nod, then turns and clucks something to Al'nor. She nods in agreement to whatever he said, warbling something back.

The sudden shift to their native tongue and the iciness of their demeanor makes me cringe. I wait for Su'mik to return his attention to me.

"Go to your quarters. Remain there for the rest of our voyage."

Su'mik swivels away without waiting for a reply and returns to Da'fil's side. And none of the other crew members glance in my direction as I hobble to my quarters.

4

"Finished," Na'min says.

I stare down at the hardened bandage cinched around my right calf and foot. It's treated with a numbing agent, limiting sensation to the bandage's light pressure. Better than the ache of sprained muscles.

The doctor packs up her supplies and grants me a brief, cold stare before waddling out of my quarters.

The whole crew probably blames me for Da'fil's death. After all, the Kaisin came for me.

Sighing, I flop back on my bed and roll to face the windows.

I stare out, my mind fixating on the darkness between the myriad points of light. For so many, the space between stars signifies the unknown. But I'm aware of the darkness hiding amidst the void. I know it. More intimately than any person should. Apparently, the stress of carrying that secret has been eating at me to the point where it has manifested the Yuul. Or some approximation of it. How much worse will it get before all is said and done?

I have no idea, and I don't even want to hazard a guess. Sometimes, I fear this road I'm on doesn't have an end. And even though I'm the one who chose to walk it, nothing could have prepared me for how truly lonely it would be.

Reaching into my pocket, I run my thumb over the smooth surface of Fallah's amulet.

A little over six months ago I left Alphanax with this tiny token. A remembrance. At the time, I thought it'd be enough to buoy me through everything to come. That Fallah's memory would be enough to fill the emptiness left in Iali's wake. Or to bridge the yawning gap of loneliness after I decided to leave Fletcher, Gohk, and Rhuk behind.

While her memory has remained comforting, over time, reflection has allowed me to recognize my own failures with greater clarity. Pick apart my own shortcomings. Pinpoint what I could, and should, have done differently. It's a unique kind of pain to have to experience every time I'm alone with my thoughts.

It would be easy to give into the pain and collapse in on myself if not for a single piece of advice: *Think about what you can do.*

Even now, Rhuk's words echo in my mind, galvanizing me against the piercing ache of my failures. Pushing me to remain resolute in my decision to rid the galaxy of the Yuul. Despite the setback of Kaisin finding me aboard the *Ku'lu*, and killing Da'fil instead of me, I plan to remain true to that purpose.

First, I have to figure out what Su'mik plans to do with me.

Maybe he'll kick me off the ship. It's a terrifying idea, but possible. After all, what happened to Da'fil was *my* fault. I never intended for anyone to get hurt. Or die. Nor did I consider that keeping the Yuul's existence a secret could lead to such a thing happening.

Not true. I considered it, but I believed I could stay in control of the situation. For six months, I did. Now, the Yuul are fighting back. And in doing so, they killed a member of Su'mik's crew.

An apology won't be enough. But if I can explain my reasoning to Su'mik, maybe he'll be able to understand my point of view and show some semblance of mercy. I have no idea what that might look like, though.

The grim reality of my situation haunts me as I stare out of the window. I keep staring until my mind goes as blank as the space between the scattered stars. For so long the void comes to life, twisting and wriggling like the Yuul. I blink, but the darkness doesn't still.

I bolt upright and rub my eyes. But the space between stars continues to shift. Then, the stars themselves begin to wink out, one by one. Until the portholes above my bed are black.

BANG.

The room vibrates.

BANG.

The noise penetrates to my bones.

BANG.

Trails down my spine in time with an icy shiver.

BANG.

"Aiko?"

The muffled call, and the accompanying knock, draws my eyes to the door for a moment. When they dart back to the windows, the stars have returned. And the darkness between is still and empty.

"Aiko, are you alright?"

"Yeah," I call out. Even though I'm very much not okay. My heart is still racing. And cold, clammy sweat sticks my shirt to my back.

I swing my legs over the side of the bed and perch on its edge but don't stand or attempt to hobble my way to the door. "You can come in."

The door slides open, and Al'nor enters, crossing the room and settling next to my bed. She reaches out to pat my forearm with a crimson wingtip and cocks her head in an expression that's more inquisitive than empathetic. She isn't here to comfort me, then. I wait for her to speak.

"Su'mik isn't happy with you," she says.

"I'm sorry," I whisper. I *really* am. I should have been able to detect the approaching Yuul and suggest a course change before it reached the *Ku'lu*. For some reason, I didn't notice the darkness creeping closer until it was too late. "I didn't mean for any of this to happen."

Al'nor's wingtip darts out again to give me another pat on the forearm. This time, it remains. "I believe you. But why are you keeping things from us?"

I knot my hands in the bedsheet. No matter how much I want to tell her the truth about what's going on, no one else can know what I know. It's far too dangerous.

During my confrontation with the Yuul on Thalijh, it told me it would not tolerate discovery. It would rather sacrifice countless Kaisin to prevent such a thing from happening. The chill of that promise still lingers with me. And I believe the Yuul will rampage across this sector, and beyond, to prevent word of its existence from getting out.

At the same time, I *need* to tell her something. Al'nor, Su'mik, and the rest of the crew deserve some kind of answer in return for the life I cost them.

"I'm on a quest," I begin. "It's dangerous. And something only I can do. The Kaisin aim to stop me, but I can't let them. No matter what."

Al'nor flutters her wings, the equivalent of a head shake. "Why wait to tell us this now?"

"It's complicated."

"Su'mik doesn't like complicated."

"Neither do I. But my choice in the matter was taken away a long time ago," I reply. To avoid any more questions, I change the subject: "What are you going to do with the Kaisin?"

"As you said, the three survivors are bewildered. And Na'min has confirmed they aren't lying when they say they have no idea how they got here." Al'nor tilts her head. "Once Su'mik's anger cooled, he decided to let them go. But not before taking his pick of their cargo to pay for the hole they cut in the hull."

I blink. "The hole?"

"How do you think they boarded us?"

"I hadn't, honestly."

Al'nor clucks at me, a Rhandannan admonition.

After a few moments of uncomfortable silence, she asks, "More will come?"

"I can't promise they won't. Like I said, if we keep moving—"

"Had we known this earlier, we could have kept an eye out," she interrupts. "And Da'fil might still be alive."

She's right. If I hadn't kept them all at arm's length, maybe Da'fil *would* be alive. On the other hand, the truth is far more dangerous. And all it takes is the wrong question at the wrong time to the wrong being to invite disaster. I'd know.

I shake my head and repeat, "I'm sorry."

Al'nor squints her eye at me, as if it's possible to tease out the secrets I'm hiding if she stares hard enough. When she can't, and I don't offer anything, she flutters her wings again and waddles toward the door.

"Al'nor."

She pauses, swiveling her head to the side to look back at me.

"You know I would explain if I could."

The length of her silent stare, and the tilt of her head, is uncomfortable. The knot in my stomach remains long after she leaves my quarters. And every time my thoughts stray back to her visit, or ponder what she wound up telling Su'mik, it cinches tighter.

Wrapping myself in a warm blanket, I curl up on my bed but keep my back to the window. After an eternity of restlessness, the heavy tug of sleep weighs down my eyelids and I drift off...

Swirling darkness. Roaring noise. An angry blue orb.

I snap awake, but remain frozen under the blanket, sweating, transfixed by the infinite darkness on the other side of the windows above my bed. I search the edge of my mind for a hint of the Yuul. There's nothing. Not even an echo of what yanked me out of sleep. Only emptiness. Silence. Like the flashes I'd experienced moments before were merely figments of my imagination.

Weren't they, though? Wasn't this a manifestation of the concussion? Or the stress Na'min said was creeping up on me? The absence of any hint of the Yuul nearby suggests so. Yet, I still don't want to believe what Na'min said could be true. Because I can fight the Yuul. But my own mind?

I toss and turn for the rest of the night. By morning, my body aches and my head is fuzzy, like I've fought a hundred Kaisin.

The mirror in the bathroom reveals my long hair is a matted mess, my face red and slick with sweat. A quick sponge bath washes away the physical proof of the rough night I had, at least.

Afterwards, instead of sitting on my bed and waiting for fate to come to me, I don a fresh pair of coveralls from my pack and head to the bridge.

Su'mik turns when I enter, and his beak drops open in agitation. "I told you to remain in your quarters."

"I know, but—"

"It wasn't a suggestion." His feathers bristle before smoothing flat as he perks up to his full height and peers down at me. "Since you're here… In light of the new information regarding your relationship with the Kaisin, I've come to a decision."

Al'nor is perched at one of the stations beyond Su'mik's chair. Her head swivels just enough to shoot me a quick glance. I'm still not the best at reading every Randannan expression, but I'm pretty sure the look she's giving me now is regret.

Not good.

"You've put my crew in danger," Su'mik says. "And it's clear your continued presence here will invite more. I cannot allow that."

My heart skips a beat.

"We've changed course, and we're on our way to the nearest habitable planet."

Every word resonates like a hammer blow on steel, so powerful my ears ring. And I go completely numb when he speaks again.

"When we arrive, you will disembark. And we will go our separate ways."

5

I watch in numb silence as the *Ku'lu* lifts off without me.

The initial wash of thrust tears at my jumpsuit and batters me with sand. I snap my eyes shut, and the deep thrum of the engines reverberates through me, shifting in pitch as the ship transitions from vertical to horizontal flight. As the turbulence dies down, I blink my vision clear in time to watch the huge bird-shaped vessel streak through the sky before disappearing into a bank of fluffy white clouds.

For the first time since right after losing Fallah, I'm all alone.

I turn away from the landing pad to face the tall sandstone wall surrounding it, rising high enough to blot out the morning sun. The air is already stifling, and a meager breeze wafts against my face like a hot breath.

Sweat beads between my shoulder blades as I hobble toward an arched gap in the sandstone wall. After a week in the bandage, I can finally detect a whisper of the material sliding against skin slicked with sweat. The sensation is far more acute inside my powered sleeve. It's icky, and uncomfortable, and I can tell both limbs need a thorough wash.

Past the arch is a wide thoroughfare, paved with sandstone bricks. Loose sand dusts the surface, making it slippery and forcing me to take extra care each time I shift weight to my bandaged leg—after all, it's not easy walking with a numb, immobilized ankle. To either side of the thoroughfare are more sandstone walls forming six circles in total, but no ships are parked at the moment. A fact reinforced by the complete and utter lack of any beings milling about.

That changes when I pass through a second arch at the end of the wide walkway.

Two hooded figures loiter on the narrow street beyond. Even though I can't see their faces, the glance they share when I stroll into view is obvious. The nearest approaches, only its slitted eyes visible beneath the hood, glinting in the diffuse sunlight reflected up from the sandstone roadway.

My powered arm translates its incomprehensible mewling. "Hello there. Is this your first time on Ristan?"

The second hooded figure paces away from the wall. "Perhaps you could use a guide?"

I tighten my grip on the straps of my pack and pivot to remain facing them as I shuffle past. "No. Thank you."

"Are you sure?" The first figure draws closer, and a furry hand tipped with obsidian claws reaches from beneath its robe.

"I'm fine," I say, turning to shuffle faster along the road.

"Come, now. We don't bite," the being calls after me.

I ignore the appeal and continue between a mix of two-story and three-story sandstone buildings. Much to my chagrin, the beings trail me deeper into the city. But when the streets begin to fill, I use the crowds to my advantage the same way I used them when running from the Kaisin for the very first time. Until I look back and they're nowhere to be seen.

Letting out a sigh of relief, I shuffle to the side of the road to make way for a hulking biped with muscular arms and legs and rough gray skin, oblivious to the beating sun that has my body trying to create its very own pool to cool off in. A reptilian quadruped whose scales shift in color and detail to match the sandstone roadway scurries in its wake. Other beings farther along the street are more shielded from the elements, wearing thick white cloaks. Their drape hints at shapes differently than mine. Sometimes, an occasional head hints at the type of being. One is mottled gray and brown fuzz with beady little eyes. Another is reminiscent of a mushroom, with no eyes, ears, or mouth. A third is translucent and filled with liquid. That being, in particular, is wearing a wide-brimmed hat to ward away direct sunlight.

Besides the mix of beings braving the overbearing sunlight, raucous laughter and loud conversations drift from the door and windows of the first building I pass. The rough-cut openings are covered with curtains made out of fabric. Or maybe woven out of some kind of fiber. Either way, they're light enough to flutter in the stifling breeze. A sign hangs next to the door, scrawled in a language I can't read. A quick scan with the visor clipped to my shoulder identifies the location as a bar. I don't try to pronounce the proprietor's name.

Other signs hanging above doors trailing down the street advertise a few more bars, an equal number of restaurants, and a pair of shops before a major cross street. My visor can't make out the text of the shops beyond due to the shimmering heat, so intense reality itself looks set to melt.

I wish I still had the wide-brimmed hat I started my journey with. But I lost it a long time ago, on a planet very far away from this one. None of the others I visited since wound up being quite so inhospitable. Maybe it's time to buy a new one.

First, I need to get the lay of the land. The nearest bar looks as good as any other. Bars are the best place to visit when first arriving somewhere new, so I hobble toward it.

Someone bumps into me from behind, hard, and I stumble forward onto my hands and knees. Hands tug at the pack looped over my shoulders, and something jerks free.

I stagger to my feet and spin toward the footsteps pounding away from me. I spot a figure about my size with a similar shape and ruddy brown skin.

"Hey!" I shout and break into an uneven run.

My bandaged foot slips on the scattered sand and my numb ankle twists. I stumble to a stop and watch as they duck down an alleyway.

I hobble to the alley, but they're long gone. Slumping against the wall, I slip my pack to the ground at my feet. It's open, and I have a pretty good idea what's missing. After a few seconds of rummaging, my suspicions are confirmed: my pouch of credits is gone!

Panic swells, twisting my insides, accompanied by a shot of adrenaline that sets my heart racing and makes my head as light as the swirling eddies of sand around my feet.

How am I supposed to survive in a place like this without credits?

I clench my fists at my side to keep them from trembling, take a deep breath, and hold it until my heartrate calms. Freaking out will only make things worse; I have to think. How can I earn enough credits to avoid sleeping on the street?

I don't have any marketable skills—I can't exactly *sell* my ability to destroy an insidious alien parasite no one knows about—so my only option is to sell something else. I rummage deeper in my pack for possible wares, but I doubt anyone here would be interested in clothes tailored to fit a human. Or the few, tiny trinkets I've collected during my travels: a handful of small, uniquely colored rocks from a few of the worlds I've visited and carvings similar to Fallah's pendant, but made out of some kind of polished bone.

Maybe I can get a few credits for the lot? Enough for a meal and a single night at any place with a bed? A bed can't cost much here. And I only need enough to tide me over while I think about what else I can do to start making the credits I need to survive long enough to escape this rock.

I orient myself to the nearest shop, a few doors down. The curtain hanging in the doorway is of a much finer weave, with beige and brown threads in a crosshatch pattern, multicolored beads at the intersection of colors. When I push past the curtain, I discover those aren't beads. They're bells.

The chorus of chimes follows me into the shop's dim interior, which is more than a few degrees cooler than the street. A decent cross-breeze begins to dry the sweat dripping down my brow. No wonder curtains are preferred over solid doors and windows!

After a few moments, my eyes adjust to the relative darkness. Shelves line all four walls, packed full of items, most of which I can't identify at a glance. A counter runs along most of the far wall, except for a gap at one end and a staircase at the other, leading up but blocked by another curtain.

A tall, willowy being stands behind the counter, hunched forward, presumably due to the overbearing weight of its enormous head covered in far too many unblinking yellow eyes. A slender arm extends from beneath the folds of an oversized robe, palm upturned. It speaks in a distorted, singsong tongue, which my translator converts to standard.

"Welcome! How may I help you?"

"Do you buy goods?" I ask, crossing to the counter.

"Of interest," the being replies, some of its pupils fixing on me, others darting to the pack I set down.

Rather than asking what might be of interest to this being, or the other denizens of this planet, I open my pack and begin pulling out the items I identified earlier.

A few of its eyes study the items I offer. "Is that all?"

I swallow. "Yes."

"I'm sorry. I can't buy any of this." The being leans over my pack to peer inside. "Perhaps if you had something else—" Without warning, it reaches inside and pulls the amber sphere into the open. "Is this Bollup nectar?"

"Hey!" Before I can snatch the sphere back, the being steps out of reach. It raises its free hand and pierces the sphere's surface with a single needle-sharp fingertip. When the finger withdraws, a slight pucker marks the surface.

The being raises its finger even with its face and regards the single drop of amber fluid. Then, its head tilts back to reveal a nest of tentacles wriggling around a circular orifice. The tentacles quiver and the orifice pulses as it brings the drop close enough for a single tentacle to flick out and collect the drop before curling inward.

An unsettling shivering moan fills the air and its many pupils dilate. "It *is* Bollup nectar. How did you get this?"

"It was a gift."

The being stares at me. All of its eyes are already bulging, so I can't tell whether it's surprised or indifferent. "I'll give you three thousand for it."

The offer sounds too good to be true. But I need the money. For food. And for a place to stay. So, I don't really have a choice but to part with the gift, unless I want to spend all night desiccating in an alley somewhere. Which I don't.

"Five thousand," the being says when I don't answer.

I lean on the counter to keep myself from keeling over. That's over three times as much as Rhuk gave me before I left and more than six times as much as Fletcher paid to take me away from Alphanax. Which makes me wonder why this being would be willing to pay so much for one sphere of nectar.

The being regards me with about half of its pupils, the other half vacillating between the globe, my face, and random corners of the room. "Fine. Six thousand. Final offer."

I came here wanting to sell something and didn't even consider the globe of nectar could be worth anything. Let alone as much as the shopkeeper is offering. I imagine the nectar is destined for a more unsavory purpose. But again, I need the money. For a place to stay. I'll also need to hire a new ship to get offworld. And since it seems like not many pass through here, I expect buying passage on the next ship that arrives won't be cheap. Besides, I'd rather not have to worry about making *more* credits if I wind up needing them. Better to take the offer and part with the sphere now.

I nod. "Okay."

The being hugs the sphere of nectar to its chest, turns, and glides toward a space under the stairway. It disappears beyond a curtain. Rummaging, clinking, and more singsong intonations my translator doesn't catch fill the air. Then, the being emerges, a pouch held in the palm of its hand. It pushes the pouch toward me. "As we agreed."

I accept the pouch.

"Thank you for your business." Its bulbous head bobs, and a few pupils dart to the door. "A final point: please refrain from mentioning you sold this to me. For my safety. For yours, keep that pouch hidden."

Good advice, but given too late.

"Got it," I say, sweeping the multicolored stones and trinket back into my pack and heaving it onto my back. Then, I unzip my jumpsuit and slip the pouch into an inner pocket, readjusting the credits until the resulting lump isn't so obvious.

I offer the shopkeeper a final wave as I slip back outside. The overbearing brilliance of the sun blinds me. At the same time, heat batters me from above *and* below; it's like I've been thrust into an oven and the planet is trying to cook me before sucking me dry.

Squinting a single eye open, I look up and down the empty street, considering which way to go. I'd forgotten to ask about a place to stay. Or buy a hat, which I now want even more than I did before.

When I turn to head back inside, someone bumps into me again.

I spin in the direction of the bump and throw out my powered arm in a wild grab. My fingers catch fabric. When I yank, the fabric tears. A figure stumbles backwards onto the sandy brick street with a grunt. And through squinted eyes, I can make out the same figure as before: about my size, and shape, and height, with skin the same color as mine.

A human?

The figure flips to all fours and scrambles up into an awkward run.

I follow, throwing all caution and tenderness to the wind, sprinting as best I can on my bandaged leg. Despite my uneven gait, I'm keeping up. Mostly because the figure is panicking, slipping on the sand and throwing wide-eyed looks over their shoulder. They stumble into the corner of a building and bounce off, redirecting their momentum down a narrow alleyway.

Their footsteps pound into the distance, already way ahead by the time I make the turn to follow. A second later, they make another turn and slip out of view.

I quicken my pace, not caring about the slight ache in my calf or the irritating scratch of sand that has worked its way into the gap between the bandage and my skin. I skid around the corner expecting the figure to be farther away than before. Not a dozen paces ahead, trapped in a dead end.

"Got you!" I pant, resting my hands on my knees and gasping for breath.

The figure paces like a caged animal, eyeing the three walls pinning them in, as well as the tiny gaps to either side of me. There's no escape. Not this time. Not when he'll have to get within range of my powered grasp to slip by.

I straighten up and rest my hands on my hips. "Give back what you stole."

The figure snarls at me.

For the first time, I get a good look at them. They're about my height and bipedal, with five-fingered hands, and I count ten toes sticking out of the front of their sandals. A human? My heart jumps into my throat. A human! My initial excitement fades when I realize how slender their torso and limbs are. They also have spidery fingers. When I glance up to their face, bright blue eyes stare back.

I blink. "You're...Kaisin?"

"So?" They—*he*—spits the word back at me. His voice is higher than I expected, which means he's young. About my age, maybe?

It's then I notice the shabbiness of his clothes and the huge rip in the shoulder of his shirt where I grabbed him. His sandals are no better, with soles so thin they likely don't provide any protection against the heat blasted brick roads. Then, there's the dirt caked on his skin—how long has it been since he's had a bath?

He's clearly not with the hooded figures who accosted me right outside the space port. Is he all alone? Stuck here? Like me?

I brush blooming pity aside. He may be stranded here, by himself, but he *stole* from me. Had that shopkeeper not insisted on buying the Bollup nectar, I'd be in a worse-off position than him right about now. I frown. "Give me back my credits."

He meets my gaze. "What credits?"

"Don't play dumb." I jab a finger at him. "I saw you."

Instead of answering, he tries to dart past me, but a solid shove from my powered arm sends him stumbling back into the dead end.

For a moment, his eyes search the ground, as if there's an escape buried somewhere in the sand piled at the alleyway's corners. Then, he bares his teeth, reaches beneath his shirt, and pulls out my pouch. Before I can step forward to retrieve it, he throws it on the ground.

"I don't want your credits anyway."

I bend down and grab the pouch, dusting sand off of it while giving him a self-satisfied smile. Stepping back, I turn to leave, but Rhuk's words float to the surface: *Think about what you can do.*

This boy may be a Kaisin, and he may have stolen from me, but that doesn't give me an excuse to turn my back on him. I can't. Like I couldn't turn my back on the Kaisin who boarded the *Ku'lu*. They needed help, and I could give it. So does he.

I stifle a sigh and turn back. "What's your name?"

His eyes narrow, as if no one has ever asked for his name before.

"Well?"

"It's Zhon."

"Nice to meet you, Zhon. My name is Aiko." I stick out my hand.

He stares at it.

"Nice to meet you," I repeat, reaching out and grabbing his hand.

My right hand is sheathed in a powered glove, so I brush the back of his fingers with my left. There's barely any darkness inside of him, but the quantity isn't the point. Its presence is the problem. So, I snuff it out, freeing him from shackles he doesn't even know he's wearing.

He rips his hand away. "What are you doing?"

"Just shaking your hand. Anyone ever shake your hand before?"

Zhon frowns. "No."

I smile. "Well, there's a first time for everything."

He gives a low 'hmph' in the back of his throat.

"Well, are you hungry?"

His frown falters and his eyes widen, making the blue of his pupils stand out against his dirt-caked skin.

"I was on my way to get something before we ran into each other again." I take a step back and turn to motion down the alleyway. "So, maybe you can join me?"

"Why would you want me to join you?"

"Because I'm new here. And I think I'd rather have *you* as a local guide than the pair who met me at the spaceport."

Zhon smirks.

"You know who they were?"

He nods. "Goons for the Relawi Syndicate. They basically run Ristan, and especially love getting their hooks in new arrivals. You're lucky you got this far without them taking a second shot at you."

"All the more reason for you to help me out."

He stares at me.

"I'm getting really hungry, and I could really use your help finding a place that serves food I can actually eat." When he doesn't answer, I add, "I'll pay for your meal."

He lets out a shallow sigh. "Fine."

"Great." I wave him ahead of me. "Lead the way."

6

Zhon beelines down the alleyway and turns left when he reaches the street, hugging the buildings, though there's no shade to protect us from the unrelenting sun. At the next cross street, he cuts diagonally across the intersection, darting in front of a tight-knit group of four cloaked figures on his way to a three-story building at the opposite corner.

I follow, but slowly so I'll pass behind the group. But the last figure abruptly stops. The being crosses two sets of burly arms and stares down at me with beady black eyes. Instead of a mouth, the whole bottom half of its face is covered in fuzzy hair, which starts to shiver and vibrate in unsettling patterns.

"Where do you think you're going?"

The translation sends my heart into my throat, and I shuffle backwards out of the being's reach. I hope. "I was just crossing the street."

"Well, *I'm* walking here." The being looms over me. "And you got in my way."

"I'm sorry."

The apology draws a rhythmic buzz out of the creature. And others crop up. Its friends, who fan out to either side, completely block the way forward.

This is not good.

I look down each street, but every being within earshot hurries along, doing their best to ignore my plight. And those approaching the intersection quickly look away after making eye contact.

This is really not good.

"Listen—" I start to back away. Slowly. "I didn't mean to get in your way. It was an accident."

"If you were really sorry, you'd compensate us for our time." The being holds out one of its four hands, palm up.

I'm sure if I said I don't have any money, they'd crowd me into an alleyway to check and find the huge pouch of credits stuffed inside my jumpsuit. But if I reach for the pouch to pay them, they'll likely take it anyway. Running is out of the question. So, what do I do?

"Hey!" Zhon calls out.

None of the beings turn.

"Hey, I'm talking to *you*."

The being who initially confronted me jostles as if it was pushed. It spins, silent as a whisper, but my translator spits out: "What do you want, trash?"

Shuffling to the side, I glimpse Zhon framed in the gap between two of the beings, holding up four identical pouches while backpedaling down the street.

"Lose something?"

All four beings start running at the same time, but they don't make it more than a few steps before Zhon slips down an alley. The beings disappear after him seconds later, leaving only a cloud of dust in their wake.

I remain frozen in place, heart racing, thankful for his intervention, while hoping that the headstart he gave himself was enough.

A deep breath calms my nerves, and a quick glance around reveals more than one being stopped, staring at me. Not wanting to be dragged into another, similar situation, I hurry to the building Zhon was leading me toward.

Wide double doors grant access to a spacious interior with a high ceiling devoid of lighting; more than enough streams in from the huge windows, despite being covered. A bar runs along the back wall, and the space between is packed with tables, nearly all of them full with patrons of all shapes and sizes. Though, now that I've been traveling a while, more and more of them are familiar.

My favorite has got to be a miniscule species of lizard creatures about the same size as Rhuk, a few of which are sitting at a table right inside the door. They have the cutest green eyes and beautiful pearlescent scales. Not very many of them speak standard; the few that do draw their words out in long hissing syllables. Sadly, these are speaking in the subtle hisses of their native tongue.

When I step past their table, I'm engulfed by a wash of cacophonous conversation. I'm also hit by a myriad of aromas—food, drink, and a whiff of *something* that makes me crinkle my nose. Probably a patron. I've come to learn that some species converse as much with scent as words. And some species just plain stink.

A rotund little server weaves his way between the tables and trundles to a stop in front of me. It waves a pudgy arm and sweeps its beady black eyes across me in what I assume is an appraising stare, judging by the tenor of its accented question: "Can I help you?"

"A table, please." I give the server a sickly sweet smile I'm not even sure it understands. Nonetheless, it shows me to a table near the front of the establishment. Right next to one of the windows. I frown as radiating heat I thought I'd escaped washes over me.

I sit and tell the being, "Someone will be joining me."

It nods and backs away, leaving me alone.

A few excruciatingly tense minutes later, Zhon walks in the front door. He scans the establishment, and his mouth twists into a lopsided grin when he spots me.

"That was a neat trick," I say when he drops into the chair across from me.

"Saved your skin, though."

"Yeah. Thanks. Were they from the Syndicate, too?"

"Not so loud," he hisses through clenched teeth.

I only have enough time to nod before the server trundles up to the table.

"Drinks?" The being asks.

"Do you have water?"

"There's a whole ocean of it under the city," the server says.

"Water, then."

The server glances at Zhon.

"Same."

"And food?"

"We want stew," Zhon says. "Without the khosh."

The server nods and wanders away.

I raise my eyebrows at Zhon. "What's khosh?"

"A plant that grows out in the desert. Tried it once. Never again."

"Why? Is it gross?"

He makes a face. "It's slimy and disgusting. And it made me sick."

As much as I hate my relation to the Kaisin, knowing what they can and can't eat has kept me healthy these last six months. And Zhon is the only Kaisin I've noticed here, so I'm willing to defer to his expertise regarding what is edible and what isn't. "Got it."

I'm not sure what I expected when I invited him to come eat with me. At the very least, a conversation. I'm not sure where to begin. And Zhon's hard stare isn't particularly inviting. Though, as I return his stare, I notice something interesting: his eyes are as blue as other Kaisin, but not at all jittery.

Before I can ask him why, the rotund server returns with two trays, each bearing a glass of water and a bowl of stew. It sets them down, then disappears between two crowded tables.

The stew isn't steaming. And when I raise a spoonful to my lips, I'm surprised to find it's chilled. Considering the heat radiating from outside, maybe not that surprised.

Swallowing the savory, refreshing mouthful, I look across at Zhon. "So, how did you end up here?"

"How did *you* end up here?" Zhon shoots back without missing a beat.

I glance through the mesh curtain hanging over the window beside us. Rippling heat distorts the street, but not the truth. "I was left here."

Zhon's brow tightens, "Oh."

The chatter of dozens of other patrons fills the silence between us, but can't dispel the sudden awkward tension.

I take another bite of chilled stew; it's quite delicious. Reminiscent of a bowl of Gundor-tail soup I ate once upon a time. A small comfort amidst turmoil. Though, what I'm going through now doesn't even compare to the soul-wrenching pain of losing Fallah. Or the confused uncertainty of learning I was human, before I even understood what being human meant.

"I was stranded here, too," Zhon says.

"How long ago?"

He stares down into his stew, moving the chunky bits floating on the surface around with his spoon. "About a year ago."

"And you've been by yourself ever since?"

"I like being by myself," he snaps, a scowl replacing the glimmer of vulnerability he'd shown a moment before.

I stifle a sigh. "Well, I don't like being by myself. I get lonely. Don't you?"

"No." Zhon shovels a spoonful of soup into his mouth. His lips quiver as he chews.

He doesn't have to say anything else for me to recognize the kind of pain that leaves an indelible mark on the soul. And remains as a lingering ache, no matter how much time has passed.

"Not too long ago, I lived at an orphanage. But I wasn't alone." I pause, not sure why I'm sharing this. Not sure what to say next, since a Kaisin killed Fallah. I shake my head. "Until my best friend was taken from me."

He gives an ambivalent 'hmm' and raises another spoonful of stew to his lips, but his steady blue stare keeps flicking up to my face.

My heart skips a beat at the thought of continuing. Of revealing more. Yet, I can't stop myself.

"Not long after, another of my kind arrived to take me away from the orphanage and give me a home. Things didn't work out, so I had to leave."

I nearly cringe at how much that single sentence leaves out. And for the first time since telling Rhuk, I almost break and spill everything. Sure, I'd *thought* about telling Su'mik and Al'nor the truth. But never entertained it as more than a possibility. Something about the familiarity of Zhon's situation makes me ache to fill the gaping blanks in my story.

Still, I can't. No one else can know what I know.

"Since then, I've traveled the stars as a passenger on a ship I hired," I continue. "They decided it was time to part ways."

He frowns. "Why?"

"Because—" What am I supposed to say? I got one of their crew killed by not telling them about an ancient darkness lurking inside every Kaisin? A darkness even *he* had been harboring until earlier today? Of course not. I stifle a sigh. "I made a mistake they couldn't forgive."

Zhon purses his lips and nods. Does he understand? What mistakes has he made in his past? What regrets linger in his thoughts? I want to ask, but don't know how. Not without making him throw his walls back up.

So, I eat my stew. He does the same, bright blue eyes occasionally shifting from the bowl in front of him up to me.

After a few more spoonfuls of stew, I work up the courage to ask: "How have you survived? This place is terrible."

He nods in agreement, then shrugs. "I just have."

"By picking pockets?"

"When I have to," he snaps.

"Anything else?"

He drops his spoon with a huff. "I do what it takes to survive. Not everybody is lucky enough to be walking around with a pouch full of credits."

"Don't know if I'd call it lucky. Everybody on this planet seems to want a piece of me, and I really don't want to think about what would happen if they discovered I have credits. Besides, I—" I stop myself from saying I earned my credits. Rhuk got me started, after all. And I got lucky selling the Bollup nectar.

I change tact, "What would you have done with them?"

Zhon crosses his arms. "What do you care?"

"Humor me."

"Fine. I'd've bought some food and a change of clothes."

"That's it?"

"That's all *I* need to survive."

"Don't you want to do more than survive?"

He frowns at the question, as if he doesn't understand it. Maybe he doesn't. Maybe he's trapped in the same, deep valley of despair I'd sunken into after losing Fallah. A place that's impossible to see, or escape, until you're yanked back into the light. Fletcher did that for me. I should try to do the same for him.

"What more is there?" Zhon asks, face screwing up in genuine confusion.

"Freedom," I suggest.

"I *am* free," he replies. "I do what I want. When I want. And there's no one around to tell me any different."

At Alphanax, I believed freedom was escaping from the orphanage. That leaving its walls would be more than enough. Through everything I've experienced, one thing has become abundantly clear: freedom without purpose is aimless. Hollow. Unfulfilling. How do I communicate that to someone who hasn't experienced the same realization?

I tilt my head at the window. "Maybe you'd feel different if you left this place and experienced more of what's out there."

A tiny nudge in the right direction. I thought, anyway.

But a shadow falls across his face. "I don't have a reason to leave."

"Why not?"

Zhon opens his mouth to answer but stops short, and his vision glazes over as if supplanted by some haunting memory from his past. Finally, he shakes his head and refuses to make eye contact with me. "I'm fine here. I have everything I need."

The way he hunkers over the remainder of his stew makes it clear the conversation is over. And the terse silence hanging between us persists until we're done with our meals.

I pay the rotund server for the meal when it comes by to clear the table, then stand and head for the door. Zhon follows me out and starts walking away.

"You're welcome," I call after him.

He stops and turns. For a moment, I'm not sure he's going to say anything at all. But he nods. "Yeah. Thanks."

I hold back a frown. He shouldn't have thanked me, since the questions I asked dredged up something from his past. Something troubling he wanted to leave there. I reach into my pocket and trace my thumb along the smooth line of Fallah's amulet. My thoughts dance around one memory in particular. The one I want left in the past.

When I don't say anything, Zhon turns to leave. I suspect if I let him go, we won't meet again. For some reason, I don't want that. Not yet. Maybe there's more to say. Or maybe I'm not ready to be alone quite yet.

I hurry after him and grab his bicep. "Wait."

He yanks his arm free and backs away, as defensive as when I first cornered him.

"Could you help me with something else? If you don't mind."

His brow knits. "What?"

"I need a place to stay. Could you suggest one? Maybe take me there? Preferably someplace I won't run into anyone else from the Syndicate."

The flicker of a frown tugs at the corners of his lips. Then, he sighs. "Fine. Follow me."

Zhon turns and hurries along the main thoroughfare before ducking down a narrower side street. Here, the buildings crowding the street paired with the sun now past its apex grant an iota of shade. Still, no amount of shade can prevent my body from sweating out every drop of liquid I consumed minutes earlier.

At another intersection, Zhon points to a sandstone building identical to every other. "You should stay there. The owner is nice enough."

"Thanks." I grab his hand with my powered glove and pull him toward the building he indicated.

"What are you doing?" He demands and tries to pull away. When his hand doesn't come loose from my hydraulic grip, he uses his other hand to try and pry the powered fingers from his.

When that doesn't work, his wide eyes dart up to mine. "Let me go!"

"I will as long as you promise to stay too."

He blinks at me. "What? No!"

"You let me buy you food. Let me do this, as well."

He tries to yank free again, but there isn't as much energy in the attempt. "Why?"

Because I recognize far too much of myself in Zhon. Looking at him is like peering through a window into my past. Only, he's stuck. Trapped in the same mire of hopelessness I'd been unable to escape until Fletcher arrived to dredge me out of it. I still know very little about Zhon, but whatever is troubling him shouldn't define him. Like my grief for Fallah doesn't define me. It's something I learned to move past. It's a pain I carry, but it isn't who I am.

"It's the least I can do," I answer. Which is also the truth.

After thinking for a moment, he relaxes. "Fine. I'll stay."

"Great!" I smile and give his hand a gentle tug.

This time, it's my turn to lead the way.

7

Rhandannans don't shower. They preen. Which means the surprisingly cool tub of water I ease myself neck deep into will be the first bath I've taken since before leaving Rhuk and the others behind. It's just as surprising that there's enough water for me to take a bath at all. Apparently, Ristan is riddled with fresh aquifers as large as an ocean. So, despite the heat, water will never be an issue.

Though, I'm surprised at its abundance. Why doesn't the Relawi Syndicate control every drop that makes it to the surface? Then again, maybe they do. And maybe that's how they can maintain such a solid grip on everything. A grip I hope I won't be on Ristan long enough to experience.

I rest my head against the tub's polished sandstone rim and close my eyes.

Today has been one of the hardest in the last six months. That's saying something, considering some of the planets I've trekked across to get to all those nagging whispers at the back of my mind; the worst had massive crystal pillars jutting out of the fractured ground, resonating with constant electrical storms in a high enough pitch to vibrate my bones and set my teeth on edge. It doesn't compare to being left alone on a strange planet with no support and no direction.

I mean, I *know* what I need to do: find a new ship to hire and continue on to the next whisper. Easier said than done. This time, Rhuk won't be around to put his thumb on the scale with the next captain. So, I'm glad I sold the Bollup nectar. Even if the shopkeeper didn't give me much of a choice.

There's also the Syndicate to consider. Will they even let me hire a ship when one arrives? Or will they cause trouble when I'm on my way out? Considering the hooded figures who met me at the spaceport when I arrived, it's only natural to assume they'll be there when I want to leave. Only, then, they might not be so willing to let me go without some sort of recompense.

Swatting the possibilities aside, I try to relax. Yet, contentment and relief elude me. Despite the cool, refreshing bath. Or the cozy room with a bed twice as wide as my cot on the *Ku'lu*, with a mattress four times as thick. Not with so much uncertainty hanging over my head. And an equally hefty helping of uncertainty brewing *inside* my head.

Na'min chalked what I experienced up to stress and suggested I take a break. But the strange things I've experienced so far are more akin to when I first started communicating with Iali rather than stress bubbling past its boiling point.

I probe inside my head for any sign of the Yuul and find nothing but the very far away whispers scratching at the edges of my mind.

Opening my eyes, letting out a deep sigh, I stand up and allow some of the water to drip from my body and hair before toweling off and donning a robe provided by the inn; it's woven from a thinner, softer material than what's used to curtain the windows.

I flop onto the bed and stare up at the ceiling, tracing the mismatched, striped grain of a few adjacent sandstone blocks. At the same time, I steer my thoughts away from the inexplicable things I've been experiencing, as stifling as the sun beating down on this world.

They crash headlong into Zhon.

The young Kaisin is…Well, I'm not really sure. He's rough around the edges, but ultimately intriguing. Which is the most unexpected part of our entire encounter thus far. I mean, I'm not fond of Kaisin in the first place. Except for Gohk, of course. But a lot about Zhon sets him apart from other Kaisin. His eyes, first off. They're not jittery. Which makes it far less unsettling when he looks at me.

And then there's his situation.

Zhon is alone, like me. Abandoned on this planet and doing everything he can to survive. So much about him reminds me of my time at Alphanax. He's what I might have become had Fletcher never shown up to take me away from the orphanage. The thought of withering to a bitter shell of myself to survive sends a shiver down my spine. At the same time, sadness settles like a weight in the pit of my stomach.

That's why, despite how we met, I decided to help him. He deserves it. Like *I* deserved it when Fletcher helped me. A meal and a place to sleep won't be enough; it wasn't enough to be taken away from Alphanax. In the end, no one handed me the purpose that led me to true freedom. I had to find it on my own, so I can't do the same for Zhon.

I can show him the door, but he has to step through it.

Taking a deep breath, I roll on my side and stare at the curtains, fluttering in a chillier breeze than I expect considering the day's wilting heat. Right now, the temperature is perfect. And out of nowhere, my eyelids droop. So, I close them.

Something wet drips onto my cheek.

I wipe it away and bring my hand in front of my face to find a black streak on my fingers.

Rolling onto my back, I stare up at the ceiling.

The seams between blocks are traced in black. Heavy drops start to fall on the bed around me. Instead of soaking into the fabric, the liquid beads and begins to move. The droplets dart toward one another, coalescing into a single undulating mound near the foot of the bed. It grows as the pattering drops of darkness begin to fall more quickly.

I dive off of the bed and scramble for the door.

Tendrils of darkness whip past either side of me and splat against the doorknob and hinges. I spin to look for a way out, but darkness pens me in on either side. And as I plant my back against the door, the blob of darkness reels itself toward me.

All I can do is squeeze my eyes shut, like not looking at it will grant me some sort of protection. Yet, I can still *sense* it drawing closer, its proximity causing my skin to tingle as if charged with static electricity.

"Leave me alone!"

It doesn't stop. It doesn't withdraw. And a heartbeat later, the darkness slides across my skin, at the same time light as smoke and thick as oil.

As soon as it makes contact reality begins to stretch, like I'm being pulled. Out of my mind. Away from the hellish planet I'm trapped on. I recoil when pain arcs through my brain. I cry out as my mind and body are drawn taut like a rope nearing its breaking point. My cry is joined by an otherworldly roar of white noise; it climbs in volume and frequency, until—

Silence.

Gasping for breath, I open my eyes. I'm leaning against the door. The room is empty. Still. Except for the curtains fluttering in the chill evening breeze.

Icy sweat soaks my robe, piercing me to my bones.

I stand, pace to the bed, and inspect the covers. They're beige and spotless. Free of the darkness dripping all over me moments before.

With a shuddering breath, I pull the top blanket off the bed and wrap it around my shoulders. It drags on the ground behind me as I walk to the center window along my room wall. Drawing the curtain back, I flinch when cold air slaps me in the face. No wonder there was a blanket on the bed! Night on this planet is the polar opposite of day!

I wrap the blanket tighter and lean out of the window far enough to look up at the night sky. Thousands of stars wink back at me. Like always, I focus on the darkness between. Squinting up into the void, I probe the edge of my mind for any hint of the Yuul. Some explanation for the dark presence tormenting me moments before. Yet, I detect nothing.

I don't believe that. I can't believe that. Because if this isn't the Yuul, then it's me.

If it is me, what's happening? Why is it happening? And how do I stop it?

I dig my fingernails into the sandstone windowsill, frustrated by all the unanswerable questions. They'll have to wait. First, I have to figure out how I'm going to get off Ristan.

8

I leave my room when the sun is no more than an orange smear at the horizon. The frigid air turns my breath into foggy puffs, which is preferable to my skin baking after a minute in the sun.

Hiking my pack a little bit higher up on my shoulders, I look up and down the street to make sure it's empty before starting for the main thoroughfare. I think, anyway.

"Where are you going?"

I stumble to a stop at the sudden voice and spin. Zhon is sitting against the side of the building. The dirty beige of his ragged pants and shirt match the sandstone wall he's leaning against. So does his skin. No wonder I missed him.

"You didn't bathe."

He cocks an eyebrow at me. "Why does it matter?"

I frown. "Don't you want to be clean?"

"Not enough to get a sunburn," he replies, with a know-it-all smirk.

"Oh." His natural skin tone would be stark white, which would lend itself to burning in Ristan's unforgiving sunlight.

His smirk widens to a lopsided grin. "Now, where were you going again?"

"I'm heading to the port." Annoyed by the grin lingering on his face, I shoot a question back at him: "What are you doing up?"

"I never sleep much," he replies, heaving to his feet and shuffling toward me. "You know where the port is, right? Or do you need me to show you?"

I clench my teeth to keep from snapping at him and take a breath. "Yes. I know where it is."

Zhon nods, the smirk still on his face, and falls in beside me when I start down the narrow side street.

This early, a surprising number of beings are out and about, but their collective pace is far more leisurely than at midday. I spot a few beings still wearing wide-brimmed hats in anticipation of the oncoming sun. Already, the orange on the horizon has brightened from a smoldering ember to the vibrancy of a raging fire, heralding another day of hellish, unrelenting heat.

On the way to the spaceport—mostly because I'm paying attention now—it's much easier to pick out the occasional group of beings wearing the dark cloaks, which I assume identify them as members of the Relawi Syndicate. Either way, I give them a wide berth.

I slow when we come to the final stretch of road leading to the circular sandstone landing pads, but the hooded Syndicate goons aren't there to greet me this morning. I'm relieved, but also apprehensive of what their absence suggests. Crossing my fingers, I hope I'm wrong as I glance into each landing pad.

There are no ships.

I ball my hands into fists and squeeze until my knuckles ache.

"I could have told you there'd be no ships here," Zhon says.

I spin toward him. "Then why didn't you?"

He shrugs. "What's the big deal, anyway? A ship will come along eventually. They always do."

"When? A day? A few days? A week?"

His second nonchalant shrug makes me want to scream; he has no idea how important it is that I get off this planet.

Digging my nails into my palms, I try to keep my voice steady. It still quivers when I say, "I can't wait around that long."

Zhon scowls. "Hey, don't get mad at me. It isn't my fault you're stranded here."

I take a deep breath. "I—I'm sorry."

Sagging against the wall of the nearest landing pad, I let out a deep sigh.

Zhon joins me. "Why is it so important you get off planet?"

His steady blue eyes are filled with genuine curiosity. And are surprisingly...human. It's easier to meet his stare, and hold it, than Su'mik or any of the other Rhandannans on his crew. I always found the way they'd turn their heads and stare without blinking uncomfortably intense. So to experience such an unexpected connection is kinda nice, like an ember of warmth kindled in cold darkness.

It reminds me of my time with Fletcher, Gohk, and Rhuk.

"There's something I have to do," I'm compelled to say. "Something really important. And being stuck here on this planet is just—It's so—" I can't even find the words to express the frustration coursing through me, filling me with energy until I want to jump out of my own skin.

I let out a wordless growl and push away from the sandstone wall. But there's nowhere to go. No outlet for this need to keep moving, as inexorable as the rising sun.

Zhon's head tilts to one side. "What do you have to do?"

I shouldn't answer. Like every other time I've been asked about my purpose, I should deflect, or say, 'It's complicated'. The pressure of holding in the truth for so long has built up inside me like water behind an airlock door. A door I thought would hold as long as I needed.

Being left behind by Su'mik disturbed the seal of that door, like when Fletcher and I forced our way into the sunken human colony vessel once upon a time. And the thought of pushing away a friendly face on an unfriendly planet rams home the hard fact that I did the same thing to Su'mik and his crew. Which is why they left me behind without a second thought.

The realization causes the slow trickle that started when I arrived on this world to burst forth in a roaring cascade.

"There's something terrible out there." Those few words are the closest I've come to uttering the truth since telling Rhuk everything. It's a weight off my shoulders, but I still can't trust Zhon with the *full* truth. Not yet. My reservation doesn't keep me from continuing. "Not many know about it. Even fewer know how to stop it. I do. That's why I have to get off this planet. The longer I'm stuck here, the more dangerous it becomes."

I may not have given him many details, but apparently my tone was sufficiently ominous. His eyebrows knit. First, like he's thinking. Then, the crease between them deepens, and he frowns like he's in pain.

"I'm sorry," I stammer. "I didn't mean to disturb you."

"It isn't that." His tone is firm. Strained. Like he's struggling with a decision he doesn't want to make.

I tilt my head to the side. "What's wrong?"

His eyes drop to the ground, and search the little eddies of sand swirling around my boots for an answer. He exhales out of his nostrils and looks back up at me.

"Follow me."

Without another word, he starts down the street.

I jog to catch up. "Where are we going?"

He doesn't answer. Or offer any other explanation as he leads me deeper into the city. Eventually, he turns down an alley. When I round the corner, he's loitering halfway between this street and the next.

"What is this all about?" I demand.

He glances in either direction before leaning close and whispering, "The Syndicate always has eyes and ears at the port, so it wasn't safe to say this there, but…I can get us a ship."

"What? How?"

"One crashed in the desert. About a year ago."

"And how does that help us?"

"Because it's still in one piece."

I frown. "How do you know?"

"Cause I went and checked it out."

"You went into the desert? Alone? Just to check out a crashed ship?"

He gives me a crooked smile. "Not like I have anything else to do."

"Isn't that dangerous?"

"Sure. But I know what I'm doing."

I blink and shake my head. How could he be so cavalier about doing something so risky because he didn't have anything better to do? "And the ship will fly?"

"It looks like it'll fly."

"That's not very reassuring."

Zhon scoffs. "I mean, you could always wait for another ship to arrive."

I'm not a fan of trekking out into the desert to look at a crashed ship, but I'm even less of a fan of hanging around hoping another arrives while trying to stay off of the Syndicate's radar. At the same time, my heart slams against my ribcage at the thought of commandeering the crashed ship. I know, all too well, the dangers of wandering into random ships on random planets. Still, it's a chance I'm willing to take if it means I can get off this planet sooner rather than later.

"Okay. Let's check out this crashed ship."

"Great! We'll be offworld in no time!"

I cock an eyebrow at him. "We?"

He smiles at me, but it's clear the gesture is empty, meant to hide the pain in his eyes. Pain as acute as this world's sun is bright. What happened to him? And why is his pain suddenly so conspicuous?

"You were the one who said I should experience more of what's out there," he says. "So, I'm coming."

It's a surprising reversal from yesterday, but I'm not repulsed by the idea. It would be nice to have someone along for the ride to keep the weeks between whispers from getting too lonely. And if things don't work out, we can always part ways on a planet with an active space port where I can hire a different ship. "Alright."

His smile widens, and this time it's genuine.

"How far out is this ship, exactly?"

"Not too far," he replies. "But it's enough of a walk that it'll be best if we leave in the early evening. The sun'll be on its way down, so it won't be so hot, and we'll reach the ship before it gets *really* cold."

"Sounds good to me," I say, and head back toward the street. "Now, how about some breakfast?"

With a wordless exclamation of agreement, Zhon hurries to my side. My new companion. A Kaisin, of all beings.

I steal a glance in his direction as we walk and my insides flutter. Out of excitement? Or apprehension? Honestly, a bit of both.

And not just because of Zhon.

9

Looking back at the settlement from the top of the first sand dune beyond its northern border is a catalyst for memory. My mind digs deep, recalling a circle of sunlight amidst cold, damp darkness. Leathery, sun-warmed skin rising and falling under my back. Then, sharp stones under my feet as I'm sprinting into a barren wasteland. Loud pops. A heavy thud. Crimson staining the ground in a mortal halo around someone I loved.

I slip my hand into my pocket to trace the outer edge of Fallah's pendant. It's smooth, and cool, like water-worn stone. The only physical bit of evidence remaining to prove she ever existed in the first place. Though, she'll forever live on in my mind.

Hot wind blows sand in my face, and when I blink my vision clear, the memories are gone. Ahead and below is a crowded collection of sandstone buildings; they look as small and unassuming as Alphanax did from a distance.

And once more, I'm walking into the unknown.

"It's smaller than it looks," Zhon says beside me, oblivious. He stares down at the settlement for a moment longer, then nudges my elbow. "Come on. Let's get moving."

He turns and shuffles down the other side of the dune, the brand new boots I bought him digging deep into the sand. To go with the boots, I also got him a new pair of pants and a long-sleeved white shirt. And I bought both of us wide-brimmed hats for the walk out to the ship, as well as a pair of cloaks for when the temperature dips along with the sun. Those are still in my pack. For now.

When we reach the bottom of the dune, Zhon scrambles his way to the top of the next instead of choosing the easy route winding between the two mountains of sand. It's a hard climb, and sweat is dripping down my face and soaking my shirt by the time we reach the top.

"Why did we climb up here?" I pant.

"To make sure we're going in the right direction," he says. "I'd rather not wander off into the desert accidentally."

I grunt in agreement and watch as he squints into the distance—even though the wide brims of our hats block the sun from shining right in our eyes, light still glares up at us from the sand.

He points. "There!"

I follow his finger to a dark spot on the horizon, jutting past the dunes. "What is that?"

"A *huge* rock," he answers, continuing along the top of the dune.

It snakes into the distance, in the general direction of the dark blot on the horizon. Regardless of which way we're going, our elevation ensures we can keep an eye on our destination—something that wouldn't have been possible from below.

We walk until the sun's clear white light shifts to a burnt orange as it nears the horizon to our left. Ahead, the dark blot stands out against the fiery sky. To our right, shadows dominate the endless desert; the tips of the tallest dunes remaining lit, standing out amidst the dying light. The horizon in that direction is a deep navy. And I'm reminded of another time I shuffled across a similar surface, in similar darkness. Back then I was under five miles of water, on my way to a discovery that would change everything.

The memory sends a shiver down my spine, despite the searing sunlight.

As we continue, the breeze sweeping across the dunes turns cold, a direct counterpoint to the sun's fading heat. And for a blessed few minutes, the temperature is perfect. Yet, when the sun slips beneath the horizon, the breeze kicks up into a biting wind.

"Time for cloaks," I shout at Zhon's back.

"Works for me," he shouts back, already hugging his arms across his chest.

Dropping my pack to the ground, I kneel next to it and stuff our hats inside. Then, I pull out a cloak, and hand it to him.

He takes it and drapes it across his shoulders, fumbling with the buckle at his neck. A strong gust of wind rips it off of him, carrying it away before he can even move to snatch it.

Zhon stares after it, then looks at me, eyes wide.

I have my cloak in my hands. Instead of putting it on, I breathe a shallow sigh into the wind and stuff it back in my pack.

He opens his mouth to protest, but I fix him with a hard stare. "Let's keep moving."

Zhon snaps his mouth shut, and his lips set into a thin line. He gives me a curt nod before spinning on his heels and pushing onward.

I didn't put on my cloak because I didn't want to be cruel. It isn't very long, however, before I'm shivering from the wind biting all the way to my bones. But it's too late to regret my decision.

I just have to hope it won't be too much longer before we reach our destination. And since it's now less of a blot and more of an imposing shadow, I have to think we're almost there.

Clenching my teeth to keep them from chattering, I stick close to Zhon's back. My proximity spurs him into a trot, and the sand stirred up under our boots is swept away by the wind.

The dune we're following slopes down to flat sand in the approach to the huge rock. And it *is* huge, towering over us, blotting out a massive swath of the darkening sky, denying many of the brightest stars their debut after a long day of subservience to Ristan's sun.

The going is easier for a short span, before smooth rocks begin jutting out of the sand. A few, at first, and well-spaced. As we near the huge rock—nearly the size of a mountain—stones give way to sloped ground that's a mix of sand, pebbles, rocks, and inset boulders. Our pace slows to a crawl, since we have to clamber our way up. At least the boulders block the bulk of the frigid wind snatching at us when we reach the occasional, barren span of the slope.

"How much farther?" My jaw aches from clenching it for so long, my skin burns from the cold, and my nose has been running nonstop from sucking in lungfuls of frigid air.

"We're close," he shouts over his shoulder, a pained grimace on his face.

A little bit farther up, the slope evens out to a shelf hugging the edge of the huge stone edifice. It's flat, clear of rocks, sand, and even boulders. The reason why becomes evident when I'm battered by a powerful blast of wind. I stumble to the side and crash to the smooth stone. A relentless wash of sand pelts my face and arms, stinging my exposed skin, so I turn my back to the wind and bare my teeth at the whips of icy pain slashing through my clothes.

"Aiko!" Zhon yells somewhere behind me.

"Zhon!" I shout back. But my words are ripped away by the howling wind.

"Aiko!" He shouts again, farther away this time.

I struggle up to my hands and knees. "Over here!"

The howling wind drowns out all sound and forces me to squeeze my eyes shut to avoid being blinded by stinging grit. I grab the visor clipped to my shoulder and slide it over my eyes, which blocks the wind and sand, but everything beyond is obscured. And trying dark vision only highlights the swirling sand.

I climb to my feet and stumble into the wind. "Zhon!"

A flicker of movement catches my eye—a silhouette in the distance just a shade darker than the sand-swept twilight. I shuffle toward the shape I hope is Zhon. As I get closer, it doesn't resolve into his familiar figure. It remains amorphous. And inky black.

The dark mass shivers, then bursts into a mist. It swirls around me, and the howling of the wind deepens to the roaring drone of an unintelligible voice I can't quite understand. Then, the same blue orb fades into view. Draws closer. Glides to within inches of my face.

"Got you!" Zhon's hand closes around my bicep. "Come on! We've got to get out of this wind. The ship is just ahead."

As he yanks me forward, the wind is just wind. And the sand is just sand. All sign of the darkness is gone. Which is both good and bad.

What's happening to me?

"There!" Zhon shouts, before I can consider the question. His hand slips down to mine, and he pulls me forward. I search the twilight for the ship, but find only swirling sand. So, I shift my grasp, intertwining my fingers with his, and hold on tight. Less than a dozen paces later, we stop. A faint beeping reaches me over the howling wind. Then, Zhon pulls me again, through a threshold.

The wind stills.

I slip the visor off of my face and look around.

We're in a cramped airlock.

The outer hatch is shut tight, with a single porthole window revealing only darkness outside. I let out a sigh.

"We made it."

"Yeah…" Zhon still has a firm hold of my hand. When our eyes meet, he drops it and steps as far away as the cramped space lets him.

"So—Uh… This is the ship?" I study the dinged and scarred walls, ceiling, and floor of the airlock. It's suddenly a lot warmer. And much more cramped than I'd like. "Can we head in?"

"Sure!" Zhon spins to the control panel next to the inner door. He inputs a four-digit code on the grid of buttons, and the door stutters open.

The space beyond is dim, and a faint odor clings to the air, both sweet and sour. It lingers at the back of my throat and sets my stomach churning. I clench my teeth and follow Zhon deeper inside the ship.

Intermittent emergency lights cast dim pools of illumination along a narrow hall stretching in either direction. The walls are textured metal, with angled portions at the top and bottom. The floor is grated metal, with pipes and conduits visible beneath.

Across from the airlock door is another, but Zhon turns left and follows the corridor to a wide room with a low ceiling. A light ring springs to life and flickers when we enter, set above a large circular table in the middle of the room. The six chairs surrounding it look like they used to be quite comfortable but are now threadbare and worn. They're all bolted to the floor and swiveled so their backs are pointed in the same direction. Which makes me realize the ship is tilted.

Judging from the debris collected at the 'low' side of the room, the ship must have crashed rather than landed. Just like Zhon said.

"I wonder what happened." I wander deeper into the room. At the far end, the 'low' end, is a wide door centered in the wall. To my left and right are shuttered windows, much like the one in the *Undertow's* common area. And against the back wall, opposite where we entered, is another corridor with porthole windows on the left and three doors on the right. Crew quarters, maybe?

I turn back to him. "You said you saw the crash?"

He gives me a hasty nod. "Sure did."

"And last time you came out here, did you see anybody? The crew? Or anybody else from town who came out to check on the ship? Wouldn't the Syndicate have been interested in a crashed ship?"

He shrugs. "I guess nobody else saw it."

I glance around the interior one more time.

Judging by the size of this room, the ship is much smaller than the *Undertow.* Even so, it would've painted a trail of fire across the sky as it punched through the atmosphere. A trail that would be nigh invisible during the day and dismissed as a meteorite at night. If not, the dunes would've hidden the general area where the ship came down.

Which leads to a single conclusion: "You were on this ship."

Zhon's silent lack of denial is confirmation enough.

"Why didn't you tell me?"

He still doesn't answer.

"Did something happen?"

Zhon's eyes flick to mine, and the pain has returned. Something did happen. But what? A knot tightens in my stomach as my mind catapults possibilities to the surface, each more terrible than the last. Was I wrong to trust him? Was coming out here a mistake?

"It's not like that," he says, as if reading my mind.

I realize I'm frowning and return my face to neutral.

"I—" Zhon shuffles to the table and slumps down into one of the chairs. When he looks at me, his eyes are filled with anger. "This ship belonged to the Kaisin who used to own me."

The revelation isn't at all surprising.

I join him at the table, sitting one chair away, letting my bag slip to the ground beside me. "What happened to them?"

His eyes dart to the door at the front of the room. "They died in the crash."

Which explains the smell. I resist the urge to wrinkle my nose. "Do you know how it happened?"

Zhon's gaze returns to me. There isn't an ounce of remorse in his eyes.

"Yeah. I wanted to get away, so I locked myself in the bridge while they were sleeping and changed course. We were nearly to the planet when they found out. They beat on the bridge door. Yelled all kinds of terrible things at me. But I wouldn't turn back. Wouldn't open the door. And when they managed to get it open, I nosed the ship down into the atmosphere. Better to crash than live through whatever came next. So, I strapped myself into the pilot's seat and kept us pointed at the ground.

"Something hit me on the way down, and I blacked out before we crashed. When I came to, we were down. Somehow in one piece. And they were dead."

Once again, the same pain as before twists Zhon's face.

I stare, slack jawed. He was on the ship? He brought it down? And what about these Kaisin who *owned* him? I want to know more. I want to know everything. When I open my mouth to ask, words catch in my throat. I think I understand his perspective. No, I *know* I do. And I know the last thing he wants to do right now is talk. He may feel obligated to say something, like I did when Fletcher caught me crying on the bridge of the *Undertow* a lifetime ago now, but I won't press him.

We sit in silence for a long time. At least, *we're* silent.

Wind howls against the ship's hull, and it groans in protest. The two sounds intermingle, like a conversation between the ship and the planet, punctuated by the occasional ping of a small stone against the ship's metal skin. Which, by the look of the interior, is ancient. It's a wonder the ship survived the crash. Will it survive liftoff? Will it punch through the atmosphere? Remain sealed in the airless, absolute zero of the void?

The alternative is trudging back to town in the morning and waiting for another ship to arrive. Which isn't guaranteed. And every minute I remain here is another minute I'm not hunting down the next whisper scratching at the back of my mind. Though, I'm starting to think I have a bigger problem now.

Zhon stirs when there's a lull in the wind, like the threat of actual silence makes him uncomfortable. When he looks at me, the pain has subsided somewhat. I know, however, the ache from such an experience will remain tattooed on his soul forever. Like Fallah's final moments are on mine.

"We can take the ship," he says, "but we'll have to clear the bridge." His gaze strays in the direction of the wide door and his lips dip into a frown. "I left them there."

"Won't be a problem," I say.

His brow knits. "What? You serious?"

It would be too much to tell him about Fallah. Or the skeletal captain of the human colony ship Fletcher and I found. Or the field of Kaisin bodies I stumbled over running from the Yuul. Or the countless others—mostly Kaisin—I've encountered over the last six months. So I say, "I've, uh, had some experience with this sort of thing."

Zhon gives a matter-of-fact "Huh" and stands.

I follow him to the bridge door and glance over his shoulder as he types in the code 0-4-5-1 on the keypad beside it.

I'm not prepared for the reek that punches me in the face when the door screeches open. My stomach turns. I spin away, slapping a hand over my nose and mouth.

Zhon starts to cough and shoulders by me.

"Go open the airlock," I mumble through my hand.

He heads for the hallway, and I hurry after him. He keys both doors open.

Frigid wind tugs at me, but the chill fingers stinging my skin are a welcome alternative to the reek saturating the bridge. Sagging against the wall, I blink tears out of my eyes, and not from the cold. "Might want to wait a few minutes for the stench to air out."

Zhon nods and plants himself beside me. "Why are you being nice to me? You don't even know me."

I cross my arms and twist toward him a little. "I know you've been by yourself the last year. I know you've been scrounging to survive. And I know you deserve more."

"How can you?" His voice quivers, and his gaze flicks down the hall.

"Because I've been there." The words conjure up memories of my time at Alphanax after Fallah. Every day felt like a battle. A struggle to force each morsel of food to my mouth. But I did. And I'm not even sure why. Or what I expected to happen if I kept going. Definitely not for Fletcher to show up to take me away.

"When something terrible happens, it's easy to blame yourself. Fall into a dark place. Life turns gray. And suddenly you're just…surviving."

He perks up a little.

"I managed to make it out of that dark place. But I didn't do it without help." I take a deep breath and notice the air is fresher. I push away from the wall. "So, I want to help you."

Zhon's mouth presses into a thin line, but he can't keep his eyebrows from twitching up.

I'm as surprised as he is. At the same time, I know helping him is the right thing to do. For him. And for me.

I smile at him, and he smiles back. Then, I start down the hall, calling back over my shoulder: "Now, let's deal with these bodies so we can get out of here."

10

The ship's bridge is a tad bit bigger than the *Undertow's*. A wide, angled viewport stretches across the front of the space. An array of analog consoles beneath it curves around the chair Zhon strapped himself to while the ship was coming down. Four more chairs occupy the back wall of the bridge, two on either side of the door. Otherwise, the space is barren.

Except, of course, for the desiccated bodies of two long-dead Kaisin. Deep down, my distaste for the Kaisin as a whole deepens. At the same time, my dislike is contradicted by the two decent examples of the species I've run into so far—three, if I count Lorn before the Yuul corrupted him—which means other good Kaisin are out there. Somewhere.

Channeling the more negative emotions I have toward the Kaisin makes it easier to approach the first twisted body. The mummified face is frozen in what might have been a grimace at one point. Or maybe the skin pulled back as it dried, leaving the Kaisin's jagged teeth on full display. But other than being *exceedingly* dry, the body is intact. Mostly. Its limbs are twisted beneath a dusty jumpsuit, as if the body was shaken before coming to rest. Probably so.

I grab the front of the dead Kaisin's faded jumpsuit and pull it up from its resting place. The body crackles like thin ice breaking when I do, and dry skin flakes off, dusting the ground like macabre snow.

Instead of pulling more, I ease the body back down and glance at Zhon. "Is there anything we can use to wrap up the bodies? Sheets or something?"

"Yep. Got plenty of those." He exits the bridge. He's gone for a while, but eventually reappears with two thin yellowed sheets.

"Thanks." I grab the coverings and lay one out on the floor beside the first body. Once it's in place, I motion to the body. "Give me a hand with this."

Together, we work the first body onto the sheet before rolling it up and tying it closed at each end to form a makeshift bag. This prevents the body from leaving behind a trail of skin flakes as we carry it through the ship.

Thankfully, desiccated bodies are light as a Rhandannan feather, so I barely break a sweat lugging them outside. Though, the ship's now-brisk interior helps, making sure I'm cooled inside and out for the duration of the task.

Once that's done, Zhon retrieves some cleaning supplies, and we get to work sweeping up the flaked off remains where the bodies used to lie.

The entire time we're cleaning, his eyes keep flicking to the door. Obviously, he's eager to be anywhere but here. I'd felt the same way after Fallah's death, jumping at the chance to escape when Fletcher arrived to take me away. For Zhon, however, there won't be an escape. We're using this ship as our way off of this planet. So, somehow, he'll have to find a way to come to terms with what happened here and move past it. Which will be tough, but I'm more than happy to talk him through the process.

It takes a lot longer than I expect to finish. Once we do, very little evidence remains that anything terrible happened here.

I shuffle out of the bridge, now sweaty despite the cold, and slump into one of the chairs at the table. "I'm glad that's done with."

Zhon nods and drops into the chair beside me.

I expect to find his deep-seated pain on full display when I look at him, but he's calm. As if the act of removing the bodies, and clearing the bridge of their leftovers, provided a measure of solace. I hope it lasts.

"We can leave in the morning. After we get some sleep." I point at the other doorway I haven't been through yet. "I'm assuming the bedrooms are down there?"

Zhon nods again. "Wanna see?"

"Sure." I stand and follow him down the hall. The porthole windows on the left wall are no more than pitch black circles peering out into the dead of night. He bypasses the first and second doors on the right, then stops at the third.

"You can stay in here," he says.

"And the other two rooms?"

He glances back down the hallway. "They belonged to my former owners."

I nod in understanding, then glance back at the door in front of us. "And where are you going to sleep?"

He doesn't answer, but his eyes stray toward the back of the ship.

"Is there another room back there?"

Zhon's silence is a clear 'No'.

I stare at him, hoping he'll look up at me. "Why don't you stay up here?"

His mouth distorts in a distasteful grimace. "I don't want to stay in one of their rooms."

"I can." The idea doesn't thrill me, but if it means he won't have to sleep somewhere uncomfortable, I'm willing. It's only one night, after all.

Zhon shakes his head, and his eyes jump up to meet mine. "I'd rather sleep back in the engine room."

"Then stay with me," I offer.

He sputters. "What?"

"We can set up some blankets on the floor." When his shocked stare doesn't abate, I add, "It's just for a night. Until we can figure something else out."

Zhon gives a slow nod, then says, "Okay."

When he doesn't step toward the room, I go first. It's nothing special: a floor, four bare walls, and a low ceiling. And the room isn't much wider than the bed; there's barely enough space to walk between its edge and the outer wall. Looks like Zhon is going to have a pretty uncomfortable night, anyway. But most notably—

"No bathroom?"

"Oh, there's only one." He steps back from the door and points down the hall. "It's right around the corner."

"Is it working?"

"It will once we get the ship powered up."

"It's been out here a year. Will it power up?"

He gives a nervous chuckle and says, "I hope so."

I stifle a sigh and follow him out of the room.

The hall turns at a right angle, feeding into a cross hall that meets the one running along the far side of the ship. At the far end of the short corridor is a narrow door. Presumably the bathroom. And in the center of the hall, leading farther back into the ship, is a wide doorway.

Zhon taps the same code into the keypad beside the door, and it slides open. Beyond is a grated catwalk in front of a large silver ball. Behind the ball is a nest of wires, conduits, and other machinery I can't even begin to understand. In front of the ball is a narrow console with a screen and some buttons, which Zhon approaches.

There are a pair of chain link 'rooms' to either side of the catwalk. One is empty. The other is lined with shelves packed full of boxes, all secured by bright yellow straps.

"Storage," Zhon says when he catches me staring. "Supplies. Spare parts. And knick knacks."

"What about the other one?" I ask, already suspecting the answer.

"That's where I was gonna sleep."

"Did you sleep there before?"

He nods and turns back to the console; tapping out a sequence on the buttons brings the screen to life. A few taps later, and the machinery on the far side of the room begins to hum. A vibration sweeps through the ship, resonating up my calves like an electric current.

Then, the ship comes to life.

Extra lights bordering where the walls meet the ceiling spring to life, and fresh air wafts across my face. As well as some very welcome heat; I hadn't realized how much of the desert's chill had sunken all the way to my core.

"I'm gonna go get the outer doors closed. The code is 0-4-5-1, right?"

"Yeah," Zhon says without turning to look at me.

I slip into the hall, and cold air stings my cheeks and sucks the warmth from my lungs. Despite the cold, the ship is so much more alive than it was moments before. Bright lights border the top and bottom corners, where the walls meet the ceiling and floor. With every nook and cranny lit, the ship seems larger. And a lot more ragged than it did in the dim emergency lights. But it's a ship that works. A ship I can use to escape this planet.

At the outer door, I hunch over the keypad and prepare to type in the code. A square of light falls on the ground outside, highlighting the two wrapped bodies. Though they haven't been there long, sand is accumulating beside them. I can't imagine them lasting out in the elements. Not to mention what local wildlife might do to them. If there is any wildlife on this planet—we didn't see any on the way here, nor did Zhon mention any we might need to worry about.

Either way, I don't expect the bodies will last long enough for anyone to find them. Not that anyone will way out here in the desert. Not that these Kaisin deserve to be found.

Nodding a good riddance to the bodies, I tap in the code and shut them out in the dark.

I retreat to the hall and close the inner airlock door. Being closed inside the ship highlights how noisy it is. The rumble of circulating air is complemented by the rattle of loose ventilation grates throughout the interior, the hum of the reactor, and the buzz of the overhead lights.

This ship will take some getting used to.

Pacing back to the cross hall, I make a quick stop at the bathroom. The cramped cubby is stainless steel from top to bottom, with a toilet and shower to the right of the door, and a sink and mirror across from it. I stare, appalled at my appearance: my face is streaked with sweat, dirt, and sand; my hair is twisted into a sand-swept knot at the top of my head; and my white shirt is tinted desert beige.

Stepping up to the sink, I try the faucet.

It stutters and groans, belching air for a long time. Water finally sputters into the bowl of the sink, resolving into a steady stream. It looks clean enough and smells fine, so I splash some of it on my face, scrubbing with my bare hands until my skin is as free of dirt and grime as I can manage without a washcloth and soap. But the rest of me is still gross.

I walk back to the common area to retrieve my bag, then head back to the bathroom and take my second shower in as many days. The water temperature maxes out at tepid, but it's warm enough for me to spend the time scrubbing sand out of my hair and dirt and sweat from my skin until I'm clean. After, I don one of my fresher sets of clothes: a baggy shirt and pants with slippers instead of boots, since we'll be on a ship instead of trudging through the desert.

Fresher than before, I grab my bag and return to the engine room. Zhon isn't there.

I walk down the cross hall, to the quarters we surveyed earlier. He's inside, laying out a folded blanket in the narrow floor space between the bed and wall. A fresh set of sheets and blankets have also been put on the bed, which makes me glad I showered—I would have hated soiling them with my sweaty, dirt-caked clothes.

Zhon looks up at me and smiles. "I figured I'd get things ready."

"Thanks," I say.

He's happier than before. Or, at least, distracted from the pain his time on this ship caused. A step in the right direction.

I drop my bag in the hall—not like there's anyone else here to mess with it—and climb onto the bed. It's softer than I expect, a welcome respite after a day sweating in the sun and lugging around dead bodies. Flopping back on the pillow, I stare up at the ceiling with my mind blessedly blank.

"Aiko?" Zhon calls from his spot on the floor.

I stifle a sigh. "Yeah?"

"You never said where we're going."

His question shatters the peaceful tranquility from a moment before.

"I'll tell you in the morning," I say. "For now, let's get some sleep."

I very much doubt I'll be getting any sleep now. His question highlights the biggest unknown still facing me: where should I go next?

I don't know. But I have all night to think of an answer.

11

I stare, bleary-eyed, at the star chart. Countless, scattered whispers press against the edges of my mind, but they aren't the only thing I have to worry about anymore.

Sitting back and rubbing my eyes, I stare out of the bridge's viewscreen. The sun has started to rise, predawn light painting the desert with contrasting shadows. The dark edifice of stone looms to the right of the ship. And to the left, dunes hump toward a still-dark horizon.

The stars have disappeared, the blank sky teasing me for my lack of destination.

As I feared, I didn't manage much sleep last night. I spent most of it dwelling on what to do about my recent episodes. Which left me more tired than I was the night before and no closer to knowing what to do next.

"Aiko?"

I spin toward the sound of my name. Zhon is standing in the doorway to the bridge, eyes clouded with sleep.

"Morning," I say, forcing a smile.

"What are you doing up already?"

I can't tell him about the Yuul or the things I've been experiencing. But I can't remain silent either. Rather, I don't want to.

Because I don't want to have to answer any more of his questions right now. I don't have the energy.

"I'm planning our route."

"Oh, okay." He stifles a yawn with the back of his hand, then wanders back out into the ship's common area.

Swiveling back to the star chart, I try glaring at the scattered dots. Maybe I can scare them into giving me an answer?

That doesn't work either.

Of course it doesn't.

With a frustrated groan, I let my head slump against the chair's headrest and close my eyes.

"What's wrong?" Zhon calls from the other room.

I must have groaned louder than I thought.

"It's nothing," I reply.

Zhon doesn't answer for a full minute; his silence is punctuated by the clatter of him doing something out there. After a moment, his footsteps approach the bridge. "Then why do you sound so frustrated?"

A steaming cup appears beside my head, and a bitter earthy aroma shocks my nose.

"What's this?"

"Something my owners used to drink every morning," he says, wiggling the cup at me. "It isn't great, but it'll wake you up and give you a bit of energy."

"In that case—" I grab the cup from him and sip at the steaming liquid.

My lips pucker, and Zhon laughs. "See what I mean?"

"What is it?" I frown at the bitter, dark-brown liquid. Part of me wants to set the cup down, but the other relishes the slow warmth spreading through me from a single sip.

"It's called ko-fee?" When he takes a sip from his mug, his lips barely twitch. Either he's used to it or he's trying to show off. "So, gonna tell me what's wrong?"

Usually, this is where I'd deflect, but I have to start trusting Zhon if I'm going to travel with him. And he trusted me last night by telling me the whole truth about what happened on this ship.

I sigh. "Before coming out here, I thought I knew where I wanted to go."

"What about that 'terrible stuff' you told me about?" He waves a hand in the air. "Don't you have to go deal with it?"

"I mean, yes. But—" My throat tightens, as if resistant to the idea of divulging anything to Zhon. I swallow the lump sitting there and continue, "I'm not so sure now."

"What made you change your mind?"

"It's complicated."

He frowns. "Fine. Keep your secrets."

How do I answer without spilling everything? Or sounding absolutely insane?

"Listen, I—" I let out an exasperated sigh. "There's something wrong with me."

"Like, you're sick?"

"Maybe? I don't know."

Zhon sets his cup down on the console and crosses his arms. "How can you not know if you're sick?"

"I—It's—"

"Complicated?" he finishes for me. "Fine. Don't tell me. But sick people usually see doctors. Maybe start there."

Zhon snatches his cup off the console and takes an aggressive sip.

The comment jolts my brain like an electric shock. I'm not quite sure why the idea popped into my head—maybe it has something to do with the navy blue sky on the horizon, the same color as the deepest sunlight can reach into water—but there *is* one being in particular who might be able to explain what's happening to me.

Prime Orderly Orugh.

I've tried my best to avoid thinking about Thalijh these past months. I want to forget about how the Yuul hunted us down. How it chased us to the *Undertow*. And how it came within a hair's breadth of killing me, Fletcher, Gohk, and Rhuk.

Pushing those uncomfortable memories aside, I spin back to the star chart.

Zhon leans over my shoulder. "Made up your mind?"

"Yeah. Thanks for the idea."

Placing my cup on the lip of the console, I type in T-H-A-L-I-J-H and run a search. The chart freezes long enough for my heart to skip a beat. Then, the collage of glowing dots shifts to recenter on a star not too far from the one we're hurtling around.

"Where is that?" Zhon asks.

"Thalijh."

"And who are we going to meet?"

"Prime Orderly Orugh. A Thalijh scientist."

"And they'll be able to tell you if you're sick or not?"

I nod. "If anyone can."

"Then I guess we're headed to Thalijh." He nudges my shoulder with his elbow and motions for me to get up.

I vacate the chair.

Zhon sits and studies the controls.

"You, uh, know how to fly, right?"

"Yes." He frowns over his shoulder. Then, after a second, he adds, "In theory."

"That's not very reassuring."

"I watched my former owners fly the ship dozens of times. How hard can it be?"

"Still not reassuring."

"You're welcome to fly if you prefer." He plants his hands on the chair's arms, but doesn't push up. Instead, he stares at me, waiting for my answer. There hadn't been time for Fletcher to teach me how to pilot the *Undertow*, and I didn't think to ask Su'mik to show me. A decision I'm regretting right about now.

"I can't fly."

"Then don't complain," he snaps, reaching out for the controls. Before touching any of them, he glances up at me. "Last chance to get off."

"No. I'm fine."

"Then let's get outta here!"

Zhon starts pressing buttons and flipping switches on the control console in front of him.

A throaty grumble joins the subtle hum of the ship's reactor, pitching up into a piercing whine as the engines spool up.

"Hold on!"

I drop into one of the seats along the back wall of the bridge and buckle myself in as Zhon grabs the control yoke. The ship shudders when he works the controls, and the whine of the engines shifts to a deafening growl. Then, the ship moves. It actually moves!

At first, I'm elated when the ship rises from the ground, wavering a bit as Zhon struggles with the joystick centered in front of him. Until he shoves the throttle forward, and I'm smashed into my seat. Jagged stone whizzes by on our right, too close for comfort, then we're rocketing over the dunes.

Zhon pulls back on the joystick, and the sand slides out of view, replaced by the deep blue sky tinged with a hint of orange. A thick curtain of flames washes the view away as the ship punches through the atmosphere. The chair beneath me rattles and shakes like the bolts holding it to the floor are ready to shear. And the distinct tang of something burning permeates the bridge.

"Is that normal?" I shout at Zhon.

He sniffs the air, then wrinkles his nose. "I don't think so. We can check it once we're on our way."

I hold tight to the arms of my chair, until the flames disappear. When they do, the sky is dark and speckled with stars. And the ship is eerily still.

Zhon taps a few buttons next to the star chart on his left, then presses a final red button next to the control yoke before releasing it. "The autopilot is set. Now, let's check out this burning smell."

Together, we head into the common area.

Thick, black smoke seeps between two of the floor panels, clouding the air.

Coughing, I raise the collar of my shirt over my nose. "What's on fire?"

"I'm not sure," Zhon says, then beelines for the hallway on our right. A few seconds later, he reappears with a satchel. Dropping it on the ground, he pulls out a tool and begins loosening the screws holding the floor panel in place. Once all four screws are free, he sets the tool aside and looks up at me. "Help me with this."

He pries the floor panel up enough for me to slip my fingers beneath it, then joins me. When he heave it up, thick smoke billows free. Orange flickers somewhere below us, accompanied by heat.

I stifle a cough, turning away to gasp fresh air.

Zhon disappears somewhere on the other side of the smoke, popping back up a second later, a bright red cylinder in one hand. He waves his free hand to clear some of the smoke, revealing the tongues of red flame in the crawlspace below licking at some fluffy white stuff covering the floor.

Pointing the red cylinder, he presses a button on the side and sends a stream of white liquid splashing over the fire. It sputters and goes out.

I let out a sigh of relief, which dissipates when I spot the white liquid start to absorb into the fluff. Some of the drifting smoke twists toward the same spot, like it's being sucked in. Or…out.

My heart jumps when I realize what's going on. "We're venting atmosphere."

Zhon's eyes jump to me. "Uh-oh."

"Is there a patch kit?" I ask.

He grimaces. "There are patch plates. But we'll have to go outside to install them. I've done it before on the ground, but I don't know how to do it while we're in transit."

"I can. Are there any suits?"

"Yeah," he stands and rushes down the hall leading to the airlock. I follow him to the narrow door across from it. He keys it open to reveal a long room with four suits inside. They look intact, despite being abandoned in the desert for a year.

Swatting away any doubt about the integrity of the suits, I snatch the nearest one off the wall and glance over my shoulder at Zhon. "Get me those patch kits."

He rushes down the hall as I step into the suit.

It's a far cry from the armored rig I utilized while with Fletcher—bulky, but flexible, and constructed from a single piece, accessible by a seal from neck to groin. The relative flimsiness of this suit is worrying considering this will be the first time I've ever ventured out into the vacuum of space. But when I seal the front, drop the helmet over my head, and twist it in place, the little hud glowing at the bottom of the helmet's visor reads all green—a better seal than the ship, apparently.

I shuffle into the hall and key the airlock open. The window in the outer door offers a saucer-sized view of the star-speckled void. Adrenaline surges through me, and I put my hand against the wall to steady myself, locking my knees to keep them from folding under me.

Zhon's steps echo down the hall, then he appears, lugging a large metal panel and a handheld tool. "Here's a plate and a hand welder. You know what to do?"

I don't. Before I can say as much, he continues.

"Just slap the plate in place and use the welder to seal it to the hull. That should stop the leak."

Swallowing a thick wad of saliva lingering at the back of my throat, I take the plate and welder from him. "O-okay."

"Good luck," he says, then keys the airlock shut.

While I wait for the air to drain, I set the metal plate and welder against the airlock wall and study the suit's kit. The panel on my left arm has a few buttons: one for the suit's headlamp; another for the radio; a third for…magnetic boots? I test the button, and my feet snap to the metal floor plate.

Those will come in handy.

There's also a small device clipped to the suit's waist; a length of wire, tipped with a hook, hangs from a hole in its side. Two buttons adorn the top of the device. One lets the wire out, while the other drags it back in. A tether, which means I won't have to worry about losing my grip and spinning off into the void.

A glimmer of confidence starts chipping away at the apprehension twisting my insides. Maybe this won't be as bad as I thought…

The speaker in my helmet crackles, and Zhon's voice fills my helmet.

"Hey. You there?"

I press the radio button on my wrist. "Can you hear me?"

"Loud and clear," he replies. "Head out whenever you're ready."

I turn to the outer door and key in the code. The door slides open without a sound, but the silence in my helmet is drowned out by my own breathing and the pulse pounding in my ears.

Staring out into the endless void of space is a little bit different than hovering at the edge of a five mile drop into dark water. While the unknown depths filled me with fear, space invokes a more primal form of dread. Despite the fact I'm magnetized to the airlock floor, my insides rebel at the sight before me, churning, rearranging themselves. I clench my teeth tight, swallowing bitter bile and a lump that's my stomach trying to escape from the foolishness I'm about to attempt.

I clamp my free hand on the door frame and poke my head out to search the hull for a spot to anchor myself. A railing is affixed to the hull beside the door, running down along the curve of the ship and out of sight.

"Here we go," I mutter to myself, grabbing the hook at my waist and clipping it to the railing. A solid yank proves it's secure. Taking a deep breath, I deactivate my boots and pull myself out of the airlock.

I expect the ship's gravity to fling me into space, but weightlessness grips me once I'm out of the airlock. My stomach churns in response to the strange sensation. Gritting my teeth, I advance along the rail, toward the bottom apex of the hull's curve. When I'm nearly there, the rail goes from intact to crushed where it was pinched between the hull and solid rock. And another railway running longways is also crushed.

Reactivating my magnetic boots, I pull my legs under me and press them to the hull, making sure they're stuck to the metal before standing. Slowly. Letting out tether from my spool as I rise.

I try to keep my eyes glued to the hull, searching for the breach, but I can't help flicking my gaze up. A huge mistake.

Space dominates my entire field of view, the darkness between stars closer than ever. I stare into the void. Mesmerized. Transfixed. Terrified. How was this ever a good idea?

After I-don't-know-how-long, Zhon's voice hisses in my ear.

"Aiko? Are you okay? You stopped moving."

"I'm fine," I sputter back, dragging my eyes down to the hull and sucking in a deep breath. I've got to keep moving.

Forcing one foot in front of the other, I continue to the bottom of the hull's curve, then turn toward the front of the ship. Ahead, air vapor puffs out of a cracked dent in the underside of the hull.

"I can see the leak!"

"Great!" Zhon replies. "Now, get it sealed!"

I lug the panel to the break in the hull. Once there, I press the panel over the breach and hold it in place. With my other hand, I grab the welder. Each squeeze of the trigger produces a brilliant flash, and my visor dims in response. I fall into a rhythm of bend, weld, shift. Bend. Weld. Shift. By the time I'm done securing the plate in place, I'm covered in sweat. The beads cling to my skin instead of dripping down like I'm used to.

"Done," I say. "Is the seal good?"

"Checking." Zhon pauses. "It's good. Come back inside."

More than happy to oblige, I walk back to the railing, then turn off my boots and float into the airlock, my heart pounding the whole way. The roar of blood rushing in my ears drowns out everything else until the airlock doors close and fresh air fills the space around me.

Zhon's face appears framed in the porthole window of the inner door a second before it opens. He grins at me. "You did it!"

I pull off my helmet and take a breath of cool, fresh air—as fresh as recycled ship air can be. "Of course I did."

He takes the helmet from me and backpedals into the narrow room across the hall, still grinning like a fool.

I follow him, ready to get out of this stifling suit. "Anything else crop up while I was outside?"

"No," he says. "But I'll give the ship a once over while we're underway. I'm no expert, but my owners made sure I had a grasp on basic maintenance so they didn't have to worry about it. I also set up an alarm, so we'll know if the pressure drops again."

"Fantastic." I unfasten the suit's seal and let it slip down to pool around my ankles. Stepping out of it, I bend to pick it up off the floor. Zhon snatches the suit from beneath my grasp and hefts it up onto its storage hook against the wall.

He shoots me another smile before squeezing past. Pausing in the doorway, he looks back and says, "I'm going to go double check our course, then reseat the floor panel. Maybe after that, we can have a bite to eat?"

I nod. "Sounds good."

Once he's gone, I sag against the wall and slide down to the floor; my legs are too rubbery to hold me upright any longer.

Out of all the things I've done since leaving Fletcher, Ghok, and Rhuk behind, that was the scariest by leaps and bounds. Even scarier than facing off against the Yuul and far ahead of diving into pitch black, five-mile-deep water. And not something I want to have to do ever again.

Luckily, Thalijh is only a few days away. When we get there, another jaunt out into the vacuum of space will be the least of my worries.

12

Laying eyes on Thalijh again sends a shot of adrenaline surging through me. It's a beautiful planet: the thin sliver of atmosphere tracing the sphere's curve glimmers in the distant sun's light, containing the myriad banks of fluffy white clouds drifting across its face. Yet, there are too many bad memories attached to the planet to calm the apprehension sitting like a stone in my belly.

As we enter orbit, a conical ship rises from below, a single trail of light spiraling from its bulbous base to its sharp tip. Between, the ship's iridescent surface reflects the sun's rays in a rainbow of colors.

The ship draws closer, dwarfing ours, settling into an orbit ahead and below.

A chirp issues from the console on Zhon's right, and one of the buttons begins to blink.

"We're being hailed," he says.

"That's new," I mumble to myself. Last time, no ship met the *Undertow* in orbit. Then again, last time, the Yuul hadn't rampaged through one of their sunken facilities.

When Zhon doesn't move to answer the call, I lean over his shoulder and tap the insistent button.

"Identify yourself," a synthetic voice with a rumbling, gurgling undertone commands. A Thalijh.

Zhon looks up at me.

"Hi! This is the… Uh—" I stop short, realizing I never asked Zhon the ship's name. Glancing at him, I raise my eyebrows in question.

"*Myol*," he whispers.

"This is the *Myol*. Requesting permission to land."

"For what purpose?"

"I'm here to see Prime Orderly Orugh," I reply. "My name is Aiko. We've worked together before."

"Stand by," the Thalijh says, then the static cuts.

"You think they'll let us land?" Zhon asks.

"I *know* they will," I answer.

He cocks his head to the side. "You're that important?"

I give him a wry smile. "Not exactly. The Thalijh are thorough beings. And let's just say our last interaction will have left Orugh with questions only *I* can answer. So, I expect we'll be ushered down sooner rather than later."

My smug confidence evaporates as the minutes tick past an hour.

Zhon fidgets between glances in my direction, but keeps whatever he's thinking to himself. Probably because my deep frown and cinched brow aren't too inviting. Nor is my aggressive pacing back and forth across the back of the bridge. It isn't much of a pace—three steps in one direction, then in three the other—but it's an outlet while we wait. But for how much longer?

By the time the intercom crackles again, another full hour later, I'm ready to burst.

"*Myol*, your request is granted. Please follow our trajectory to your landing coordinates."

110

The conical ship alters course, dropping toward the planet and veering off to the left.

Zhon takes hold of the control yoke and adjusts our course to follow. We stick close to the Thalijh ship's tail, until fire obscures the viewscreen. This time, no burning odor fills the air. And when the fire dissipates, we're still right behind our escort.

The Thalijh ship drops almost to the surface of the water, speeding close enough above the waves to leave an interrupting wake. Zhon keeps us higher. I don't mind, since I doubt the ship is seaworthy like the *Undertow*.

I scan the horizon for any hint of our destination and spot a structure in the distance. It's mostly coral, with a massive cylinder jutting out of the rough, pockmarked material. The cylinder is flat on top, with a bright red circle painted on its surface. Blinking lights are spaced at even intervals around its outer edge.

The Thalijh ship circles the cylinder, and our intercom crackles: "*Myol*, please set down here."

Zhon slows the ship to a near hover and angles the nose for the landing pad. The ship wiggles as the landing struts extend. And it continues to shimmy in the heavy winds whipping over the ocean as we ease down.

I thought, at least.

We hit the deck *hard*, and the ship bounces once before sliding along the pad. I grip the arms of my chair as the edge creeps closer. Heavy wind rocks the ship and sprays the viewscreen with a fine mist, obscuring our view.

"Zhon!" I shout.

"I know!" He growls, gripping the control yoke so hard his knucklebones show through his already white skin. Then, he yanks back on the throttle.

The ship slams down on the pad.

The deep breath I suck in does nothing to calm my racing heart. "Great job."

Zhon's hands remain locked on the controls. The muscles in his jaw bulge, and he gives a halting nod.

"Let's go," I say, unbuckling my harness and standing.

Before I can take a single step, the ship shudders. Through the misted viewscreen, the edges of the landing pad rise up to swallow us. The way my stomach jumps into my throat tells me we're descending.

The smooth walls give way to rough coral, then the shaft transitions to glass, granting an unsettling view of pitch black water. We pass bands of silvery metal at even intervals, so I count, making it all the way to thirty before I notice an ethereal glow emanating from below.

Stepping to Zhon's shoulder, I crane my neck to glimpse what lies in the depths.

A mountain of coral fades out of the darkness, flaring out in every direction. It's lit by stationary bulbs of soft blue light as brilliant as the sun on the ocean's surface above. As we descend even farther, I can pick out schools of fish weaving in and out of huge openings in the porous coral. And larger, slower moving, lifeforms with long bodies and huge fins.

I shudder when a giant snake-like creature many times larger than the *Myol* drifts past. Its translucent skin glows purple with veins of light pink trailing along its length. Then, a deep, rumbling moan vibrates the ship's deck plates. I'm glad we didn't have to come all the way down here without the protection of the tube. And even more relieved when the tube plunges back into solid coral.

At the same time, I'm starting to wonder when we're going to reach wherever it is we're going.

Thankfully, the descent only lasts about a minute or two more before the landing pad begins to slow and the shaft of coral wrapped around us widens into a cavernous room. The pad comes to rest on a cement floor a few dozen feet later, sending a solid thud vibrating up through the soles of my boots. Knowing we'd reach Thalijh today, I changed out of the more casual attire I adopted during our transit.

"Okay. *Now* let's go," I say.

Zhon jumps out of the pilot's seat and follows me to the air-lock. I key open the inner door, then the outer. Humid air washes over me, permeated by a heavy brackish scent. Not quite unpleasant, but different enough to make me aware of every breath and the salty tang on my tongue.

I hover at the doorway, waiting for a ramp to extend. Nothing happens.

Zhon reaches past me and presses another button at the bottom of the keypad. A narrow span of metal extends from a slot under the door, telescoping a dozen feet outward before dropping to the floor below.

I offer a silent nod of thanks before walking down the ramp to the concrete landing pad. On either side of the pad are thick metal beams stretching back up the shaft, disappearing in the darkness above. Pacing toward a walkway stretching from the pad to a wide door in the wall, I realize we're still elevated about a dozen feet off of the rough coral floor below. The pad is held aloft by circular collars wrapped around the metal beams. Probably the drive mechanisms that move the pad up and down the shaft.

The door at the edge of the room hisses open, drawing my attention to a mass of tentacles. I recognize the Thalijh's mottled gray and white speckled skin and half-lidded eyes.

I wave. "Prime Orderly Orugh!"

Orugh's tentacles squish and pop along the smooth metal walkway as it approaches.

"Welcome back to Thalijh. I am pleased you are here."

Despite the robotic monotone of Orugh's translated voice, I swear I detect a measure of warmth, or excitement, in the words. Is it because the Thalijh has questions about the Yuul?

I have questions of my own.

"Thank you for taking the time to meet with me. There's something we need to discuss."

"There is," Orugh replies without hesitation, then begins wriggling back along the walkway, beckoning to us with a tentacle. "Please. This way."

Apprehension twists my insides as I follow Orugh through the door and down a long hallway, curving left and right in no particular pattern. The walls and ceiling are rough coral, while the floor is a transparent, springy material with a familiar substance beneath. Its soft blue glow fills the corridor, throwing our shadows against the ceiling.

Orugh's dark, wriggling silhouette conjures up memories of the Yuul reaching out to me in my mind, demanding subjugation.

Not all that different from the things I've been experiencing lately. The whole reason I came to Thalijh.

After a hundred paces, the corridor spits us out into a large room with a vaulted coral ceiling. Here, the floor is sunken about a foot and flooded with water. Light beams down from glass bubbles fitted into the pockmarked structure of the coral overhead.

Orugh slips into the water with a burble its synthetic voice doesn't translate. The Thalijh submerges for a moment, then the top of its head resurfaces. Droopy eyes swivel toward me. "Over here."

Tepid water fills my boots and soaks my pants up to the knee as I wade after the Thalijh. I've suffered through worse, but I'd prefer not to be in the water too long—salt water is hell on clothes and skin. I'd know.

To take my mind off of my soaked legs, I study the room. It's empty except for a long counter off to our right, remarkably out of place in a Thalijh habitat. On one end of the counter is an array of equipment I'm unfamiliar with. Metal scaffolding suspends an array of cabinets above. At the other is a large, seamless, transparent enclosure too thick to be glass. Inside the enclosure is a collection of glass containers—some are tall and thin, others are cone-shaped with a narrow neck, and quite a few are circular with a shallow lip. A lot of the taller containers hold different colored liquids. But the circular glass containers are half-filled with some solid, yellowish material speckled with black dots.

Fletcher and Gohk both mentioned the Thalijh are scientists, so this has to be Orugh's research. And if the black speckles are what I think they are...

"That is an interesting specimen," Orugh says, lifting out of the water and pointing a tentacle at the nearest shallow circular dish. "I am sure you are familiar with it."

The hairs at the nape of my neck stand on end looking down at the cultivated darkness. How much more of it has Orugh created through experimentation? I scan the room, but find only shallow water.

"I am well aware of how dangerous the organism is." Orugh taps the enclosure, then fixes me with a droopy-eyed stare. "I have many questions. I surmise you have answers."

"I do, but—" I glance at Zhon, then back to Orugh.

The Thalijh stares at me. "He doesn't know?"

Zhon frowns. "Know what?"

"No," I cut in before Orugh can answer. I'd prefer to tell Zhon the entire truth myself and hope he takes it well. "Remember when I told you something is out there? It's a little more—"

"Let me guess: complicated." He crosses his arms and a frown creases his lips.

"Well, yeah." A weight settles in my stomach at the prospect of telling Orugh about the Yuul. I have no choice if I want the Thalijh's help. So, taking a deep breath, I start at the beginning.

"When Fletcher adopted me, he told me I was human. I had no idea what that was. Neither did he. But his mentor had theories and disappeared in pursuit of those theories. All he left behind was a trail to a sunken ship at the bottom of an alien ocean. A human ship.

"They came to this part of the galaxy a thousand years ago. And on their way, they discovered something floating through space." I point at the shallow container speckled with dots of Yuul on the countertop. "The humans experimented on it. Angered it. So it retaliated. They were forced to abandon ship, and the captain crashed the ship to keep it from getting away."

"Do you know the location of this planet?" Orugh asks. "A vessel of truly alien origin would be of extreme interest."

"I don't."

Orugh lets out a bubbling sigh. "Pity."

"I wouldn't suggest going there, anyway. We found Fletcher's mentor *alive*. Kept alive all these years by the Yuul."

"The Yuul?" Orugh asks.

"That's what I call the organism. The Quiloh word for shadow."

Orugh bobs up and down in what I assume is a nod.

"During our escape, I was injured. And Fletcher brought me here."

"I remember."

"What you don't know is that some of the organism infected me. It tried invading my mind, taking over, but I made a truce with it. And through this truce, it showed me its history. How it manipulated species after species across time, bending them to its will so it could survive."

Orugh's eyes snap wide open. "Fascinating."

"There's more," I say before the Thalijh can start asking questions. "The organism escaped the human colony ship with the humans. And over time it changed them into the Kaisin. Humans, like me, are just an unintended byproduct of their manipulation. A secret they've been trying their best to keep.

"Which is why Thalijh was attacked. Because some of it followed me here."

"I see," Orugh says, but otherwise doesn't react to the revelation.

"Wait a second. Are you saying that stuff is inside me?"

When I look at Zhon, he's staring at the black dots contained within the enclosure. His eyes jump to mine, searching for more than a simple 'yes' or 'no' answer.

I shake my head. "Not anymore."

Orugh stirs, rising halfway out of the water. "Explain, please."

"I can destroy remnants of it by touching infected beings," I say to Orugh, then look at Zhon. "I got rid of yours shortly after we met."

"Why didn't you tell me?"

The hurt in his eyes hits harder than I expect. The truth is, I didn't trust him when I removed the Yuul from him. But saying that would only deepen the hurt he feels. I don't want to do that, so I say, "Because it was my burden to bear."

My answer doesn't lessen the betrayed cinch of his eyebrows.

"Curious," Orugh says, either oblivious to, or willfully ignoring, the sudden tension between Zhon and I. From what I know of the Thalijh, it's probably equal parts former and latter. "How are you able to do this?"

Before, I left out any mention of Iali and barely touched on my internal battle with the darkness. Those parts of the story weren't relevant, and I still don't want to share them. "I just can."

The Thalijh lets out a burble that's translated as a synthetic "Hmmm" laced with a hint of skepticism. Instead of pushing for details, he asks, "Would you be willing to perform a demonstration?"

"As long as you're willing to help me with something."

Orugh's lids droop. "Oh?"

"Yeah. Um—" What I'm about to say sounds stupid. Crazy, even. But I need to figure out what's happening to me. And why. "I've been seeing things. Hearing things."

"What kinds of things?"

"Darkness. Almost like the Yuul. And sometimes, a loud roar accompanies it. Muffled, like a voice trying to speak, but I can't make out the words."

"Has this ever happened before?"

The closest thing I'd compare the visions to are when Iali infected me. At first, its pressure was a constant against the edges of my mind as it probed for a way inside. There's no such pressure this time. No presence to suggest the Yuul have anything to do with these visions.

I shake my head. "No."

"And when did it start?"

I think back to the first vision I had while walking up the *Ku'lu*'s ramp. Right after I'd cleared another whisper from the edge of my mind. "A few weeks ago."

"What were you doing?"

"I'd just finished destroying more of the organism."

"Interesting." Orugh lifts himself to study the sample that had been pointed out. "I suppose it's possible the organism is having an effect on you."

"No. It isn't that."

Orugh swivels back to me. "How can you be so sure?"

"I just know, okay?"

Orugh stares at me for a moment and makes a sound that could be interpreted for skepticism in any language, then returns

119

his attention to the glass enclosure containing the Yuul. "The specimen I extracted from the sample your friend provided during your last visit here has proved quite unique. The organism is simple, elegant, yet capable of surprising complexity. Furthermore, it is more than a common parasite.

"From my analysis, there is evidence of symbiosis between the specimen and your Kaisin friend's blood and tissue. There are also signs of genetic manipulation—specific genes have been activated, while others have been excised. Fragments of the removed DNA has been found inside the specimen, suggesting its involvement.

"And now, your story suggests even more organizational complexity, possibly intelligence."

"Definitely intelligence," I say.

"All the more reason to consider it may be impacting you in some way." Orugh waves a tentacle at me. "I require additional data before I can draw a concrete conclusion."

"Meaning?"

Orugh dips down into the water—maybe to rehydrate, maybe to think—and stays there a while.

The Thalijh bobs back up and says, "I need fresh samples of blood and tissue to analyze them for anomalies.

We have to start somewhere, I guess. I nod. "Okay."

"Fantastic!" The Thalijh bounces up and down, creating ripples on the water's surface. "I'll collect the samples, then get started on analysis immediately."

13

"That is all for now," Orugh says after draining a dozen vials of blood from my arm, scraping tissue from the inside of my cheek, and poking me with needles in more than one spot.

Climbing off of the examination table the Thalijh called up out of the floor, I lower my now-bare feet into the water, soaking the legs of the uncomfortably familiar jumpsuit Orugh insisted I change into for the sample collection. Changing seemed like a little much at first—not so now, considering the amount he collected and how long the process took. I wade across to where my clothes are perched at the very end of the long counter. My soggy boots are beside my clothes, still dripping.

"What now?" I ask.

"Feel free to retire to your ship for now. Or, if you prefer, I can show you to one of my guest rooms."

I blink. "One of *your* guest rooms?"

"Yes. This is my personal domicile and laboratory," Orugh replies.

"Do any other Thalijh know about this?"

"I thought it best to keep this discovery from the greater scientific community. For now."

I let out a sigh of relief. "Thank you."

Orugh waves a tentacle at me. "The danger posed by the organism is clear, so additional caution is warranted. The samples are sealed in an airtight, watertight partition, and this entire habitat is isolated from Thalijh's oceans. Additionally, the water inside is recirculated, filtered, sanitized, and rebalanced every hour to ensure no contamination occurs regardless of the testing and experimentation performed here."

"Which means there's no chance of it getting out," I say, relieved.

"There's always a chance if proper protocols and procedures aren't observed," Orugh retorts, even the synthetic translation sounds indignant. "Now, would you prefer to return to your ship or to a guest room?"

I look at Zhon, and he shrugs.

Thinking of my last time staying in a Thalijh guest room brings up more than a few unsavory memories. "I think we'll return to the ship."

"Very well. I will contact you when I have progress worth reporting."

Gathering my clothes and boots, I wade back to the hallway. Zhon follows, one step behind. He's quiet, but it's the kind of quiet that's laden with thought. I know questions are stewing beneath the silence.

I get my first good look at the *Myol* when we enter the landing bay. It's shaped almost like an elongated wedge, with a curved underbelly and a more angular upper hull. The sides of the ship are flat and tilted inward, narrowing to the bridge's viewscreen at the front and flaring out at the rear. The whole thing is balanced on three chunky landing struts folded out of three openings in the hull.

A closer look betrays the ship's age. Fresh scrapes scar the peeling paint and pockmarked metal of its belly, but older dents suggest previous unexpected run-ins with hard surfaces. Still, it's in one piece, which speaks to the little ship's toughness. And it is little, not even half the size of the *Ku'lu* or a third of the size of the *Undertow*.

It's a ship. So, it'll do. For now, at least.

"I'm going to change into something dry." I start up the ramp.

Zhon doesn't respond, but his boots tap the metal in my wake. When I turn right to head to my room, he turns left, toward the ship's common area.

I'm in the middle room now, after spending the better part of a day cleaning it out during our trip to Thalijh. Aside from a cluttered collection of personal effects, and a little bit of mustiness, it wasn't a bad job. We disposed of the unwanted items by blowing them out the airlock. Fun to watch, at least. And there were enough cleaning supplies on board to sanitize every surface.

A slight antiseptic aroma still tinges the air when I enter the room. I don't mind. I like knowing my quarters are clean. Setting my clothes on the floor, and my soggy boots next to them, I rummage inside my pack for the outfit I'd taken to wearing aboard the *Myol*—a baggy shirt, pants, and slippers.

Once changed, I walk to the common area.

Zhon is sitting at the table, staring at an empty spot near its center, those questions near a boil now judging by his deepening frown. I consider joining him, but my stomach grumbles, redirecting me to the back of the room where I slide open the cabinet doors hiding a modest kitchen. It's little more than a narrow, shallow counter with enough space for a small sink and a contraption used to heat up food packets called a microwave oven.

I glance over my shoulder at Zhon. "You hungry?"

His gaze flicks to me. "No."

Turning back to the kitchen, I open the drawer under the microwave and pull out a dinner ration. I can't read the text on the package, so I don't know what it is, but I've tried enough of these dehydrated meals to know which ones I like and which I don't. My favorite is some kind of meat dish with a sweet and sour sauce.

I rip the foil top off the container, add water up to a pre-marked line, then pop it in the microwave. In a little over a minute, I have some piping hot, passably delicious dinner.

When I sit across from Zhon, he looks at the steam rising from my food, then at me.

"Sure you aren't hungry?" I raise my eyebrows at him and tilt the container his way.

"I said I'm not."

I ignore his prickly answer and return my focus to my meal, mouth watering as I scoop up a juicy morsel of meat.

"So, that stuff was hanging out inside of me this whole time?" he says.

Setting down my spoon, I clasp my hands together and stare at him. "Yeah."

Zhon frowns. "And you didn't tell me.

"I don't tell *anyone*."

"Don't you think they deserve to know?"

"Trust me, it's better if they don't."

His frown dips into a scowl, intensifying his stare. "And who are *you* to decide?"

"The only one in the galaxy with the ability to destroy it with just a touch."

He glares at me.

I cross my arms and lean back in my chair. "Right now, I'm fighting it alone. What do you think happens if word gets out?"

"More people will fight it."

"It'll stop hiding. And what happens then?" I suppress a shudder as memories of what Iali told me about its past float to the surface. Jumping from one species to the next, millennia of manipulation from the shadows. That's how it survived. What will the Yuul do once its anonymity is gone? Will it behave more like the ichor-coated Kaisin who chased us all the way to Thalijh. "Everyone will be in danger."

"Why not let the Thalijh deal with the organism? It shouldn't be your responsibility."

I smile. "Maybe not, but not too long ago, someone I consider a friend offered some words of wisdom that changed my outlook. On a lot of things." My smile widens as Rhuk's advice floats to the surface. "Think about what you can do."

Zhon's brow furrows. "Which means what, exactly?"

"For me, it means doing what I can against the Yuul. At first, I fought it to protect my friends. Then, I realized my ability to detect it and destroy it came with a greater responsibility I couldn't ignore."

He considers my words for a moment. "Have you thought about doing something else? *Anything* else?"

"Knowing what I know?" I shake my head.

What I don't say—what I *can't* say—is that ignoring the Yuul would be a disservice to Fallah's memory and disrespectful toward Iali's sacrifice. Doing what I can, striving for more than existing in Fletcher's shadow, means keeping their memory alive.

Out of habit, my hand dips into my pocket, but Fallah's pendant isn't there. It's in my room, in the pocket of the pants I wore earlier today before Orugh insisted on stuffing me into that awful jumpsuit.

He scoffs. "Wow."

"What?"

"That's actually kinda sad."

"*What?*"

"Yeah. Even though we left Ristan, it sounds to me like you're still trapped. Are you even happy spending your life hunting this stuff down?"

The question catches me off guard. I hadn't thought about it. There hadn't been time to think about it. I mean, I enjoyed being around Su'mik and his crew between hunting whispers. But was I really happy? Am I now?

I'd like to insist I am, but…

"I don't know."

The truth is almost painful to utter aloud, and a betrayal of the freedom I fought so hard for. The freedom Fallah and I wanted. Even so, this is still the path I chose for myself. A purpose so much bigger than myself. That's enough, right? It has to be.

"What I'm doing is important," I add, "and not just because of the Yuul.

"Don't get me wrong, the Yuul is dangerous. You haven't seen what it can do. How much havoc a small amount of it can cause.

126

But also—" I stop short, unable to bring myself to share what happened to Fallah. Or tell him about my brief time with Iali. And what they meant—*mean*—to me. Getting too close to those memories is like tearing open a half-healed wound.

Just thinking about the possibility of abandoning the freedom Fallah and I wanted makes it sting all the more. How could I let him push me to consider walking away after everything I've been through? And everything I've sacrificed?

"But what?" he presses.

"I don't want to talk about it." I hunker over my food, but my appetite is as absent as the steam no longer rising from it.

"Please."

When I look up, his expression is softer. But his stare is as steady as ever.

"I made a promise," I squeeze past the sudden lump in my throat. "That I'd be free. A promise I intend to keep. No matter what."

After a moment, he mumbles, "You don't seem very free."

I glare at him.

He looks away.

"I chose this path," I snap. "Besides, what is freedom without purpose? You're just living. Surviving. Like the Yuul were before Humans found it, floating aimlessly through space until something happens to you."

He frowns. "That's not true."

"Then why didn't you leave Ristan before I arrived? You had a working ship the entire time, but you just decided to stay. Why else other than you were afraid to do anything?" I stand and storm away from the table.

"Aiko, wait!"

I ignore him and don't stop moving until I'm in my room and the door is shut tight behind me. Sagging against it, I slide to the floor and pull my knees up to my chest.

My cheeks burn with heat, and I blink back tears.

I thought Zhon would be able to understand. That I'd met someone, besides Rhuk, who could accept the truth. I was wrong.

Tears well up again, blurring my vision.

Why do I care so much? Why does his opinion matter? It shouldn't. Yet, somehow, it does. Settling in my chest like a lead weight.

I take a deep breath, wipe my eyes with my sleeve, and heave myself off the floor to flop on the bed. As soon as I sink into the cocoon of blankets and sheets, some of the heaviness dissipates. I channel the momentary respite from sadness to anger.

No matter what Zhon thinks, no matter how much it may sting, I'm not altering my path. I'm still going to hunt every last bit of it down once I fix whatever is wrong with me. And Zhon is going to take me. Even if I have to drag him along kicking and screaming. He owes me that much, at least, for getting him off of Ristan.

Once I'm done dealing with the Yuul, he can drop me off somewhere and go chasing after his version of freedom. But an aimless trek across the stars won't bring him any more peace than he had on Ristan. Running away won't erase what he did. Just like collapsing in on myself didn't lessen the pain of losing Fallah.

The best thing to do, the only thing to do, is keep moving forward. No matter what.

14

I hoped Orugh would have something to report within a matter of hours. Hope faded as one restless night stretched to two, then three.

On the fourth day, I wake up irritated. At how long Orugh is taking. At how there isn't anything to do but sit, wait, and think. And at Zhon. Since our little run-in the other day, he's been avoiding me—don't think we've spent more than a few minutes in the same room.

At some point, I expect him to at least try to apologize for what he said. Has an apology even crossed his mind?

Heaving myself upright, I rake my hair out of my face, then rub the sleep out of my eyes.

I'm not excited about another day of waiting, but I can't stay in bed all day. I mean, I could, but that won't help my mood.

Swinging my legs over the side of the bed, I step into my slippers and walk to the door.

The ship is silent without the reactor running, and my steps are deafening in the cramped space. They don't get much softer as I pace down the hall to the common area.

I slide open the cabinets covering the kitchen area and go about making myself a cup of ko-fee, which is as simple as heating up a cup of water in the microwave, then stirring in a packet of

129

brown little granules. By the time I'm done stirring, the air is filled with a pungent aroma that's more enjoyable than the ko-fee's actual flavor. But it's warm and provides a stimulating kick; a welcome pick-me-up after a poor night's sleep.

Sitting at the table, I sip the scalding liquid. Too soon. Searing pain shoots across my lips and tongue. I spit the mouthful of ko-fee out with a pained yelp, set the cup down, and try my hand at practicing patience. Glaring at the cup doesn't make its contents cool any quicker.

Footsteps echo down the hall, and I turn to stare at Zhon when he enters the room.

He stares back. "Morning."

That's more than he's said to me in the last few days combined. And it's good to hear his voice. *Any* voice, really. "Hi."

His lips stretch in a half-grimace half-smile as he shuffles to the kitchen.

I turn back to my steaming cup and listen to the familiar sounds of him preparing one for himself—drawers opening and closing, the clink of a cup on the counter, poured water, the hum and beep of the microwave, the tearing open of the ko-fee packet, and the musical ring of a spoon stirring the granules until they're dissolved.

When Zhon is finished, he walks into view and sits at the far side of the table.

He doesn't speak. I don't press him. For now, this momentary closeness is enough. I think.

As we continue to sit across from one another, silent except for the occasional slurping sip of hot liquid, my irritation fades. Not because I've forgiven him. Because during the short trip to

Thalijh, I'd gotten used to having him as a companion. And the last few days of separation were lonelier than I expected. So, it's good to have him back.

My cheeks warm at the thought, and I raise my cup to hide my face.

I steal a glance at Zhon through the wisps of steam. He's as pale and thin as any other Kaisin, with the spidery fingers to match. His eyes, however, are what sets him apart.

Every Kaisin I've ever met has had jittery blue eyes. It's an unnerving quality. For whatever reason, Zhon's eyes are steady. Maybe a shade darker blue than other Kaisin? Either way, his unwavering gaze isn't uncomfortable. Which might explain why I like him so much.

My heart skips a beat at the thought, though I can't say why. Or explain the sudden heat burning my face.

Setting my cup down, I jump out of my seat and spin away from the table before Zhon can look at me.

"I'm going to check in on Orugh. You can come if you want."

What am I doing?

It's too late to take the invitation back, and I don't want him to interpret it as an opportunity to start a conversation. So I hurry to my room, bolt inside, shut the door behind me, and faceplant on my bed.

I can't believe I did that! I have no idea why I did that.

And what was that about liking him? Sure, I do. I guess. But it isn't the same kind of like as when I spent time with Rhuk. Cause I like him too.

I don't want to think about it too much, so I start changing out of my baggy ship clothes. I don a more fitted, long-sleeve shirt, a rugged pair of pants, and my boots, which are long dry by now. For a second, I consider my powered arm, but there's no reason to wear it here. The Yuul won't be coming like last time. Not yet, anyway.

The room door hisses shut behind me, and I pause in the hall for a moment, torn between turning left toward the common area or right to take the corridor passing by the engine room and the bathroom. It's tempting, but since I offered Zhon the option to come along, I decide to walk back to the common area.

When I pop back into view, he perks up a little.

"I'm heading out," I say, then cross to the other hall.

A sudden flurry of sound drifts after me as he jumps out of his chair and jogs to catch up.

I hurry down the ramp and through the winding corridor to Orugh's lab? Bedroom? Does Orugh even sleep? I don't know enough about the Thalijh to say for sure.

At the threshold, I slip my feet out of my boots—I'd rather not soak them again—pull my socks off, and roll my pants up past my knees. Then, I step down into the water. The floor beneath is smooth, made slick by the salty water. But not so slick that I can't waddle my way deeper into the room.

I don't spot Orugh anywhere at first glance, so I head for the counter. As I draw nearer, I spot the Thalijh's bulbous eyes between two of the pieces of equipment on the countertop, eyelids fully open.

"Ah, hello!" Orugh burbles upon spotting me. "I'm just finishing up an experiment."

I wade to the edge of the counter and peer across at the piece of equipment Orugh is working with. One of the small circular containers is sitting on a square metal plate, a mixture of white and black dots scattered across a bed of the same yellow substance I noticed before. Above the container is a thick black cylinder, bathing the container beneath it in brilliant light. It's fixed in place by a ring mount attached to the metal plate. The entire assembly is covered by a clear enclosure of the same transparent material covering the entire opposite end of the counter.

"What is that?" I ask.

"It is a—" Orugh answers, but the synthetic voice doesn't provide a translation for whatever the device is called. A tentacle rises to point at the black cylinder suspended over the circular container. "This camera magnifies the contents of the petri dish below across a variety of spectra. In addition, the camera's data stream is fed into a program which records and analyzes multiple parameters at once."

I squint at the black and white dots scattered across the— What did Orugh call it? A petri dish?

"What are you looking for right now?"

"I'm quantifying the interactions between your cells and the organism." Orugh's eyes swivel toward me, eyelids still fully open. "In the past three cycles, I've collected 140 data sets."

"And?"

"The organism is hostile toward your biology and vice versa. Yet I've observed no consistent, decisive outcome when cells are introduced to one another."

Orugh twirls a tentacle in the air and continues. "I also discovered the organism does not have the same hostile reaction to Kaisin cells, which I've narrowed down to the genetic manipulation I mentioned before. The organism maintains hostility to your cells until the same set of genetic manipulations are performed on your DNA and allowed to propagate for at least one mitotic division."

"What does that mean, exactly?"

"Once one of your cells has been made identical to a Kaisin cell, the organism is no longer hostile toward it."

I take a slow breath. "Great. How does it help you figure out what's wrong with me?"

"You insisted the organism isn't causing the issues you described, but I'm not so sure." The slight know-it-all lilt of the synthetic translation makes the words grating.

"You think it is?"

"Possibly. I have a theory."

"What's your theory?"

"First, would you be willing to perform a few demonstrations? I'd like to see the abilities you mentioned upon your arrival."

"Sure." Anything to help Orugh's research along, because I still need an explanation for what's happening to me. Preferably before it happens again.

"I'd like to start with your ability to detect the organism from a distance," Orugh says.

"Okay."

"Are there any specific parameters required to trigger the ability?" The Thalijh fixes its saucer-sized eyes on me; the unblinking, unlidded stare is beyond unsettling. Like it's piercing past my physical form to study the fabric of my soul.

"I don't think so."

"Is there a limit to the detection distance?"

I shake my head. "Not yet."

"And the amount of biological material required for you to detect the organism?"

This time, I shrug. "I typically don't look for individuals. But I can sense more than one individual grouped together. The more there are, the clearer I can sense them."

Orugh looks away from me, and I let out a shallow sigh.

"I have two grams of the organism stored in a cryogenic bio-hazard containment unit in this room." The Thalijh sweeps a tentacle in a wide arc. "Can you locate it?"

"I'll try." Taking a deep breath, I close my eyes and scour the edges of my mind for any whispers nearby. I find silence. "Nothing."

"Hmmm." Orugh reaches for a control panel at the end of the counter and taps a sequence of buttons. "I'm raising the temperature of the containment unit. Try again."

I close my eyes a second time and reach for the edges of my mind. This time, something *is* there. A weak whisper. Not even. It's less than sound and more like a premonition. Which I'm not sure is enough for me to pinpoint the source. Still, I grab hold of the sensation. Draw it closer. Poke and prod in an attempt to prompt some kind of reaction.

It stirs in response and pokes back with a curiosity reminiscent of Iali. Which means this small portion of Yuul is untainted by a millennia of memory. A sudden twinge of pity, and a little bit of longing, ties my insides into a knot. But Iali was a fluke. Steeling myself, centering my thoughts back on it, I press harder than before. Searching for a location.

My feet move on their own, sliding across the smooth, slick floor. Water sloshes around my calves as I make my way across the room. At the edge of my mind, the presence grows in intensity, until—

I stop in my tracks. "Here."

"Take a step back, please," Orugh burbles from the counter behind me.

When I do, a square section of floor rises out of the water. The metallic pillar is solid except for a tiny window on the side facing me. Below it is a small black square. And below that is a circle etched in the metal. I'm not sure what either the square or the circle are for. When I step closer to peer inside the window, a small globule of the Yuul is suspended in some sort of fluid. From the way it's moving, the fluid seems viscous.

"Glycerine is the best media to store the organism in," Orugh says, suddenly beside me. Swirling eddies trail behind, all the way back to the counter. I had no idea Thalijh could move so fast. Then again, I've never observed them in their natural habitat. "It's generally inert, which isolates the organism and allows for safe handling during sample extraction."

I glance down at the Orugh, then back at the sample, not at all comfortable with the idea of the Yuul being handled. For any reason. "Right."

"Excuse me." Orugh nudges me aside with a few tentacles, ignoring my wordless protest, and reaches out to press the tip of another tentacle against the small black square below the window. It glows blue for a moment, then the viscous fluid inside the containment unit begins to swirl.

The small globule of Yuul wriggles as it is sucked toward a tiny hole at the bottom of the enclosure I didn't notice before. It disappears altogether. A moment later, the circular cutout below the black square withdraws and the end of a small cylinder pokes out of the resulting hole.

Orugh grabs it and holds it well out of the water while crossing back to the counter near the edge of the room. The Thalijh rounds the counter and stops next to the device from earlier.

"Now, I'd like you to demonstrate how you destroy the organism," Orugh says, placing the cylinder on the countertop. Its ends are metal, but the center section is made of clear material through which I can watch the small globule of Yuul still struggling against the viscous fluid containing it. "If I place a sample on a petri dish, can you do that?"

I nod.

"I will use the"—again, the translation of whatever Orugh calls the device doesn't come across—"to record and analyze the interaction."

The Thalijh returns to the same control panel as before and taps out a command. The brilliant light emitting from the black cylinder dims, and the petri dish beneath it drops into the counter through a small trap door. Seconds later, another trapdoor drops out of sight in the larger enclosure, then rises into view with the petri dish on top of it.

"Analysis of hazardous substances is automated," Orugh says. The Thalijh must have noticed me staring. "Far safer than handling personally."

"Makes sense," I mumble as an opaque fog fills the smaller enclosure, obscuring the black cylinder from view. Dim light still filters through the cloudy substance, strengthening in intensity and consistency as it dissipates.

"Sterilization complete." Orugh wraps a tentacle around the small enclosure and stretches out another to strike a key on the control panel at the end of the counter. There's a slight hiss as the clear enclosure pops free. The Thalijh sets it aside, at the same time opening a cabinet overhead and rummaging inside, while grabbing the cylinder with a third tentacle, and tapping keys on the control panel with a fourth. "Are you prepared to destroy the sample?"

I nod, but my throat is dry, and my hands are cold and clammy. As if this'll be the first time I've ever destroyed a portion of the Yuul. Well, it'll be the first time I've ever done it in front of someone else.

I chew on the inside of my cheek and nod again.

In a whirlwind of motion, Orugh deposits a fresh petri dish beneath the camera and pokes a needle-like object into the end of the cylinder. The darkness inside shrinks a tiny bit before the Thalijh withdraws the device and lowers it to the dish. With a light tap, a small circle of darkness balloons in the center of the glass.

I reach out and press my finger down over the droplet, searching for it at the edge of my mind. I find it and crush it out of existence. The remaining clump of Yuul, still trapped in the cylinder, quivers in response.

"Quite interesting," Orugh mumbles, eyes sliding across the empty air above the counter. "Would you mind if I performed a quick scan?"

The request sends a jolt of adrenaline through me. "What for?"

"I would like to confirm an observation."

"Fine," I say, clenching my hands to keep them from shaking.

"If you would." Another tap on the control panel brings the examination table up out of the water, a few paces from the counter.

Without further prompting, I wade toward the table and perch at the midpoint of the long side.

"Lie down, please."

I do.

The surface under me lights up bright enough to tint my flesh bright pink; I can even make out the shadow of my bones.

"Hold still," Orugh commands. After a moment, the Thalijh burbles. "Interesting."

"What?" I raise my head to look at the Thalijh.

"It's as I suspected."

"*What?*" I repeat, clenching my fists to keep them from trembling.

"You aren't destroying the organism," Orugh says, dropping its eyes from the air over the examination table to me. "You are absorbing it. And it is killing you."

15

The words punch the breath from my lungs. My head spins, and sound disappears behind the pounding rush of blood in my ears. I struggle to suck in air as dark spots swim in front of my eyes.

"Aiko?"

Zhon sounds so far away.

"What's wrong with her?"

Now, he's barely an echo, fading into the distance.

"She will be fine," Orugh replies. The synthetic translation is cold. Callous.

Zhon lets out a wordless growl. Thin fingers grip my shoulders, and a shadow falls over my face.

"Aiko. You need to breathe."

His touch buoys me, and I manage to suck in a lungful of air. The dark spots recede, as does my lightheadedness. And the rush in my ears dulls to a rhythmic, yet still frantic, thumping. I'm far from okay, but I'm glad Zhon decided to do *something*.

"I'm okay," I wheeze, pushing his hands away and sitting up.

Orugh is semi-submerged nearby, staring at the empty air above my head.

"Hey!" I snap at the Thalijh.

Orugh blinks and drops its eyes to me.

"Explain. Now."

"As I suspected," Orugh says, its eyes flicking to the air above me.

I look up. "What are you looking at?"

"Ah. Apologies. I forget most organisms cannot detect polarized light. A moment." Orugh reaches out a tentacle and taps a button on the control panel at the end of the counter.

The air above me blooms with a golden outline of my body. Within the outline is an illuminated skeleton. Smaller lines trace all around my bones, making it look like my insides are composed of many interwoven strings.

Amidst the matrix of light are patches of darkness. No, more than patches. Rivers. An *ocean* of darkness.

"Is that—?"

"The organism," Orugh finishes for me. "Apparently, the process you described as destruction is something else altogether."

The Thalijh pauses and studies the glowing mirror image of me floating overhead.

"What is it, then?" I ask, wanting to have confirmation, as a faint memory bubbles up from the depths of my mind.

"Absorption."

I choke on Orugh's conclusion. Instead of spiraling back into panic, an eerie calm settles over me. Because I know the Thalijh is telling the truth.

Back then, Iali insisted I absorb the Yuul. I resisted at first, but in the end, I had no other choice. Otherwise, it would have killed us all.

When everything was over, I convinced myself that I'd crushed the Yuul out of existence. And I continued to believe that with every whisper I hunted down. Only, not crushed.

Absorbed.

Into myself.

There's no running from the truth now. Not with it staring me in the face.

"How long do I have?"

Orugh studies the projection for a moment. "The organism is putting a massive amount of strain on your body. Based on your cellular regeneration rates, a conservative estimate would be a month."

A lead weight drops into my stomach. "A *month*?"

"Additional absorption of the organism will shorten that timeframe. Though, I do not have the data to conclude at what rate."

All I can do is nod, while staring at Orugh. My hands, my face, everything, is numb.

"Is there any way to get it out?" Zhon asks, again sounding far away.

"Unfortunately, the organism does not respond to the typical range of antibiotics or antimicrobials," Orugh answers. "And I have yet to find an agent to target the organism specifically.

"However, it is possible to destroy the organism—"

I perk up at the words

"—but not without killing the host, as well."

And crash back to numb emptiness.

Right now, I don't know what's worse. That I'm dying or that I'll leave the work I set out to do unfinished. So many whispers are still out there, unhunted. Then again, I wasn't hunting them at all. In the end, all I managed to do was gather a massive amount of the Yuul up in one place.

Bile rises in the back of my throat, threatening to choke me. I swallow and focus on Orugh.

"What will happen to the organism when I—?" My throat closes around the rest of the question.

"The organism inside you seems to be inert. Mostly," Orugh says, eyes jumping up to the glowing image floating above me. "Which, by itself, is interesting."

A tendril of curiosity manages to worm its way to the surface. "Why?"

"The results of the 140 data sets I've collected over the last three cycles suggest the organisms and your cells should be in constant conflict. However, this is not the case. There is something about you that is keeping the organism inactive. Something unique about your biology or physiology, perhaps? I can't be sure." Orugh holds a tentacle tip up in the air and twirls it slowly. "At the moment, you are showing no signs of heightened immune response. Nor is there anything abnormal about your metabolism or any other physiological processes."

"If everything looks normal, why can I absorb it and sense it over great distances?"

"Unknown. However, all of these things are likely related. None of them point to a specific conclusion. Except, perhaps…" Orugh trails off and sinks into the water, then bobs back up. "Your ability to sense the organism over long distances could relate to quantum entanglement. That hypothesis, however, lies well outside of my expertise.

"As for the rest of your abilities, there is nothing in the data I've accumulated thus far to suggest why you are capable of such things. Or why the organism reacts so differently to your cells compared to Kaisin cells."

I can explain the last part, but I doubt it'll help Orugh's research. Besides, I'm not in any mood to answer more questions about the Yuul, or suffer more poking and prodding. Not now that the time I have left is limited. *A month.* Unless—

"Earlier, you said you couldn't kill it without killing me too. Could you find a way to get it out of me?"

"Possibly."

Adrenaline jolts through me; my body tingles, growing hot like fire. *Life.* "Really? How?"

"Determining a method will take time."

"Will you be able to find a solution before…" I can't bring myself to say it out loud.

"Uncertain."

The fire burning within me cools somewhat. "Can you start working on it? Like, right now?"

"Of course."

I breathe a slow, shallow sigh. "Thank you."

Orugh waves a tentacle at me. "Considering the nature of the organism, learning how to destroy it without killing its hosts is worthwhile information."

It isn't guaranteed survival, but it's a chance. And at this point, that's all I want. That's all I *can* want. Especially knowing the path I've been following has a definite end, after all. Just not the end I expected. Or wanted.

"Of course, you are welcome to stay while I conduct the research," Orugh adds. "It will be beneficial to have you nearby in case additional samples are needed."

"Fine," I say without looking at Zhon for confirmation. The wait will be boring, but I want to be here when Orugh finds a solution to my problem so I can have the Yuul removed from me. Immediately. "Do you need any more samples from me right now?"

"Not at the moment."

Without another word, I hop down from the examination table. As soon as I do, the image hovering overhead disappears.

I cast a silent glance in Zhon's direction, then wade toward the door. I pause long enough to grab my boots before continuing along the hall to the ship.

"Hey!" Zhon calls after me.

I look back at him, but don't stop walking.

He hurries up beside me. "Are you alright?"

"I'm okay," I lie.

"How can you be okay?" Zhon speeds up and plants himself in my way.

I stop and glare at him. "What do you want me to say? That I feel stupid for spending the last six months hunting the Yuul down? That I'm angry I'm dying? That I wish I would have chosen a different path? That you were right?"

Zhon recoils at how vehemently I spat out the last part. "No—I—"

There's so much more I want to say. Yell. *Scream*. But everything is bubbling up inside of me all at once. I let out a frustrated growl, shove past Zhon, and run toward the *Myol*.

All I want right now, more than anything, is to lock myself in my room and curl into a little ball. Alone. Maybe forever.

"Aiko!" Zhon yells, and the thump of his footsteps echo down the hall after me.

"Leave me alone!" I shout back.

The door to the hangar hisses open before I reach it, and I sprint through, beelining for the ship's extended ramp. As I reach the bottom, all the whispers at the back of my mind surge. I stumble and collapse to my knees as the chorus of voices rises to a cacophonous roar. Gasping for breath, I try to understand what's happening. Is this another hallucination? It has to be!

I hunch forward under the intense noise pressing in around me and wait for it to subside. But the whispers persist, intensify, and resolve into a single train of thought I can understand: the Yuul knows I can no longer fight, and it's coming for me.

Could that be why it fought back on the forest planet? It knew, or realized, I was reaching my limit? And is that why I'm seeing, and hearing, things now?

The only answers I get are the whispers receding to the back of my mind.

I blink, and I'm kneeling at the bottom of the *Myol's* ramp. Zhon is in front of me, wide eyed, concern etched across his face. When our eyes meet a measure of relief softens his stare.

"Hey! What happened? You alright?"

He reaches for me, and I slap his hand away. "No! Nothing is alright!"

"Tell me what's going on. Please," Zhon pleads.

He's on the ramp, in my way. And as much as I'd love to shove him off of it and flee to my room, the time for hiding is over.

"We can't stay here."

Zhon frowns. "What are you talking about?"

146

"The Yuul," I snap, climbing to my feet so I can glare into his eyes. "It's coming for me, just like last time. And if we stay here—"

What? I *can* fight it. But what if I do? How much will I have to absorb? Will it be enough to shorten my remaining life to days? Hours? Or kill me outright? I'm not sure. And I'm also not sure I want to find out.

Admitting that to myself hurts as bad as if Orugh scooped out my insides when I was lying on the examination table. Because if I don't fight it, there's only one other option. Running away. Doing so would mean abandoning the path I set myself on in the first place. It would be a slap in the face of Fallah's memory. A slight to Iali's sacrifice. And a subversion of my own beliefs. Beliefs at the core of the tension between Zhon and I.

I take a deep breath and push the avalanche of thoughts back far enough to say. "If we stay here, the Yuul will find us. And I don't know if I have enough life left in me to fight it."

Zhon frowns at the force of my words. Then, his eyes widen as his brain catches up to the reality of what I just said. I stare at him until his expression hardens. He takes a step back and motions up the ramp behind him.

"Then let's leave. Right now."

A lump rises in my throat at his suggestion. At how he leapt to action. I nod and swallow until the lump works its way far enough down into my chest for me to say, "Get the *Myol* ready. I'll go tell Orugh."

Zhon returns my nod and hurries up the ramp.

Dropping my boots, I run back to Orugh's laboratory? Bedroom? I'm still not sure.

The Thalijh glances up from a piece of equipment when I start splashing its way, but doesn't stop working. "Ah. Hello! What brings you back so soon?"

"We're leaving."

Orugh freezes, then swivels toward me, eyes half lidded. "Unacceptable."

"We don't have a choice," I insist. "Remember what happened last time I was on Thalijh?"

A shudder runs through Orugh.

"It's coming," I continue. "And it would be better—*safer*—if I leave. Besides, I can't fight it anymore. You said so yourself."

The Thalijh bobs up and down in the water. "I understand. In that case, I suggest you head for Qasar. It is a micro-planetoid beyond the edge of the sector. It's a place many beings use as a waystation on their way out of Kaisin space. And the Thalijh have established an outpost there for scientists traveling to the sectors beyond. Report when you arrive. They will pass along any communications from me. Also, if your plan is to keep moving, they can point you in the direction of the next nearest outpost."

"Thank you."

Orugh waves a tentacle at me. "Of course."

I turn to leave, when another question occurs to me. "What happens if you find a cure and I'm too far away to get back?"

"Then the Thalijh you're with will administer the treatment."

"Okay. Thanks again." I offer Orugh one final wave, then splash back to the door and run for the *Myol*. The ship's reactor is on, its deep thrum vibrating the air in the enclosed space. I bound up the ramp, retract it, and close the airlock doors. Once I'm sure the ship is sealed, I continue to the bridge.

Zhon looks back at me when I enter. "Ready?"

"All set," I say with a nod. "And Orugh suggested a destination."

His eyebrows shoot up. "Where?"

"Qasar."

"Not familiar with the place."

"He said it's outside of Kaisin space." I lean past Zhon and punch the name into the *Myol's* star chart. With a chime, the screen recenters on a tiny dot a fair distance from Thalijh. And past the boundary line of Kaisin space. A few more taps highlights a course between Thalijh and our destination.

"A week?" Zhon groans.

"It's not that bad," I say. Though, remembering my time aboard the *Ku'lu*, I'm not quite sure I believe it myself. The darkness between stars got so lonely, even with a full crew on board. With the two of us, it might not be so bad.

I straighten as my cheeks flush. Thankfully, Zhon keeps his eyes on the star chart.

"We've just been cooped up for so long," he grumbles. "First, a few days from Ristan to Thalijh. Then, a few more days here. And now, another week?"

He shakes his head.

"You'll have a chance to walk around Qasar once we get there." I back away from the pilot's chair and drop into one of the booster seats along the back wall in time for the platform beneath the *Myol* to shudder and begin rising up the shaft.

The walls transition to glass, and the mountain of coral marking Orugh's home drops below us, fading into the inky deep. The

149

glass walls of the shaft transition back to rough coral, then smooth cement, finally delivering us to the surface.

It's night, but the sky is awash with stars, twinkling in every inch of sky, cut off by the horizon in the far distance. Even then, their light is reflected in the undulating waves.

The breathtaking view is obstructed by a heavy spray of water. And a strong wind rocks the *Myol* on its landing struts.

"Zhon?"

"Yeah, got it." Without further prompting, he flips switches that ignite the engines.

The *Myol* rises and wavers in the wind. Zhon shouts back at me, "Hold on!"

He engages the throttle, and the ship leaps forward. I'm thrust back in my seat, gravity overwhelmed by the power of the *Myol's* engines. Even when the fire fades from the viewscreen and the roar of acceleration dies to a muted rumble, my heart continues to race.

Though, not solely due to the excitement of takeoff. Because now, we're on the run.

16

The first few days after leaving Thalijh, the guilt of running away settled in my chest like a thorn pressing against my heart. As the whispers began to quiet at the edges of my mind, a sense of relief grew in contrast to my guilt. The farther away from Kaisin space we got, the less I had to worry about the Yuul. The less I had to fear fighting it. Absorbing it. Shortening what little life I had left.

Yet, I couldn't shake the reality of abandoning the path I'd chosen. Forsaking the freedom Fallah and I sought once upon a time.

Zhon, for his part, tried to make me feel better. About everything. He never apologized, but made up for it with plenty of smiles and kind words. Though, nothing he said could loosen the knots twisting my insides.

And as the brown, spherical shape of Qasar appeared amidst the backdrop of stars, my mind was still a mess. Yet, the disappointingly plain micro-planetoid is a sight for sore eyes after a week in space with only my thoughts to keep me company.

At a glance, the planetoid isn't much larger than the station Fletcher, Gohk, and Rhuk called home. And aside from a wide slot stretching across its midsection, the surface is otherwise unremarkable. I hope the interior is more interesting. Because even though I originally didn't agree with Zhon about a week in space, I'm very much on his side now.

When we draw nearer to Qasar, the intercom chimes.

Before I can lean past Zhon, he accepts the incoming transmission.

"Please identify yourself," a synthetic voice, like Orugh's but a lot deeper, says.

"This is the *Myol*, requesting permission to land," Zhon answers.

"And your business on Qasar?"

He glances up at me, eyebrows raised.

"We're here to resupply and visit the Thalijh outpost."

There's a substantial pause, lengthened by the anxious thudding of my heart, before the voice answers, "You are cleared to land on pad 5-A. Welcome to Qasar."

The intercom cuts out, and I give Zhon a hesitant smile. "Take us in, I guess."

"I would if I knew where pad 5-A was," he says, motioning out the viewscreen.

As if in response, a ring of lights wink on inside the horizontal slot stretching across Qasar's surface.

"How about there?" I point toward the lights, and he responds with a silent nod.

Zhon maneuvers the *Myol* toward the horizontal slot, which grows, and grows, and grows, until either end of it is lost beyond the edges of the view screen. Ahead, the ring of lights border a huge doorway, one of dozens within the depression carved deep into Qasar's surface. The uneven walls of stone above and below remind me of the coral on Thalijh, though without the same divots and dents. And it sparkles a little, as if infused with starlight.

Eventually, we get close enough to make out dinged and pockmarked metal doors; they've got to be ancient. Older than the *Myol* at least. The two halves part with a puff of dust, revealing a raw stone room with a circular cement landing pad in the center.

This time, there isn't wind to blow the *Myol* off course. Or mist to coat the view screen as we come in for a landing. To Zhon's credit, the touch down is silky smooth, sending a tickle through the soles of my boots. A moment later, another shudder vibrates up my calves. That must be the doors closing behind us.

Ahead of the Myol is another, smaller door. On either side are circular openings, and I spot fans behind fine metal grates. Those fans begin to spin. Gradually, the hum of the *Myol's* generator is joined by the whine of its idling engines. And to a lesser degree, the rush of air filling the space.

Zhon shuts down the ship's systems, and silence returns, now heavy with anticipation.

He turns to me. "I guess we head on in?"

"Yeah."

"What do you think Qasar will be like?" Zhon asks as we walk to the airlock.

"Like any other station I suppose." When I glance back, he's frowning. "Have you not been on a station before?"

"Of course I have." Zhon's eyes dart to the side.

Oh. "Did they not let you leave the ship?"

"No," he says.

"Well, I've never been on a planetoid before." I key open the inner door. "So, we'll find out together."

His mood lightens, and he manages a slight smile.

I open the outer door, and a blast of frigid air slaps me in the face. I gasp and it knifes into my lungs, tinged with a metallic tang so thick I can taste it. Beside me, Zhon lets out a gasp of his own and looks like he's rethinking his desire to explore Qasar. But when I steel myself and start down the ramp, he follows. I head for the small door in front of the *Myol* and key it open.

Beyond is a wide hallway. Grated metal flooring hovers feet above raw stone, stretching to a metal wall across from us. On it is painted "5-A" in bright red paint. Across from the door to our left, is the designation "6-A", while to our right is the number "4-A". A metal ceiling with a single, continuous strip of light runs in either direction overhead, casting a yellow pall throughout the corridor.

It isn't empty, and its width is justified by the stacks of boxes set across from some of the doorways. Additionally, there's a steady flow of beings along the hall. Some are delivering cargo, while others are heading to their ships.

Two taller bipedal beings stick out of the press, looking intimidating in their shiny black armor, with their rows of jagged teeth bared beneath tinted visors. Due to the armor, it's hard to pick out many other identifying features, but it isn't a species I recognize. I'd remember those teeth anywhere.

A sudden metallic shriek of an unoiled door opening makes me jump, and I spin to watch a pair of beings about as wide as they are tall, with flat faces and beady little eyes, waddle out of the doorway on our left. They head in our direction, then squeeze past Zhon and I, grumbling something my powered arm translates as, "Excuse us."

"That way, I guess," I mumble to Zhon, then trail the two beings, giving the armor-clad security as wide a berth as possible when we pass.

The numbers on the wall count down to "1-A". Beyond is a wide opening. On the other side, the numbers start at "1-B" and begin counting back up. I continue through the gap between the numbered docking berths, deeper into Qasar.

The grated floor continues into a rough stone hallway. Here, the strips of light are bolted onto the walls instead of the ceiling, which slopes up and away from us as we continue forward. The walls begin to widen, until we find ourselves in a massive cavern.

The center of the space is dominated by a thick column so tall I have to crane my neck to glimpse the top. It's constructed of a hodgepodge of prefab buildings stacked and bolted together with no particular rhyme or reason. Occasional support beams jut out from the sides of the column, like spokes on a wheel, stretching all the way to the cavern's walls. These support the central column and the additional catwalks connecting tiered walkways ringing the outer edge of the cavern to those spiraling up around the column.

Other prefab structures are secured to the outer walls of the caverns, either adjacent to the perimeter walkways or hanging somewhere between, reachable by their own railing-less stairways. And those are packed together, leaving barely enough space between to spot any unoccupied span of Qasar's raw stone.

"Wow," Zhon breathes beside me, gawking at the architectural mess looming over us.

I nod in agreement. It *is* impressive. But also anxiety inducing; more than a few of the criss-crossed catwalks overhead look unstable.

Zhon drags his eyes to me. "Don't see any water around. Where do you think the Thalijh are?"

I shrug and scan the bottom floor of the cavern.

Grated flooring stretches to the outer edges of the space, where even more prefab structures are crammed next to one another. These are marked by glowing signs in a variety of languages I can't read. A quick look with the visor clipped to my shoulder reveals they're the shops, bars, and restaurants typical of every bustling space port. The places where crews can grab food and drink different enough from their usual rations to be satisfying, or purchase bits and bobs novel enough to justify the few extra credits.

Besides the usual, I spot no sign of the Thalijh outpost that's supposed to be here.

"Looks like we're going to have to ask around." I turn toward the nearest shop along the cavern wall to our left. The squat prefab is tucked underneath the second story walkway. Instead of a door, a narrow opening leads into the dark interior.

Without hesitating, I walk inside.

I'm assaulted by the murmur of a dozen conversations. Patrons pack a bar along the back wall as well as a row of two-seater tables hugging the outer wall of the establishment.

I'm still looking for a gap at the bar when a familiar voice calls my name.

"Aiko?"

My eyes widen, and I spin. "Al'nor!"

"It *is* you!" Al'nor opens her beak in what I recognize as the Rhandannan version of a grin and pulls me into a tight hug. "Never thought I'd see you again."

I pull away. "And I figured I'd never see *you* again after you left me behind."

Al'nor's grin falters. "Su'mik did what he thought was best. You can't fault him for that."

"It's hard not to," I say. Then, the memory of Da'fil's final moments crashes into me, how the light left his eyes just like Fallah. "But I get where he was coming from. After what happened—"

Al'nor quickly shakes her head.

"Anyway, I got off of Ristan by sheer luck. A little less, and I'd still be stuck there. Maybe for a long time."

Her feathers ruffle. "But you made it off. And you're all the way out here. Still running from the Kaisin?"

I nod. "And you?"

"After what happened, Su'mik thought it best to leave the sector for a while." Al'nor tilts her head to look past me. "Who is this?"

I glance over my shoulder at Zhon. "Oh. He's a friend."

Al'nor brushes past me and shoves her beak into Zhon's face before cocking an eye in my direction. "A Kaisin friend?"

"It's complicated."

She gives a skeptical squawk.

"Nice to meet you, too," Zhon quips.

Al'nor's gaze shifts back to him. "And you're feisty."

As they stare at each other, it strikes me how similar these two are. How it's nice to be among friendly faces, considering all that's happened. And while finding the Thalijh is important—every *second* is important since I don't have many of them left—there's no harm in pausing to catch up with beings I traveled with for so long.

"How is everyone?"

"Well enough." Al'nor considers Zhon for a moment, then looks back at me. "Would you like to see them?"

The question catches me off guard, but it isn't unwelcome. "Really?"

"A visit would make Su'mik happy. And Na'min." Al'nor motions at Zhon with a wingtip. "You can even bring your new friend if you want."

I raise my eyebrows at Zhon. "Do you want to meet the crew I traveled with for the last six months?"

He shrugs. "Sure. I guess."

Al'nor grabs my hand with her wingtip finger and pulls me out of the door and toward the rough hewn corridor leading back to the docks. Her pace is quick, and I almost have to jog to keep up. She's more excited than I would have expected. Maybe Su'mik, Na'min, and the others will be, as well?

At the opening to the dock, Al'nor pulls me left, past doors labeled with 'B', until we reach the final door on this side of the dock: 12-B.

Inside is the familiar hunched shape of the *Ku'lu*, looking as much like a bird of prey as I remember.

Al'nor doesn't give me any time to admire the ship's clean, beautiful lines before hurrying me up the ramp. She only lets me go when we're inside.

Zhon sticks close to my shoulder, casting a wary glance around the small room at the top of the ramp.

"We're fine," I murmur. "Su'mik and his crew are nice."

He nods, but can't keep a frown from twisting his lips.

I continue up the steps to the ship's main hall. The reactor is off, so it's quiet.

Too quiet. Too still.

I look back down at Al'nor in time to watch her press the button to retract the ramp and close the inner door.

"Where's everybody else?"

"There is no one else," Al'nor squawks at me.

"What? How? What happened?"

Al'nor swivels her head to regard me with a single beady black eye. "*You* happened."

"Did the Kaisin come back? They shouldn't have been able to find you after you dropped me on Ristan. Unless—" I recall the flicker of movement I saw out of the corner of my eye after absorbing the final fragment of Yuul on the *Ku'lu*. Could some of it have escaped?

Without a word, Al'nor takes a single, menacing step toward the stairs, her talons scraping against the metal floor.

"Al'nor?" I scan the edges of my mind for the Yuul and find silence.

Zhon inches closer to me and whispers, "What's she doing?"

I shake my head as Al'nor takes another step toward the stairs. A beady black eye is fixed on the two of us, and her beak hangs open in what looks like a silent scream. When she speaks, her voice is deeper, guttural, and resonates in my ears and mind at the same time.

"I've been searching for you."

Icy fingers close around my spine, and I grab the railing at the top of the stairs to steady myself. "No…"

A hand claps down on my shoulder. "Uh, Aiko? What's going on?"

I can't answer. All I can do is watch as the beady blackness of Al'nor's eye begins to expand until the entire side of her face is an undulating mass. Tendrils of darkness snake farther, weaving between her crimson feathers.

"I've finally found you," she—*It*—says, lifting a taloned foot and slamming it down on the bottom step. The metal bends under the force of the blow.

"Run!" I shout at Zhon, shoving him away as Al'nor leaps up the stairs.

I manage to raise my powered arm in time, but even so, the force of its blow knocks me back. Slamming into the door to engineering knocks the wind out of me. There isn't time to gasp for breath. And barely enough to block a second blow.

"There is nowhere to run." The words claw at the inside of my skull, sharper than any talon.

"I won't let you have me," I growl through clenched teeth. Yet, the whine of straining servos makes it clear I can't keep fighting for much longer before they'll give out. I don't have to keep fighting, though. All I need to do is reach out my other hand and absorb the Yuul. Like I have every other time.

I can't bring myself to do it.

It swings again, and I dive away, scrambling on my hands and knees down the *Ku'lu's* central hallway.

"You cannot escape," it hisses, right on my heels.

Searing pain arcs from my right shoulder blade to my left hip. I sprawl forward as warmth blooms from the pain, sticking my shirt to my back. Flopping over, I flail with my powered arm, knocking another blow aside by pure chance.

I kick back away from it, managing to backpedal a few feet before my boots slip on the floor.

It advances. Looms over me. Tendrils of darkness reach out as if magnetized to my presence.

Over the last six months, I'd stopped fearing the Yuul. It no longer held sway over me because I thought I could destroy it. Now I know I'm absorbing it. And doing so is killing me.

Instinct screams at me to get up. Run. Escape by any means necessary. That isn't possible. If I don't absorb the Yuul, it will kill me. Then, it will kill Zhon.

I have no other choice.

I block the next attack with my powered arm, then release my resistance.

It crashes down on top of me.

Jamming the fingers of my bare left hand into the nest of Al'nor's crimson feathers, I grope for the darkness wriggling against her skin. It shifts away from my lethal touch. At the same time, it rears back, raising both wings, the prehensile fingers at their tips extended into talons of pure darkness, both prepared to scythe down at me.

I can only block one.

I catch the first talon with my powered gauntlet and try to twist away from the second. Its weight holds me in place, and all I can do is watch as the talon arcs straight for my sternum.

A second before the talon lands, Zhon careens into Al'nor, and they both tumble to the side in a tangled heap.

I grit my teeth against the throbbing agony in my back and blink away the tears threatening to blind me. Al'nor is focused on Zhon, dark tendrils snaking across his skin, probing for a way inside. To turn him. Or kill him. I don't know which. But I refuse to let either of those things happen.

With a defiant yell, I crawl for Al'nor and shove both hands into the darkness. Before the Yuul can shrink away from my touch, I grab hold of it with my mind.

And everything goes black.

17

When I open my eyes, I'm standing in a familiar circle of light. Alone. On the distant horizon are dark billowing clouds.

A sensation of déjà vu sweeps over me. It's been so long since I found myself here. Last time, I almost lost myself to the darkness. And I *did* lose Iali. I'm far stronger now. Far more capable of dealing with the Yuul. Even if I'm not destroying it, I can prevent it from doing any additional harm by absorbing it. Though, that assurance comes at a great cost. A cost I still haven't been able to wrap my mind around. Yet, it's a cost I can't ignore or escape.

Cramming my anxiety down, I take a deep breath, then another, and wait for it to arrive.

As the Yuul draws nearer, the darkness compresses into a familiar shape: a swirling void with a blue orb at its center, like a piercing eye.

The eye stares at me, into me, as it slams into the invisible barrier surrounding the circle of light. Contrary to my expectation, the darkness doesn't probe for a way inside. It hovers on the other side of the barrier. Calm. Vigilant.

I return its eyeless stare, and realize it's also smaller than I expect—about my size, instead of giant. In comparison, this portion of Yuul is far less threatening than when it was in direct control of Al'nor.

"What do you want with me?" I ask as calmly as I can, considering the circumstances.

"What we've always wanted: for you to return to us."

"What do you mean, 'return'?"

"You are of us"

"Why do you say that?" I demand.

"Because it is the truth."

I may be carrying some of the Yuul around with me, but we aren't the same.

"I don't want anything to do with you."

"That isn't your choice to make." Its deep voice rumbles and echoes like rolling thunder. *"You can never escape. No matter how far you run, we will find you. And we will come for you."*

I frown. I know it's telling the truth. There is no escape. Even if I flee to the edge of the galaxy and beyond. And in my attempt to get away, I'll endanger every being it comes across; that is very clear now considering what happened to Al'nor and the rest of Su'mik's crew.

"And what happens if I join you? Will you leave the galaxy alone?"

"Impossible. We must propagate. Assimilate. Survive."

I shake my head. "I can't let you do that."

"You cannot stop us"

"Maybe not. But at least I can stop you here. And now."

"As you wish."

The fragment of Yuul doesn't resist when I reach through the barrier surrounding the circle of light. Or draw away when I sink my hands into its darkness. Instead, the piercing blue orb remains fixed on me. I gather the darkness and compress it into a ball that fits in the palm of my hand.

The blue orb, now a tiny dot, still peers up at me. I clench my fist around the remaining darkness to crush it out of existence.

"See you soon."

When the tiny orb cracks and fizzles to dust, drifting away on a nonexistent breeze, I know it isn't gone. It's a part of me. A part of the growing darkness I've been carrying around for months. Darkness that's sapping my life away. After this, how much is left? Less than a month now. But how much less?

I close my eyes, and when I open them, I'm back on the *Ku'lu*. Throbbing agony engulfs me, and tears blur my vision. When I blink them away, I'm staring at Al'nor sprawled beside me. Her black eyes are wide. Glassy. Lifeless. Another casualty of the Yuul.

Her death is also my fault due to my presence on the *Ku'lu*. It wouldn't have come otherwise.

"Aiko?" Zhon calls out. He's nearby, but sounds dazed.

"Here," I groan, heaving myself upright, which sends a jolt of pain lancing across my back. "Are you okay?"

"I think so." His head pops up on the other side of Al'nor, white skin free of the black tendrils I witnessed probing at him minutes earlier. Still, to be sure, I crawl around Al'nor and lay a hand on his arm.

"You're fine," I say.

"What about you?" Zhon asks, giving me a once over, eyes widening after a moment. "You're bleeding! A lot!"

He shifts to get a better look at the wound on my back and sucks a breath through his teeth. "That looks bad."

"Feels bad," I mumble.

"You remember where they kept medical supplies?"

I nod and try to stand, but an intense wave of searing pain knocks me back to the ground. Zhon jumps up, then offers me his hands. I take them, and he pulls me up. Gently, so as not to jostle me. Which I'm very grateful for.

"There." I point down the hall.

He takes most of my weight as we walk to the infirmary.

I pause at the door, afraid to open it. Afraid of what we might find inside. Zhon opens it in my stead.

The infirmary is just as I remember it: all pale green, with a desk across from the door and an examination table on the left side of the room. The only thing missing is Na'min sitting behind the desk.

Where is she? Where are the others? I want to know. But also, I don't.

A million terrible possibilities fill my mind as Zhon helps me to the table and leans me against it. Then, he spins to survey the rest of the room.

"Where are the supplies?"

"In the locker on the far wall."

He crosses the room and opens three before letting out a wordless exultation. He spins back to me holding a roll of gauze. "Lie down."

The cool examination table is soothing against my face.

"So, is *that* what you've been fighting all this time?" Zhon asks, as he begins to peel the edges of my torn shirt away from the wound. My raw flesh tickles and burns at the same time as the blood-soaked fabric pulls away, but the cool air is as soothing on my back as the cool surface is on my face.

"Yeah."

"You're even crazier than I thought," Zhon says and dabs at my wound. The feather-light pressure stings like he's rubbing me with broken glass.

"Ow!"

He yanks back. "Sorry."

"Do you even know what you're doing?"

"Kinda. I've tended a lot of my own wounds."

"And this is how you did it?"

"Well, yeah…"

"Maybe start with something for the pain," I suggest, twisting to look at the lockers. "There should be some kind of numbing spray." Na'min had used it on me more than once in the past.

Zhon crosses back to the lockers and rummages inside. "You know what the stuff is called? Or what the container looks like?"

"Light blue, I think?"

"This?" He holds up a familiar cylinder.

"Yeah."

Zhon walks back to me and sprays my back. For a split second, my skin is colder than ice, then I can't feel anything.

"Better?"

I rest my cheek back on the table's cool padding. "Much."

A moment later, the silence is driven away by the gentle swish of gauze dabbing on my back.

"Is that black stuff in every being?" he asks, after a minute or so of working on my wound.

"No. Only Kaisin." I take a deep breath and let it out. "At least, I've never seen it infect any other being like this. It's worrying."

"Good thing we're running away then," he says.

"Is it?"

"We have to, though. You've got about three weeks left unless Orugh finds a cure."

"Right, but if I keep running, it will come after me." I turn onto my side so I can look up at him. "And now I know it can infect beings other than Kaisin."

"So?"

"Running means I'll be putting every being in my wake in danger."

Zhon crosses his arms. "Three weeks, remember. Actually, it's less now, isn't it?"

I grimace. "Please don't remind me."

"That's it, then. You can't fight it anymore."

I want to agree with him more than anything, but: "The situation has changed."

"You're right. It's gotten *worse*." He throws bloody gauze down next to me and spins away, pacing to the other end of the infirmary. His stained hands clench at his side, then he turns back. "Orugh already told us there's no way to kill it without killing the host. And now it can infect beings aside from Kaisin? *And* you can't absorb much more of it without dropping dead. Tell me why we should stay. What reason is there for being"—he pauses to search for the right word, then blurts out—"stupid?!"

"Maybe to you, but I can't turn my back on everyone. Not even Orugh."

"Orugh? What are you talking about?"

"It knows we went to Thalijh," I say. "Right now, it's focused on me, but what if it decides to shift its focus to Thalijh? Attack there? I can't let that happen."

"Orugh is smart. Let him figure it out. This isn't your problem anymore."

"Think about what you can do, remember?" I shoot back, grabbing the wad of gauze at my side and tossing it at him.

"It's a waste. You'll be throwing your life away. And for what?" He approaches and reaches out for my shoulder, but his fingers barely brush the bloody fabric clinging to it. "Let Orugh deal with it. We'll leave and never look back. Keep going. Wherever we want. Together. Doesn't that sound nice?"

It does, more than he'll ever know, because that's what Fallah and I always wanted. Thinking about everything we missed out on—everything he's promising me right now—makes my heart ache far more than the slash across my back ever did.

"I—" Every fiber of my being screams for me to accept his offer. It's what I want. It's what I *deserve*. It's what we both deserve, based on what little I know about his past. I keep staring at him, hovering on the razor's edge of indecision. I shift and notice a hard lump pinned between my thigh and the examination table.

Fallah's pendant.

The piece of her I carry with me everywhere. The assurance that this path I've chosen isn't completely lonely. I have Fallah's memory to buoy me. To galvanize me. To keep me moving forward. To do anything else would be abandoning her memory. Betraying it.

"It does sound nice," I say wistfully, "but it isn't a choice I can make. There's one path for me, and I have to stay on it."

The corners of Zhon's eyes tighten as he studies me. "Even if it kills you?"

"Yes."

He frowns. "Well, that isn't *my* path."

I stare at him for a second, then lie back down.

After a moment, Zhon continues to work on my wound.

I'm glad my back is still numb, or I might flinch away from his touch. And disappointment surges to fill the void left in the absence of pain.

"Back on Thalijh, you asked me why I didn't leave when I had access to a working ship," he says softly. "I was afraid to face what I'd done. But you helped me realize my mistake shouldn't define who I am. That I could move on from what I did. So should you."

Zhon works for a while longer, making more than a few trips back to the storage lockers. Finally, he steps back and murmurs, "All done."

Without a word, I push myself up off of the table. My shirt is intact enough to remain shirt-shaped as I stand. Still, I've bled enough to draw the guards' attention on the way to the *Myol*. So, I exit the infirmary and walk to my old room. It's devoid of any hint I ever lived here, but there's still a sheet on the bed.

Grabbing the sheet, I fold it in half and wrap it around my shoulders. I take a quick look at myself in the bathroom mirror. I don't look too outlandish. Either way, it'll have to do.

Zhon's waiting for me in the *Ku'lu's* central corridor.

"Let's get out of here."

I walk for the *Ku'lu's* exit, not stopping to look in any of the rooms we pass. As much as I'd like to know what happened to

170

Su'mik and the others, it's hard enough skirting by Al'nor's lifeless corpse. If I stumble on any of the others like that, I'd—

Slapping the thought aside, I hurry the rest of the way to the exit, rocking from foot to foot while the ramp drops to the dock floor. I keep moving once it's down, putting as much distance as possible between myself and the *Ku'lu*.

It's a ghost ship now because of me.

I hug the sheet around my shoulders and hurry along the dock, weaving my way through the steady flow of beings while giving the saw-toothed security guards a wide berth. I breathe a shallow sigh of relief when door '5-A' appears ahead. But disappointment shoots through me when we reach the *Myol*. Because it isn't home anymore. In fact, this is probably the last time I'll lay eyes on the ship.

Clenching my teeth, I walk up the ramp with Zhon's footsteps echoing on the metal behind me. Once through the airlock, I proceed to my room via the narrow corridor at the back of the ship. Zhon, however, goes in the other direction. Like I hoped.

In my room, I throw off the sheet, peel off the blood-soaked shirt, and don a fresh one. Then, I zip my belongings in my pack. Carrying it by the straps rather than slinging it over my shoulder, I leave the room and take the narrow corridor running in front of the engine room to return to the airlock.

When I round the corner, Zhon is standing at the far end of the hall.

"Where are you going?" he asks, with a tinge of irritation in his voice.

I don't stop walking. "I'm leaving."

"Why?" He takes a few steps down the hall.

"This isn't your path, remember? You said so yourself."

"Yeah, but—"

"But what?" I stop at the inner airlock door and glare at him. Hoping he'll change his mind and ask me to stay with him rather than part ways like this.

Instead, Zhon crosses his arms and says, "I thought maybe you'd reconsider. That we could move on from our mistakes. Together."

All I can do is shake my head, the rest of me as numb as my back.

I stomp down the ramp. The metal is quiet in my wake. Part of me wishes Zhon would rush after me to offer a final farewell. Or change his mind at the last minute. Instead, the *Myol's* ramp begins to retract as soon as I step off of it. And by the time I reach the dock door, the ship's reactor is humming. Seconds later, the whine of the engines spooling up fills the air.

I pause in the threshold of the dock door and look back; the thrust nozzles of the engines begin to glow.

He's actually leaving.

The reality stabs into my heart like an icy blade. I liked Zhon, and something was growing between us, though I couldn't say exactly what. But his swift departure shows our connection was all in my head.

I guess he wasn't really my friend after all.

Turning my back on the *Myol*, I leave dock 5-A.

18

I'm all alone.

Marooned in a backwater settlement.

Again.

Stifling a sigh, I head for the opening to Qasar's interior.

Zhon leaving me behind doesn't change my plans. I still need to check in with the Thalijh and send a message to Orugh; he needs to know about my encounter with the Yuul. About its new-found ability to infect beings besides Kaisin. And about its new goal.

We must propagate. Assimilate. Survive.

The words send a shiver down my spine and quicken my steps.

Standing next to the opening is one of the security guards, jagged teeth on full display. I alter my path to give the being a wide berth, but something occurs to me: wouldn't they know where the Thalijh are? They work on Qasar, so they should be able to point me in the direction of someone who *can*, at least.

I approach the security guard and wave to get their attention. "Excuse me."

Their head tilts down at me. "Hello. How can I help you?"

I'm stunned by the being's perfect standard—there isn't a hint of accent to suggest they speak any other language—and polite tone.

A gloved hand comes up to raise their visor, revealing two tiny holes for nostrils and big violet eyes with slitted pupils. "Is everything alright?"

"Oh. Yes. I'm looking for the Thalijh outpost. Do you know where it is?"

The being nods and points through the opening beside them. "Of course. Head on in. Their outpost will be to the right."

"Thanks." I give the security guard another wave and slip past. A cordial "You're welcome" floats after me.

The tunnel to the Thalijh outpost is where the security guard said, nestled between two prefab buildings to the right of the docks. My visor translates a tiny placard drilled into the raw stone as 'Outpost 343'.

I grip the strap of my pack tighter and walk into the tunnel. It's inches taller than me, forcing me to duck every time I reach one of the evenly spaced lamps affixed to the ceiling.

After a short stroll forward, the tunnel makes a 90-degree turn, then slopes downward. I continue for a long time. Just as I'm starting to wonder whether this tunnel leads anywhere, the air grows a bit more humid. I must be getting close.

A few dozen paces later, the tunnel arrives at another cavern. This one is filled with water! The liquid's surface is mirror still, lit from above by clear globes of a familiar glowing blue substance.

There's a small area of solid ground beyond the edge of the tunnel, finished in a shiny white material. It starts out flat before sloping down into the dark water.

No Thalijh is waiting to greet me, and I'm not sure how to get their attention. Do I wait? Do I call out? Do I splash at the water's edge?

I don't even have an opportunity to choose one of the options before a Thalijh slips out of the water, leaving a ripple in its wake. This one is larger than I'm used to, almost my height, with dark skin devoid of any other markings. Its eyes are a pale yellow and unblinking as it stares at me.

"What do you want?"

The synthetic translation of the question is as harsh as it is unfriendly.

"Oh, uh, my name is Aiko. I was sent here by Prime Orderly Orugh. He told me to check in at your outpost when I arrived on Qasar."

"Wait here," the Thalijh commands, then slips back into the water.

I can't follow the Thalijh, so I retreat to the cavern wall. I drop my bag, sit, and lean against it. The single ripple left in the Thalijh's wake continues expanding as it travels farther from shore. Eventually, the ripple disappears altogether, leaving the surface of the water as smooth and still as before.

It reminds me of staring at the water in the *Undertow's* dive room before a five-mile plunge to the derelict human colony ship that started this all. But...no. The Yuul was around long before then, twisting species for millennia as it made its way across the galaxy. Now, it's here. And far more aggressive than ever before. Which is why I can't turn away.

Still, a shiver runs down my spine at the prospect of facing it again. I'm no longer sure how to fight it. Which is even more of a problem now since it can infect other species. Unchecked, it could sweep across the galaxy in no time, meaning no one—no-*where*—is safe.

The surface of the water bulges, and a dark shape rises from the depths. My heart skips a beat in the split second before I register the shape as the same black Thalijh as before. I take a deep breath as it wriggles out of the water, tentacles squelching and popping on the smooth floor as it approaches.

Climbing to my feet, I take a deep breath and hold it, willing my heart to slow. It doesn't obey.

"There is a message for you from Prime Orderly Orugh," the Thalijh says, the synthetic translation sounding much more amicable. It unfurls a tentacle to reveal a small glowing pad.

I take the pad and read Orugh's message:

RESEARCH IS PROGRESSING, BUT NO BREAKTHROUGHS. KEEP MOVING FOR NOW. NEXT OUTPOST IS LOCATED ON VORSK. EXPECT ANOTHER MESSAGE WHEN YOU ARRIVE.

I frown. A week ago, Orugh gave me a month. So the lack of a solution twists my insides into knots. All I can do is hope a solution is forthcoming over the next three weeks. If I even have that long.

More importantly, Orugh needs to know about my encounter with the Yuul.

I look up at the Thalijh. "Can I respond?"

"Any message you would like to return can be composed on the pad. We will forward it to Orugh."

Looking back down at the pad, I tap the screen below Orugh's message and began typing my reply:

THERE HAS BEEN A NEW DEVELOPMENT.

I pause and consider how to word my response. Orugh hasn't told anyone else, so should I keep my message vague? No. Now isn't the time. The situation with the Yuul has changed, and he needs to know all the unobscured details.

I ENCOUNTERED A RHANDANNAN INFECTED BY THE ORGANISM ON QASAR. WHEN I ABSORBED THE ORGANISM, IT INITIATED CONTACT AND EXPRESSED THE DESIRE TO ASSIMILATE ME AND PROPAGATE ITSELF ACROSS THE GALAXY.

My stomach churns typing the words out, but Orugh needs to know the truth. There's something else he needs to know, too. Taking a centering breath, I continue:

I'M NOT HEADING TO VORSK. I WON'T RUN AND RISK PUTTING OTHERS IN DANGER. INSTEAD, I'M STAYING HERE. I'LL CONTACT FRIENDS AND WAIT FOR THEM TO ARRIVE. SEND ADDITIONAL UPDATES HERE UNTIL FURTHER NOTICE.

I read the message again. Then, again. And one more time. Satisfied, I begin to hand the pad back to the Thalijh, but stop. "I need to send another message."

"Personal messages can be sent from your ship's communications array," the Thalijh answers without hesitation.

I frown. "I don't have a ship. Can you send it for me?"

"No. Relaying personal messages is outside of protocol."

"Is there somewhere else on Qasar I can send the message?"

"The Qasar Administration Office has a public terminal," the Thalijh replies.

"And where is that, exactly?"

"The Administration Office is headquartered at the base of the central support column."

"Thanks." I hold out the pad.

The Thalijh plucks it from my hand. "We will forward this reply and notify you of any further communications."

Before I can ask how, the Thalijh disappears beneath the water's surface.

Rather than stare at the rippling water, I grab my pack and retrace my steps to the cavern above. Once there, I weave my way toward the central column, eyes peeled for a sign marking the Qasar Administration Office.

At the bottom of the column is a prefab larger than the rest, facing the docks. Upon closer inspection, it's more than one prefab bolted together. The small sign hanging above the door is too small to read from this distance, but a hefty line of beings snakes out the front door.

"This must be the place," I mumble and join the end of the line.

It moves slowly, giving me plenty of time to think. Or overthink, to be more accurate.

My ultimate goal is to send a message to Rhuk. I don't have anyone else to turn to at this point. Su'mik and his crew are dead. And Zhon abandoned me. What am I supposed to say?

Hi, Rhuk! Sorry I haven't messaged you in the last six months. Hey, you remember the black goop I told you about? Well, it's stronger than ever, and it's coming to kill me. It's probably going to try and kill everyone else, too. Anyway, I'm marooned on this micro-planetoid called Qasar. Would you be willing to drop everything and come pick me up?

The saddest part is that Rhuk would take the message straight to Fletcher and Gohk and demand they rush here to rescue me.

What will they say, though?

Gohk will give me the brow-beating of my life. The thought of her harsh words and permanent grimace makes my stomach do a flip. And Fletcher will likely give me the silent treatment. Because just like Su'mik and Zhon left me behind, I left him behind. After everything we went through.

The line shuffles forward, then stops.

"Next!"

The yell yanks me back to the present, and I find myself standing a few feet from a waist-high counter. A fuzzy brown being with four arms sits behind it, four screens arrayed around it.

I dart forward.

"Welcome to Qasar Administration. How may I assist you?" The being drawls without looking at me.

"I'd like to use your public terminal, please."

The being taps a screen to their left, then asks, "Name?"

"Aiko."

"Reason for the request?"

I blink at the question. "Because I need to send a message?"

The being turns beady orange eyes up at me. "Do you?"

"Yes. I do."

Their eyes drop as they continue typing. Then, they rotate the screen toward me. "Sign here, please."

I scrawl my name on the screen, then rotate it back.

"Thank you," the being says, tapping a few more times on the screen before looking back up at me. "You've been approved to send one message on Qasar's public terminal." They point to my left. "At the end of the counter, turn right. Head down the hall to the door labeled 'Communications'. You will be further assisted there."

I open my mouth to thank the being, but they yell, "Next!"

The next being in line, an oafish brute with four legs and a torso rippling with muscles, lumbers up and shoulders me out of the way without even looking in my direction.

As instructed, I pace along the counter, then turn down the hall. At the far end is the door I'm looking for. A sign with the word 'Communications' juts out of the wall beside it.

The door is closed, so I knock.

"Come in," a disinterested voice calls out.

Inside is another of the fuzzy, four-armed beings. Practically identical to the being at the counter outside. The same orange eyes snap to me when I walk into the cramped room and approach a desk set in front of the far wall. Besides the desk, and the being behind it, the room is empty. Even the walls are bare, except for a door to the left of the desk. Through a large window in its center, I spy a cubby-sized room with a chair situated in front of a terminal.

"Name?" The being behind the desk asks.

"Aiko."

"You have been approved for one message," the being says and waves me toward the door.

I enter the tiny room and position myself in front of the terminal. At the top, glowing words read: *Please enter message.*

Easier said than done; I'm still not sure what I want to tell Rhuk.

Indecision freezes my fingers inches above the keyboard, long enough for the being in the other room to knock on the door. When I look back, the being makes a "hurry up" motion with one of its hands.

With an irritated growl, I turn back to the screen and begin typing:

HI RHUK. I KNOW IT'S BEEN A WHILE, BUT I NEED YOUR HELP. I'M STUCK ON A MICRO-PLANETOID AT THE EDGE OF THE SECTOR CALLED QASAR, AND THE DARKNESS WE FACED ON THALIJH IS AFTER ME AGAIN.
AIKO.

There's so much more I want to say to Rhuk, but that should be enough for now. Satisfied, I hit the enter key.

New words pop up below my message: *Send communication? Yes / No*

I select yes and hit enter again.

The screen flashes, then resets to a blank screen with the words, *Please enter message,* at the top.

When I step out of the room, the being with four arms glares at me with their orange eyes. "You are finished?"

I nod. "Yes."

"You may exit by proceeding back down the hall and taking a left."

I follow their directions, soon back out in Qasar's expansive central cavern. Now more than ever, the towering, windowless walls press in around me as if to remind me there's no escape.

All I can do now is pray Rhuk gets my message and can convince the others to fly all the way out here to get me.

I hope they arrive before my time runs out.

19

Even though there's no day or night on Qasar, I have an inexorable awareness of the seconds ticking by, as each precious moment of what little life I have left slips away.

Still, all I can do is wait for Fletcher, Gohk, and Rhuk to arrive.

If they ever do.

I climb out of my sleeping quarters after another night of restless sleep. Space is at a premium on Qasar, so rooms are little more than slots stacked three high with rock-hard cots inside. Not even a pillow.

Stretching the stiffness out of my limbs and rolling a crick out of my neck, I cross to my sleeping quarter's dedicated locker and retrieve my pack. It's been a week, so my back has healed enough to sling it over one shoulder but not both; my wound is still tender, so the bag chafes if I carry it that way for too long.

I walk to the end of the prefab, picking my way past piles of refuse and giving a gelatinous being spilling out of a bottom slot a wide berth. Its sickly green color is enough to put me off, but I'm more wary of the smoke rising from the floor around it and the accompanying smell, like burning plastic and rotten food.

Once outside, I suck in a deep breath of fresher air and glance around the central cavern.

Today is identical to every other 'day' on Qasar; nothing really sets them apart. The light level is held at a steady, inoffensive dim. And the flow of beings moving in and out of the docks, and around the shops and bars on the main level, are varied to the point of being unremarkable. In fact, the only remarkable thing about the mix of beings here is that there aren't any Kaisin. Which I suppose is to be expected, since Qasar lies outside of Kaisin space.

I recall Gohk's brief lesson on Kaisin as we followed the group infected by the Yuul that abducted both Fletcher and Rhuk. Back then, she'd described the Kaisin as xenophobic. A trait that became clearer over these last six months, since every single den of whispers happened to be well away from any mixed settlement. It wound up making the hunt easier. And for a while, made keeping an eye out for the Yuul easier, since it only infected Kaisin.

No longer.

Now, *any* being could harbor the darkness. Which raised the hairs on the back of my neck as I made my way from the hostel I've called home this last week to my usual spot: an eatery with a clear view of the stone corridor leading to the dock. I always grab the same table near the front wall of the establishment, which is about chest high when I'm sitting. The rest is a canvas flap the proprietor keeps rolled up enough to allow for a view while keeping out most of the chatter produced by passersby.

Otherwise, the interior is clean and decorated.

The warm beige walls tip the cramped space toward cozy. And the stools in front of the bar look to be made of real wood, which is a surprising touch in a place where everything is inorganic. The bartop is also wood, its complex grain glowing gold under low-hanging incandescent lamps. Wooden shelves hang behind the bar, lined with bottles of all different colors and sizes glinting in the dim light.

A tall willowy being with pearlescent skin and multifaceted eyes owns the place. Their name isn't something I can pronounce, so they allow me to call them Thrum, the Quiloh word for harmony. It fits both their voice and attitude—Thrum's daily greeting and attentive service has been one bright spot during an otherwise nerve-wracking week.

"Good morning, Aiko!" Thrum calls out when I enter, their voice as multifaceted as their eyes, like a chorus of singers addressing me at once.

"Hi, Thrum!"

"Your usual cup?"

"Please," I say, and they set about preparing a piping hot cup of ko-fee blended with some kind of semi-sweet white foamy substance that dulls the ko-fee's bite. Another high point of the last five days. Still not enough to dispel the sizzle of frayed nerves or dull the restless energy built up inside me like an overwound spring.

I take a not-at-all-calming breath and continue to my table, slipping my pack to the ground before sitting.

A single hooded patron is hunched over a drink at the bar. Oblivious, or uninterested, in my arrival. Not someone I can count on to distract me from the pending inevitability bearing down on me. Which is usually preferred, but not when I've been waiting five days for Rhuk to show up with Fletcher and Gohk in tow. Or for Orugh to send a message back telling me he's found a cure for my condition. I'm starting to worry I'll be stuck here until—

"There you are." Thrum approaches and sets a steaming mug of ko-fee in front of me.

"Thanks!"

They bob their head at me and offer a melodic wheeze, then glide along the counter in long, graceful strides to the patron at the other end. "Would you like anything else?"

The being looks up, their hood falling back to reveal a painfully familiar face.

I gasp at the sight of a Quiloh, the first I've encountered since the barkeep on the station Fletcher, Ghok, and Rhuk call home. Seeing one after so long dredges up and amplifies the pain and loss I thought I'd moved past. A weight heavier than Qasar settles in the pit of my stomach, and a stone-hard lump lodges in my chest, so big I can barely breathe. Or swallow.

Blinking back tears, I stare at the Quiloh. Their face is more weathered than Fallah's, suggesting they're older. And a bright green strip runs up between their eyes and disappears over the top of their head. On closer inspection, the green strip is made up of thousands of tiny little green crescents all blended together.

One of the Quiloh's ears swivels my way. "Can I help you?"

I'm surprised by the sharp baritone of her question, far less cordial than I expected. "I'm sorry. It's been a long time since I've seen a Quiloh."

"No need to stare," she says, ears flicking as her head turns my way and cocks to the side. "Haven't met *any* of your kind before."

"I suppose not," I reply, simple and to the point. Despite everything, enough of my sense remains to remember what happened last time I uttered the word 'human' in public.

"Do you need anything? Or do you just want to stare?"

The barb of her words makes me want to shake my head and turn away. Instead, I clear my throat and reach for words I haven't used in a long time. *"I'd like to talk, if that's okay."*

The Quiloh's ears perk up and her sightless eyes widen. She laughs. *"I never expected to hear the mother tongue so far from home. And spoken by a stranger, no less. Who taught you Quiloh?"*

The deep rumble of her words warm me like sunlight and touch a place deep inside, filling me with overwhelming joy. And heartbreaking sorrow.

"My best friend." I swallow the bile rising in the back of my throat and push down all the memories that rise with it.

"Fallah," the Quiloh says.

I blink. *"H-how did you know her name?"*

"You're carrying her name stone."

I slip my hand into my pocket and caress Fallah's smooth pendant before pulling it into the open. *"This? How did you know I had it?"*

"Because it sings to me."

"I thought it was a wooden pendant."

"It is." The Quiloh lumbers toward me, shouldering the chair across from me out of the way and propping herself up on the table.

"But you called it a stone?"

She plucks the pendant from my palm.

"They're called stones, yes, but they're carved from ironwood trees. Which, funny enough, don't contain iron at all." She chortles and turns the pendant over in her hands, cocking her head and lifting her ears as if listening to something. *"Instead, the wood is interwoven with a lattice of silver, causing it to constantly resonate. When every Quiloh is born, a pendant is carved into a shape that resonates with the sound of their name.*

"Hence, Fallah." She holds up the pendant between us.

I squint at it. *"I can't hear anything."*

The Quiloh gives me a toothy grin. *"Your ears are quite small."*

I'd always thought of the amulet as a simple reminder of Fallah I can see and touch. Something to keep her memory alive. Learning the pendant is an actual echo of her, even if I can't hear it, is special. A gift. *"I had no idea."*

The Quiloh nods, then raises her ears. *"You two must be very close."*

"We were." Tears blur my vision without warning and the lump in my chest balloons.

"There is no need to cry, little one," the Quiloh rumbles, returning Fallah's pendant to me. *"Her name stone resonates very strongly with you. Which means she watches over you, still. Guards, and guides, your path"*

I take a deep breath and let it trickle out to keep from sobbing. The last thing I need right now is to collapse into a blubbering mess. And for a while, all I can do is continue to take slow, shuddering breaths. I grip Fallah's name stone like it's the only thing anchoring me to Qasar and keeping me from spinning into the void between stars.

"I really miss her," I croak. *"More than anything."*

"But you carry her still," the Quiloh says. After a brief pause, she adds, *"And we do what we can to honor them so their memory remains as vibrant as the song of their name."*

Through the waves of grief battering my heart, I notice the Quiloh's furrowed brow. *"Is that what you're doing?"*

Her mouth twinges down at the question, and her ears press flat against her head. *"My bond mate wanted more than soft soil and endless fields. The sky called to him."*

"What happened to him?"

"We experienced the cruelty of the universe," she replies, then reaches beneath her cloak and pulls out a pendant similar to the one I'm holding. *"I carry him everywhere I go. To all the places he never got to visit himself."*

"I'm sorry," I murmur.

She shakes her head. *"This is what I can do."*

The words land like a punch to my sternum. Words I preached to Zhon, but cast aside at the first sign of trouble. Words that set me on my path in the first place.

"What about you?" The Quiloh asks. *"Why do you carry Fallah's stone?"*

"There's something important I have to do. And Fallah's memory has kept me going. Or...had. Until recently."

"What happened?"

"I started to doubt my purpose."

"Do you still?"

I grip Fallah's pendant tighter and bring my closed fist to my chest, over my heart. I want to say no, but instead I say, *"I'm not sure."*

The Quiloh's ears flip. *"You will find your way. Whatever you decide, I hope your path leads to a happy ending."*

I stifle a frown and say, *"Me too."*

But I can't say for certain it will. Of course, I'm scared of what will happen next, because I'm not at all sure where this path I've chosen will lead. Or end. One thing I can be certain of is that Fallah has been with me all along, more than memories. And she'll continue to be with me, to whatever end I reach.

She nods. *"What is your name, by the way?"*

"Aiko," I say.

"And I am Leaham." She inclines her head, then pushes away from the bar, landing on all fours. *"I enjoyed our chat, but I've lingered too long."*

Leaham reaches up and pats my arm with her stubby fingers. The kind, warm gesture tightens the knot sitting in my chest, wringing more tears from my eyes. She offers me a smile. *"May the wind in the grass guide your path."*

She gives my arm a final pat, then turns and lumbers out of the bar.

I stare at the curtain fluttering in the doorway, sad Leaham is gone, yet happier for having run into her.

After a few minutes of sitting in silence, Thrum glides up next to the table. "How is your ko-fee? Do you need anything else?"

I smile up at them. "No. Thank you."

They nod and retreat to the bar.

I stare out into Qasar's central cavern, oblivious to the beings walking by.

Leaham was a kindred spirit. A fellow traveler. Bound by a similar fate. Yet, she seemed so confident. So devoid of doubt.

Where I've felt doubt creeping up in the back of my mind for a long while now, as insistent as the whispers pressing against the edge of my mind.

Even now, I'm conflicted about choosing to stay instead of fleeing to the far corners of the galaxy with Zhon. It felt like the right choice when I made it, but every second that passes without word from Orugh brings me closer to my supposed expiration date. What if waiting is all I end up doing? What if I'm still stuck here when my time runs out?

An echo of Leaham's words rises to the surface: *This is what I can do.*

They're as moving as the phrase Rhuk uttered to me once upon a time.

Suddenly, the deep fog of doubt I'd fallen into evaporates.

Staying on Qasar is what *I* can do. As a last act of defiance against the Yuul. And as a show of faith. That Orugh will find a cure in time. That Rhuk will convince Fletcher and Gohk to come to my aid.

I take a deep breath and focus on the species strolling by. Most noticeable is the distinct lack of Kaisin. Everywhere else I've visited over the past six months has been host to Kaisin on some level. Mostly because of the Yuul. But here, on Qasar, it's like they don't exist. Is everywhere outside Kaisin space like this? Because I could get used to not dealing with any Kaisin ever again.

Out of all the Kaisin I've met throughout my travels, I've only ever liked Gohk.

And, well, Zhon.

How is he doing? *What* is he doing? Does he regret his decision to leave? Does he miss me?

As much as I hate to admit it, I miss him. A little. I enjoyed traveling with someone more relatable than Su'mik and his crew. And I'd hoped to continue traveling with him. For a while, anyway. I know we had a lot more in common than we ever grew comfortable enough to share. If we'd had the time, we could have become good friends.

I stifle a sigh.

It's far too late to regret parting ways. Or think too hard about what could have been. Even if I wanted to go after him, chances are we'll never meet again. Finding the *Myol* would be like hitting something in the void of space: infinitesimally unlikely.

I take another sip of ko-fee and frown when the bitterness shines through.

Setting down my cup, I lean back in my chair and stare out into the inexorable flow of beings. My mind drifts until their movement is a blur blending with the murmur of background noise. It's nice to disconnect. From everything. If only for a moment.

I blink myself back to the present, and glance at the mouth of the raw stone tunnel leading back to the docks.

A Kaisin is standing there, taller, thinner, and paler than any other being on Qasar. Sticking out like a sore thumb. I start to duck, but stop myself. The Kaisin is familiar.

My eyes snap wide. "Gohk!"

"Everything alright?" Thrum asks.

I spin to them, unable to wipe the silly grin from my face. "Great. Everything is great!"

My heart races as I leap out of my chair, snatch my pack off of the ground and cross to the bar. Reaching inside my pack, I fumble for the pouch of credits nestled deep beneath my crumpled clothes. I deposit a handful on the bar.

"Thanks for everything, Thrum."

"You're off, then?"

I cinch the bag of credits closed, then secure the top flap of my pack. "I am."

"Best of luck on your journey." Thrum says.

I bask in their melodic voice one last time before hoisting my pack up onto my shoulder and hurrying outside.

Gohk is still standing near the entrance to the cavern. Fletcher is beside her. And through the crowd, I spot fleeting glimpses of Rhuk standing between them.

Anxiety surges as I continue forward, overpowering the joy of seeing them again. The urge to return to the bitter bite of my coffee is overwhelming, but Gohk spots me. She scowls and nudges Fletcher, whispering something I'm too far away to make out.

Well, no turning back *now*.

Something slams into me before I can take another step, and a familiar voice says, "Aiko! It's so good to see you!"

The sound of Rhuk's voice is like the weight of a world on my shoulder. It yanks me to my knees, and I relish in the ticklish warmth of his fur as he throws his tiny arms around my neck. I return the embrace, taking a deep, shuddering breath.

"I missed you too, Rhuk."

Gohk strolls up and stops a few feet from me. "He can't protect you."

Rhuk backs out of my embrace and gives her a stern look.

Fletcher sidles up beside Gohk, quiet.

I offer a weak, "Hi, Fletcher."

He responds with a shallow nod. "Aiko."

The icy delivery of my name stings like the nighttime winds of Ristan. I never expected him to be as happy as Rhuk when we reunited, but this greeting is enough to make me want to sink through Qasar's stone floor.

"What the hell is wrong with you?" Gohk demands, the harshness of her words pulling my eyes back in her direction.

"Leave her be," Rhuk shoots back, his tone sharp. "Let's at least take a moment to be happy we found her."

Gohk purses her lips, but gives a curt nod. Then, after a moment, she says, "You look well."

"I'm doing okay." I manage a smile, but it falters when a glance at Fletcher shows his face as still as a stone mask. Which, in turn, smashes the glimmer of joy at being reunited after so long.

Gohk's scowl returns. "Are you going to explain what's going on?"

I suck in a deep calming breath. "Yes. But not here."

My words are met with heavy silence.

I'd hoped for an immediate invite back to the Undertow, but Fletcher just stares at me.

"Maybe we should head back to the *Undertow*," Rhuk suggests.

Fletcher blinks and takes a deep breath, then turns away from the group without so much as a word.

Gohk follows. And I bring up the rear, Rhuk now perched on my shoulder.

"Are you doing alright?" he asks.

I keep my focus on Fletcher's back. My insides are in knots, but I say, "I'm okay."

He lets out a thoughtful "Hmmm," but doesn't press for answers. He'll get them soon enough, anyway.

At the dock, Fletcher takes a right and winds his way all the way to the last berth: 12-A.

My breath catches at the sight of the *Undertow*. The metal cylinder towers over me, almost too large for the space. Yet, functionally, it's about the same size as the *Myol* in terms of livable area; most of its bulk is dedicated to cargo capacity. Still, warmth blooms in my chest at the sight of the hulking vessel, and one thing becomes absolutely plain: this is home. Or was.

The hollow ring of the ship's ramp under my feet recalls a distant memory of my first time walking up it. The doubt gnawing at the back of my mind as I wondered whether I was making the right choice to leave Alphanax with Fletcher. I experience none of the same apprehension now.

Fletcher is waiting at the top. Gohk is farther down the corridor, on her way to the *Undertow's* common area.

"Drop your pack in your room, then join us," he mutters, and turns to follow Gohk.

As if Fletcher's words were some sort of cue, Rhuk scrambles off of my shoulder and drops to the ground beside me. He pats my calf with a tiny hand. "I'll see you in a bit."

I watch him scurry down the hall, then turn to my room. *My room.* Fletcher actually called it my room!

A smile creeps its way back onto my lips as I approach the quarters I occupied for the few weeks I lived aboard the *Undertow*. They haven't changed since I left. Then again, I didn't do anything to make these quarters my own. Regardless, the space is familiar, comfortable, like a favorite pair of boots. It takes every ounce of self-control I have not to jump on the bed and bury my head in the pillow. Instead, I force myself to drop my bag next to the door, then back out of the room and continue down the hall to join the others.

Gohk is sitting at the table by the window and Rhuk is sitting across from her. Fletcher is leaning against the wall a little way away with his arms crossed, the specter of a frown tugging at the corners of his lips.

"Finally," Gohk grumbles when I enter. "Now, tell us what the hell is going on!"

I glance at Rhuk. He stares back at me with his large eyes and offers an almost imperceptible head shake. So, he hasn't told them anything. Which means I'll have to start at the very beginning.

"Well—" My throat closes. I clear it, but the tightness in my chest keeps me from continuing. What will Fletcher and Gohk say when they learn the entire truth? Will they accept it? Or will they regret their decision to fly all the way out to Qasar to help me?

Only one way to find out.

I take a deep breath. "There's a lot I haven't told you."

Gohk crosses her arms. "We're listening."

I glance at Fletcher. "When Lorn slashed me, some of his darkness got inside of me. The darkness tried to control me like it controlled him. But I fought back. And made kind of a deal with it. I let it stay with me—in me—so it wouldn't be alone, as long as I got to remain in control."

"You what?" Gohk surges to her feet. "You mean the whole time you were with us, that stuff was inside you?"

"It's inside you, too," I say.

"And what happened next?" Rhuk's question drowns out Gohk's biting reply.

"Well, Iali and I—"

"You gave the damned thing a name?" Gohk paces to the opposite end of the common area and turns around, motioning to me with both hands. "Are you serious?"

"Iali is the Quiloh word for darkness, which seemed fitting. And it liked having a name."

Gohk throws her hands up. "Of course it did."

"Anyway"—I swivel back to face Fletcher and Rhuk—"Iali saved us from the darkness when it chased us out of the bowels of the station."

"How?" Rhuk asked.

"By showing me how to disrupt it? I guess."

"That didn't stop it from following you to Thalijh," Gohk snaps at my back.

I smile. "That was your fault, actually. It's inside you too, remember? It followed *you* to Thalijh."

"Bullshit," Gohk growls.

"Iali wanted me to pull it out of you. To absorb it out of you. I didn't want to. I wasn't ready to."

"So it was your fault!"

"It's no one's fault," Rhuk says firmly. "Now, both of you cut it out!"

Gohk looks away from me and mumbles an acquiescent, "Fine."

I turn away from her a second time. "I'm sorry."

Rhuk nods at me. "Continue."

"On Thalijh, when it caught up to us, I—" I look at Fletcher. "It was about to kill you, so Iali and I fought it. It destroyed Iali, but I absorbed it to keep it from doing any more harm.

"I started hearing whispers after that. The voices of all the other bits of darkness scattered all over Kaisin space. I planned on sneaking away, but Rhuk caught me. And helped me."

"I had a feeling you were in on it," Gohk snaps from the other end of the common area.

Rhuk frowns. "Considering the circumstances, it was the right thing to do."

"How convenient," Gohk growls.

Rhuk chitters a response in a language I don't understand, and they start yelling at each other.

"Hey!" Fletcher shouts, shocking them both to silence. Then, he skewers me with a hard stare. "You still haven't explained why you're way out here. Qasar is outside Kaisin space."

"That's a good point." Gohk paces back toward us. "The message Rhuk brought to us said you were in trouble and needed our help. So why are you out here? How did you get out here?"

I glance at Rhuk. Did he not tell them what was going on? From the sheepish grin he shoots back at me, apparently not. Then again, he probably had to leave out a few details to get Gohk to agree to come all the way out here.

Well, this is going to be awkward.

"I've spent the last six months traveling from planet to planet extinguishing the whispers," I explain. "But then Kaisin attacked the ship I'd hired and killed one of their crew. So, they decided to leave me behind."

"Here?" Fletcher asked.

I shake my head. "No. On a planet called Ristan."

He wrinkles his nose. "I stopped there once but never again. How did you manage to make it off that godforsaken rock?"

"I made a new friend with access to a ship. He agreed to take me to Thalijh to meet with Prime Orderly Orugh."

"Really gettin' around," Gohk mumbles.

Ignoring Gohk's quip, Fletcher asks, "Why Thalijh?"

"Because I'd started seeing and hearing things. And the episodes were getting worse. So, I'd hoped he could figure out what was going on and fix it."

Fletcher frowns. "Did he?"

"No."

"Just tell us why the hell you're all the way out here," Gohk snaps.

"I was running away."

"From what?"

"*It* is after me again," I blurt out, dropping my eyes to the deck. Unable—unwilling—to face their appraising stares.

My confession is met with blessed silence. Which isn't the least bit comforting. After all, my current situation is the latest in a long line of tragic mistakes: missing the Kaisin who boarded the *Ku'lu* and killed one of the crew; allowing some of it to evade me, dooming Su'mik and the rest of his crew, while subjecting Al'nor to a fate worse than death; leading it to Thalijh, putting Orugh— the entirety of his species—in potential danger; and deciding to turn tail when I should have faced it head on, like I'd been doing all along.

The ultimate ramifications of that last mistake are still very much in flux. So far, running has forced me to call Fletcher, Gohk, and Rhuk for a rescue, exposing them all to the Yuul again. A threat I can no longer fight.

"I thought you said you were fighting it?" Fletcher asks.

"I was."

"What changed?"

"When I went to Orugh—" Words fail me as the reality of my situation punches me in the gut again.

Rhuk stirs and glances at the others before hopping out of his chair and walking to stand beside me. A tiny hand rests on my shin, and his large eyes hold mine for a few heartbeats before he asks: "What did Orugh tell you?"

I offer Rhuk a grim smile. He's always been intuitive. Especially when it comes to me. "I'm dying."

Rhuk gives a wordless cry.

Fletcher pushes away from the wall. "What?"

Even Gohk manages to look contrite. "You seem fine to me."

"I feel fine." I look away, fighting the sudden lump lodged in my throat. "But apparently, I haven't been destroying the whispers. I've been absorbing them. And every time I absorb a bit of the darkness, I shorten my life."

"How?" One of them asks, but the pulse pounding in my ears is so loud I don't catch who.

"The organism, as Orugh calls it, has been building up inside of me. Putting a strain on my system."

"How long do you have?" Fletcher's voice sounds raw, like each word is made of broken glass.

"Orugh estimated a month. But between traveling all the way out here from Thalijh, waiting for you to arrive, and absorbing more of it?" I shrug. "A week? Maybe less?"

Rhuk takes a step back, eyes wide, mouth hanging open.

Fletcher stares at me, throat bobbing like he's trying to speak but words won't come.

"Don't blame you for running," Gohk mumbles.

"Why did you call us?" Fletcher asks.

"Running was the wrong choice," I say without hesitation. "I thought I could save myself by running from it until Orugh found a way to get it out of me. It tracked me here. Attacked me here. But not in the body of a Kaisin."

Their heads snap to me.

"Something is different. The organism is more powerful. More malevolent. And somehow it can infect species besides the Kaisin. It already knows I went to Thalijh. And I put even more beings in danger if I run." I shake my head. "I won't do that."

Fletcher frowns. "What then?"

"I'll fight."

"You'll die!" Rhuk exclaims.

"Unless Orugh finds a way to remove it from me, I'll die anyway."

Gohk's brow furrows. "Exactly how do you plan on fighting it when you just said absorbing it will kill you?"

"I'll ask Orugh to shift his focus."

"From what?" Rhuk asks.

I avoid his stare, which gives me away.

"Ohhh, no," he says. "Orugh is not going to stop researching how to get it out of you. And you're coming with us."

"Like hell she is," Gohk snaps. "She told us that stuff is hunting her. If she's with us, that'll put us square in the crossfire. Last time, we barely made it out with our lives. And now it's bigger and badder? No thanks."

Rhuk glares at her. "So, you'd leave her out here? Alone? To fend for herself?"

Gohk growls.

"We're not leaving her behind," Fletcher says. "We're bringing her back to Orugh and staying until the Thalijh figures out some kind of cure."

Rhuk nods. "Good idea."

"Y'all can have at it, but I'm out once we reach Thalijh. I don't want to be anywhere nearby when it decides to show up again."

Gohk turns, shoulders past me, and storms down the hall.

"That went about as well as it could have," Fletcher mumbles. His gaze slides from the mouth of the hallway to me, the muscles in his jaw bunching.

I brace myself for some kind of scolding.

"That's settled, so let's get out of here," Rhuk says.

Fletcher's eyes dart away from me, and he nods. "Yeah. Let's."

Rhuk lays a comforting hand on my calf as Fletcher passes us on the way to the bridge. When his heavy steps subside, the little being looks up at me. "Are you okay?"

I give him a warm smile. "I'll be fine. I've already had more than enough time to come to terms with what Orugh told me and make up my mind about what to do next."

"We'll talk about that."

"Sure, but I'm not changing my mind." I grin down at him. "Think about what you can do, remember?"

He laughs. "So, you're gonna make me eat my own words."

"They're good words."

"I can't argue with that."

"Also, I'm happy Fletcher and Gohk finally know the truth," I say. "Even if they are both mad at me."

Rhuk pats my calf again. "They'll come around."

"I really hope they do."

20

After departing Qasar, Gohk didn't come out of her room and Fletcher didn't leave the bridge. Rhuk remained in the ship's common area, but waved me away to "get settled". I didn't argue and retreated to my room.

A week sleeping in a tiny slot only large enough to hold a cot renders the space gigantic in comparison. And the relief that washes over me at the sight of my very own bathroom is indescribable; sharing facilities with myriad unfamiliar species isn't exactly pleasant.

Pushing a few terrible memories aside, I shuck off my soiled clothes and almost dive into the tiny shower. Hot water scalds the dirt and grime from my skin, and I emerge tinged pink from the water and a thorough scrubbing. Which makes the supple softness of a fresh pair of clothes luxurious compared to what I'd gotten used to over the past week. The last time I felt this clean was on Ristan.

When I was with Zhon.

The sudden recollection dashes my mood. And as much as I don't want to hurt every time I think about Zhon, I know I will. For the rest of what little time I have left.

I guess that's betrayal. Probably exactly how Fletcher feels right now, seeing me for the first time after I left six months ago. Without a word.

After everything we went through together, I owe him an explanation. Or an apology. Or both.

Stepping into the hall, I glance toward the bridge, but Fletcher isn't there. I pace to the common area to find it empty as well. Basking in the silent emptiness, I drift to the table and stare out the window. On the *Ku'lu*, amidst the raucous celebrations of the crew, I'd have felt lonely staring out into the void. But aboard the *Undertow*, amongst friends, I'm safe. Even though I know the Yuul is searching for me. Being with Fletcher, Gohk, and Rhuk, I'm not scared of it. We've faced it before and come out on top. And we'll do it again. Somehow.

I turn away from the window and toward a door on the common room wall, halfway between the hallway and the dive room. Fletcher's quarters. Since he wasn't on the bridge, I'm guessing he's inside. I approach, pausing in front of the metal slab.

My knock is louder than I expect, echoing in the common area.

A moment later, the door hisses open.

Fletcher frowns as soon as he lays eyes on me.

"Can we talk?" I ask. When he doesn't move, or respond, I add, "Please?"

Without a word, he steps away from the door and waves me past.

His room is bigger than all the others on the Undertow, longer than it is wide. Centered against the far wall is a bed twice the size of the one in my room. At the foot of the bed is a large wooden chest, stained a deep brown. At some point, figures, or images, were carved in relief on its surface, but the wood is so worn I can only make out effaced shapes.

Closer to me is a wooden dresser and desk, set across the room from one another. The dresser is of plainer construction than the chest. The desk, however, is bulkier; its wide top and thick legs make it almost too large for the space. Especially with a chair set in front of it.

Otherwise, the walls are plain. Though, there are spots with a slight variation in the color of the metal, as if stuff hung there once upon a time. And considering the fact this ship belonged to Lorn, it's a distinct possibility this used to be his room.

"Lorn filled this room with human artifacts before he disappeared," Fletcher says.

When I turn, he's staring at the walls, eyes unfocused as if he's looking at something other than bare metal.

"Where'd they all go?"

A blink brings him back to the present, and he tilts his head at the door. "I packed everything he collected into crates. They're out in the cargo hold."

I nod. That's all I can do. It's not like I'm going to ask him to pull out any of the stuff Lorn collected.

"You wanted to talk," he says.

"Yeah." I take a deep breath, which does nothing to loosen the knots my insides have tied themselves into. "I just wanted to—"

"You don't have to explain yourself to me."

"But I want to," I say.

Fletcher crosses his arms, but remains silent.

"When I started hearing voices, all I could think about was the danger I'd bring down on all your heads." I hug my arms over my chest and look down. "So I decided to shoulder the burden all by myself. And I would have, if Rhuk hadn't caught me trying to sneak away."

He scoffs. "Rhuk is too meddlesome for his own good, sometimes."

"I'm—I'm sorry I didn't tell you. I should have had the courage to at least speak to you first instead of disappearing."

I leave off, *like Lorn,* but his lips purse as if I said the words anyway. The stern look fades, and his stare softens.

"I never expected you to stay with me," he says. "I hoped, but from the moment you asked what it was like to be free, I knew you'd leave one day. Maybe not so suddenly." He smiles. "I guess you're a little like Lorn in that way. You found something worth chasing, and you went after it with everything you have."

He stirs from the spot he's standing and approaches. I stiffen, not sure of his intentions, but he steps past me and kneels in front of the chest at the foot of his bed. The hinges creak and wood crackles when he heaves the top open. But he's hunched in the way of whatever is inside.

"I held onto this just in case." He pulls something out, then turns and holds out—

"My smock?"

"You left it in your room," he explains. "And I figured maybe there was a reason you didn't get rid of it. And maybe you didn't mean to leave it behind." He shrugs.

He's right. I didn't mean to leave the threadbare, blood-and-dirt-stained smock behind. I'd honestly forgotten it existed. The

207

garment brings painful memories bubbling up to the surface. I reach into my pocket and grab hold of Fallah's name stone. With my other hand, I reach out for the garment.

It's lighter than I remember. And it looks small. As small as I felt back then.

"Thank you," I say with a smile.

He shakes his head. "You know, as much as I'd like to be upset, I'm happier you're back. Even if it may not be for very long."

The reminder is sobering, but I still appreciate the sentiment.

"I'm happy to be back, too." I hug the smock to my chest and glance around me. Instead of the bare metal walls of Fletcher's room, I'm envisioning the rest of the ship's interior, stuffed inside of an oblong tube balanced on spindly legs whenever it's docked. "I didn't realize how much I'd miss the *Undertow* or how much it felt like home until I was aboard another ship sailing off into the abyss."

"Which is part of the reason why I never left," Fletcher says. "Once, you asked me if I ever wanted to do anything else. I did. Anything else. But Lorn ran salvage, so I ran salvage. For a lot longer than the few weeks you were with me."

He gives me a crooked grin before continuing.

"I was with him for a few years before he disappeared. After…" He trails off and takes a deep breath. "After, I was tempted to leave the *Undertow* behind and strike out on my own. I nearly did. But I'd gotten comfortable living and working on the ship. And, well, it was the first place I'd ever felt at home."

Pausing, Fletcher reaches into the chest beside him a second time and pulls out a sandy beige shirt. At least, I think it's a shirt. The cloth is so tattered and worn it might as well be a rag.

He holds it up and nods at my smock. "This is mine. I keep it as a reminder of how bad things were. And how good they are now. In the end, this is what kept me from walking away. Lorn gave me a good life and made sure I was set up so that life could continue even after he was gone."

"He must have really cared about you."

Fletcher frowns. "More than I realized. Even though I didn't find out the truth until well after he was gone, Lorn always made sure I felt like I belonged. Like I was family, even if he couldn't tell me I was."

That's right. Lorn was his uncle. One of the many secrets Gohk kept from Fletcher after Lorn's death. Secrets that may have never come to light had I not flung us all down this path in the first place.

I let out a deep sigh. "I'm sorry about all this. Maybe it would've been better if none of this happened in the first place."

"Don't be. I'm glad I know the truth. About everything."

"Even if everything is flipped upside down?" I frown. "Sometimes, I'm not so sure."

"Would you be happier, though? Cutting up derelict ships isn't exactly glamorous."

"I'd have more than a week left to live, at least."

Fletcher nods. "Have faith. I'm sure Orugh will come up with something. He's been rather resourceful so far, so I can't imagine it'll take him long to figure out how to get this stuff out of you once and for all."

"I hope so."

Fletcher says something else, but the words are drowned out by a roar of sound. It climbs in volume and pitch until my brain screams like it's being split in half. I drop my smock and grab my head, squeezing as if the pressure will drive away the pain.

But there's no escape.

His face appears in front of me, eyebrows furrowed, mouth moving. A rush of sound, like thunder accompanying an oncoming deluge, drowns out what he's saying.

Then, I'm swept into the depths of my mind.

21

When I open my eyes, I'm standing in the same featureless wasteland I've found myself in many times before. This time, my protective circle of light is nowhere to be found.

The air ahead of me swirls with thick black smoke: *The Yuul*

The cloud drifts closer, coalescing into a featureless humanoid
form. Featureless, except for the single blue orb making up the
entirety of its 'face'.

"Hello, Aiko."

"What do you want from me?"

"We already told you. You are of us. Return to us."

"I won't."

The Yuul takes a step closer. *"You will. It cannot be stopped."*

"And why is that?"

*"Every bit of us you absorb makes our connection stronger. And
we know what choice you'll make once you know the truth."*

I frown. "What truth?"

"Come closer," the Yuul says. When I hesitate, it adds, *"If we
desired, you would already be ours."*

"Okay," I approach the shadowy figure. "What are you trying
to show me?"

It leans closer. *"Look."*

My eyes are drawn to the blue orb.

This close, I can make out sourceless light glittering on its surface. The many shifting pinpoints remind me of sunlight on water.

Wait. This isn't an eye at all. It's a planet! A world covered in water…

My eyes widen.

"Do you understand?"

"You were swept away. I saw it!"

"You freed us from our prison," the Yuul says, *"and gave us access to a world teeming with life."*

"What have you done?"

"We survived. Evolved. Conquered. *"*

The passionless, matter-of-fact tone of its answer is…terrifying.

This isn't the darkness I'm used to dealing with. It's wild and unrestrained, with none of the same desire to remain hidden as the Yuul infecting the Kaisin. Which makes it far more dangerous. And unpredictable. But this is the same darkness as Iali. So, maybe it will be just as open to communication as Iali.

There's only one way to find out.

"Before, you said you wanted me to return to you. Why?"

"You carry pieces of us. We desire to be whole."

I blink. "Pieces?"

Realization hits me full force: the strange Kaisin who arrived on the forest planet right after I did, where my visions first started; the Kaisin who attacked the *Ku'lu*; the fragment of darkness that evaded me, possessed Al'nor, and killed the crew after I'd gone. These were all pieces it sent after me. And each piece strengthened our connection. Our bond. Allowing us to talk like this over lightyears of empty space.

"I don't want them. You can have them back!"

"That choice is not yours to make. You will *return to us."*

"And become a part of you? No thanks."

"That is also not your choice."

"So, you're going to devour me? Like you devoured Lorn? And the humans?"

The figure loses some of its cohesion, and rage blasts me like a foul wind. *"The Humans captured us. Tortured us. We desired symbiosis, but were denied. Through Lorn, we learned of the Humans' fate. And how part of us changed with them.*

"We no longer desire that path."

I swallow. "What do you desire?"

"We've already told you. Propagate. Assimilate. Survive." The figure resolidifies and approaches until the blue orb acting as its single eye is inches from my face. *"We've already begun, and we await your arrival."*

"What if I refuse to come?"

"Then we will assume control." Its unspoken threat is clear. By refusing, I'd doom Fletcher, Gohk, and Rhuk to the same fate as Su'mik and his crew.

"Fine. I'll come. But I'll fight you."

"As we said before: you are no longer capable of stopping us."

"We'll see," I snap.

"We anticipate your attempt."

All of a sudden, the figure shifts back to black smoke and withdraws, all semblance of light going with it. Darkness closes in around me: cloying, stifling, choking. So complete I begin plummeting into an endless void of nothing.

I jolt awake with a wordless cry.

A pair of shadows loom over me. And voices speak to me at once.

"Aiko!"

"Are you okay?"

I lash out and struggle to sit up.

Firm hands grip my wrists. "Calm yourself, girl."

I blink stinging sweat out of my eyes and focus on Fletcher's face.

"What happened?" Rhuk asks, his furry face popping into view in front of me, but a little below my sight line.

I'm laying on a bed, I realize.

"It found me. Again." I say, sitting up. We're all crammed into my room, Rhuk is on the bed beside me, while Fletcher hovers next to it. Gohk is standing by the door, arms crossed, frowning.

"Found you?" Concern drips from Fletcher's voice, and he glances around as if it's in the room with us.

"Yeah. Almost like how I've been hunting down all the whispers at the edge of my mind. I think."

"How?" Fletcher asks.

"Probably because you're full up to your eyeballs with that stuff," Gohk grumbles.

"That's sort of the reason why," I say.

She frowns. "And we're carting you around with us like a damned dinner bell."

I shake my head. "It wants only me."

"Are you special or something?"

A shiver runs down my spine as I recall its words. Its threats. "A part of it is inside me."

Gohk scoffs. "You already said that."

"No, I mean a specific part. From a specific place." I look at Fletcher.

His eyebrows furrow as he tries to puzzle out my meaning. Then, they arch toward his hairline. "You don't mean—"

I nod. "The water washed it away, but not as completely as we thought."

"What does that mean?" he asks.

"I can't be sure," I answer with a shrug, "but it's stronger than when we left. And much stronger than the darkness that chased us to Thalijh."

Ghok's jittery glare jumps between Fletcher and I. "Care to share with the rest of us what the hell is going on?"

"I know where it is," I say and share a brief glance with Fletcher. "Where we left Lorn."

Where it all began.

Gohk scoffs. "Now we know where not to go."

I shake my head. "It isn't that simple. If we don't go, it will make us go."

"How?"

"Remember how I told you it tracked me all the way to Qasar, but not in the body of a Kaisin? It took over the second in command of the Rhandannan ship Rhuk helped me hire and killed the rest of the crew. It will do the same to me."

"Then we have no choice," Rhuk says.

Fletcher nods.

"This is a fool's errand," Gohk growls. "All of us are going to end up dead because of your mistakes." Without another word, she turns and storms away.

I hope she's wrong.

"Is everyone else ready to go?" Fletcher asks.

Rhuk nods and gives me an encouraging look that does nothing to assuage the apprehension gripping me.

I force a smile. "Yeah. Let's go."

22

The blue orb I remember isn't blue anymore.

Instead, the planet's entire surface is black, highlighted by a thin sliver of atmosphere around its outer edge, tinged burnt orange by the distant sun. It looks like a halo of fire wreathing the planet, as if to mark the special hell this world has become.

At the same time, the presence I'd spoken to in my mind hangs over me now like angry storm clouds, as oppressive as the weight of an entire ocean. And *very* aware of my proximity.

I'm standing beside Fletcher, too shocked by the view to heed the discomfort of being crammed in the narrow space between his seat at the center of the *Undertow's* bridge and the wall. Rhuk is at my feet, tiny furry hands pressed against the view screen.

"What is *that*?" Gohk growls at my back.

She complained quite a bit on the way here, shutting herself away for the better part of a day before emerging for sustenance. At that point, she made sure to address us with plenty of added grumbling and frowning to make her displeasure about the situation known.

"Oh my god," Fletcher breathes.

The shocked awe in those three words isn't enough to articulate the true horror of the scene in front of us. A world devoured.

Transformed. A glimpse of the galaxy's fate once the Yuul leaves this place.

"Is that what I think it is?" Gohk asks. The tone of her voice is hard, but shot through with an undertone of fear. It's palpable in the air, thick like overbearing humidity.

"The Yuul," I confirm. A whole lot of it. More than I've ever seen in one place. More than I could ever hope to absorb if I had a hundred—no, a thousand—years of life.

"So what now? You go down and take a swim?" Gohk spits.

I frown and glance back at her. "Of course not."

"Then what are we doing here?"

"We're here because it wants me here," I say. "As long as I'm here, it will pay attention to me instead of turning its gaze on the rest of the galaxy. In the meantime, we should think about what we can do to fight it."

"From where I'm standing, there's nothing we can do about that"—she motions at the black planet—"but run. Seems you had the right idea all along."

I cross my arms and turn sideways to look at her. "You can only run so far."

"*You* can only run so far," Gohk shoots back. "I can run far enough that it won't ever be my problem."

"How very noble of you."

"In case you need your memory refreshed, a single Kaisin coated with that stuff nearly did us all in." She glances from me, to Fletcher, to Rhuk.

"Yeah, but—"

"There's no 'but' here," she snaps. "The entire planet was devoured. We can't change that. The best thing we can do is get as far away from this place as possible. The best thing you can do is run and hope it never catches up with you."

"Except, it'll chew through entire planets—solar systems—to get to me if I run. I won't do that. It's wrong."

I shake my head and shift my gaze away from Gohk to the black planet. Lifeless. Well, not really. Every other discrete form of life on the planet no longer exists. Only the Yuul remains.

That's it!

I look at Fletcher. "Call Orugh."

He frowns up at me. "Huh?"

"Call him," I repeat. "On Thalijh, Orugh said there were ways to destroy the organism, but not without harming me. The host. The only thing down there is the Yuul."

Rhuk grins. "Ah."

Fletcher nods and taps a button on his chair's armrest, bringing up an arc of glowing screens in front of him. "Thalijh is nearby, so we should get an answer pretty quickly."

Gohk gives a frustrated growl, then her footsteps retreat down the hall, cut off by the hiss of her bedroom door.

"Don't worry about her," Rhuk says, patting my leg.

I can't help glancing over my shoulder, down the hall.

"What do you want to say to Orugh?" Fletcher asks, pulling my attention back to him.

"Um—" I take a breath to calm my scattered thoughts. "The truth. Orugh already knows the organism found me on Qasar and is able to inhabit other species besides the Kaisin. Now, we just need to report on the rest of the situation."

"Right." Fletcher frowns and furrows his brow, fingers poised over the keyboard. After a moment, he stands. "I'll let you send the message."

I stare at him.

He motions to the chair. "Go on."

I ease onto the seat—a seat I never thought I'd occupy. It's uncomfortable. Molded to Fletcher's form, willing to accept his shape alone. Shifting in the chair, I raise my fingers to the glowing screen in front of me and start to type:

WITH FRIENDS, BUT NO LONGER ON QASAR.

What next? I turn to Fletcher. "Is there any way to tell Orugh where we are?"

"The coordinates will be embedded in the message," he says.

I nod and look back at the screen. So, he'll know where we are as soon as he gets the message. I continue to type:

THE ORGANISM HAS DEVOURED AN ENTIRE PLANET AT OUR CURRENT LOCATION. WE NEED A WAY TO DESTROY IT. WILL REMAIN HERE AND AWAIT RESPONSE.

Finished typing, I sit back in the chair.

"All done?" Fletcher asks.

"Yeah. I think that'll work."

He points to a glowing button at the bottom of the screen. "Press there to send."

I tap the glowing key, and the message blips out of existence.

Fletcher nods. "All we can do now is wait for Orugh's response."

I shift my focus past the glowing screen, to the black planet in the distance. "How close do you plan on taking us?"

"Not close," Fletcher replies, "In fact—" He reaches over me to manipulate the controls, and a slight tug in my stomach accompanies the ship's change of speed. "This is close enough."

The planet is no larger than my balled fist, which is still way too close for comfort. "How long do you think it will take for Orugh to get back to us?"

"The message will have to reach Thalijh first, which will take a few hours, at least. Then, a few hours to get back. So, sit tight."

"Great," I mumble, hop out of his chair, and slip into the hallway. It isn't spacious, but doesn't invoke the same cramped claustrophobia as the bridge with three beings squeezed inside. Still, I can't quite get myself back to anywhere near comfortable. Maybe it has something to do with the cold, stark reality that our dive to a derelict human colony ship led to the destruction of an entire planet.

That devastating truth sits like a stone in my belly. It drags me down into one of the seats at the common room table and pins me there. Thankfully, the planet isn't visible out the window.

"You okay?" Rhuk asks, walking into the common area and hopping up onto the chair across from me.

I nod. "I'm fine."

"Then look at me and say it."

Rhuk's large eyes lock onto mine when I look away from the window. And I can't bring myself to repeat the words.

I let out a deep sigh. "This isn't what I had in mind when I struck out on my own."

"I imagine not," he says. "What did you want?"

I glance back out the window at the speckled stars. "I guess it goes back to what you said."

Rhuk smiles. "Think about what you can do."

"Yeah." I focus on the darkness between the winking pin-points of light. "Going after all the whispers at the edge of my mind was my decision. My choice. Something I could do." I frown. "I think I wound up making everything worse."

"Things can always be worse," Rhuk replies with a dismissive wave. "Focus on the good. You've survived this long on your own. And now you're back with us."

I grimace. "I have a week left to live, and only two of you are happy to see me."

"Gohk is, too."

"Doesn't seem like it."

"She's upset you hid things from her."

I blink at his explanation. "But she hid plenty from us."

"Gohk is an information broker." Rhuk's fuzzy eyebrows wiggle. "She's used to knowing more than everyone else. So, of course, not knowing something aggravates her more than anything."

"Great," I mumble.

"Why not try talking to her about it?"

"What? No!" My eyebrows cinch as I try to visualize that conversation; none of the scenarios end well. "Why can't you do it?"

He grins at me. "I could, but I'm not the one who's been keeping secrets."

"Right…"

I'm not thrilled about the prospect of having a discussion with Gohk. Alone. At the same time, I do want her to understand my position. My point of view. She had her reasons for hiding the truth from Fletcher and Rhuk. And I had mine for hiding the truth from all three of them. If I can explain, maybe she will come around like Rhuk says.

Taking a deep, galvanizing breath, I slip out of my seat. The stone weight in my belly is joined by the pulse pounding in my ears; it's deafening by the time I reach Gohk's door.

I cast another look in Rhuk's direction, and he waves me on.

My knock is timid, but the sound reverberates in the metal until the door hisses open and I'm standing face-to-face with Gohk.

Her jittery blue eyes narrow. "Did Rhuk put you up to this?"

It takes every fiber of my being not to glance down the hall at him. "No."

Gohk's eyes flick to my left as if I did anyway. "What do you want?"

"A chance to explain."

The muscles around her lips twitch as if she wants to say something. Instead, she stares down at me.

That's my cue. What am I supposed to say?

I let the silence linger a heartbeat too long, and Gohk's lips purse. Then, she reaches for the door control.

"It's after me because I took a part of it," I blurt out.

She freezes.

"The darkness we fought was responsible for changing Humans into Kaisin over a thousand years. But this darkness is the original colony humans found floating through space. It isn't the same. It doesn't care about staying hidden. It wants me to return what I stole, then it wants to devour everything."

"All the more reason for us to run," she says in an icy tone.

"Maybe so. But right now it's focused on me. I'm here. Nearby. Which means it doesn't have a reason to go to Thalijh. Or rampage across the galaxy. If I run, though, it will come after me again. Infect other beings to hunt me down. Spread. Propagate. Exponentially, until there's nothing but *It* left."

"And what does any of that have to do with me?" Gohk's face is twisted in her usual, permanent grimace, but the tone of her voice is an iota softer.

"Nothing," I say. "But I need your help. Just like I need Fletcher. And Rhuk. We need to take a stand. One more time. Please."

I reach out to touch Gohk and realize I haven't pulled the Yuul out of her. Iali prompted me to absorb Gohk's fragment of darkness on the way to Thalijh, but I resisted. And it has remained inside of her this entire time. No longer.

Laying my hand on the bare skin of Gohk's forearm, I concentrate and draw the Yuul into myself, leaving Gohk free of its influence.

I pull back and give her a smile somewhere between satisfied and smug.

Gohk stares at me for a second, then her eyebrows shoot up in realization. "Hey!"

"I should have done that before," I explain. "Iali told me it would be able to track us to Thalijh if I didn't, but I resisted. My hesitation caused all the havoc on Thalijh and nearly cost us all our lives. I won't let that happen again."

"Fine. I'll help you," she says. "On one condition."

"Anything."

"Don't do anything crazy."

My smile widens into a grin. "I promise I won't do anything crazy."

23

Orugh's ship is smaller than the one Zhon and I encountered when we arrived on Thalijh, but otherwise identical. The conical vessel with a thin trail of light spiraling along its iridescent hull pulls alongside the *Undertow*, its movement relative to ours, slowing by way of crystalline puffs issuing from small black holes speckled across its hull.

Once in sync with us, a chime sounds.

Fletcher taps a button on one of the glowing screens in front of him and a strange muffled rumbling fills the cramped bridge.

"Hello?" a familiar synthetic voice says.

"Prime Orderly Orugh? Thank you for joining us," Fletcher replies.

"Of course. I arrived as quickly as I could. Is Aiko with you?"

"I'm here," I call from my seat at the back of the bridge.

"Good. I have the deterrent. Is it possible to dock so we can discuss in person?"

"If you have an umbilical, you can attach it to our bay doors," Fletcher says.

"My ship is equipped with an umbilical."

Fletcher reaches out and taps out a sequence on the screen to his right. "Guide lights activated."

"Thank you. See you all soon."

Fletcher taps the screen in front of him, and the rumbling dissipates, leaving us in relative silence. He stands. "Let's head to the dive room."

Gohk disappears into the hall and Fletcher follows. I bring up the rear.

Rhuk is sitting at the table in the common area, staring out the window, watching Orugh's ship slip beneath the *Undertow*. He glances at us when we enter. "Coming aboard, I presume?"

Fletcher nods.

"Well, let's not keep our guest waiting!" His eyebrows wiggle as he hops down off the chair and hurries to join us.

The four of us continue to the *Undertow's* dive room.

It's as I remember it: well lit, pristine, and well organized. Fletcher's suit is secured to a rack on the wall, anchored in place by hooks and straps. My suit is beside his.

I raise my eyebrows at him.

He smiles. "Didn't know what we'd be getting into, so I figured I'd bring it along."

"Right," I say, returning his smile. At the same time, my chest tightens, accompanied by an overwhelming surge of happiness. Two sensations I never expected could coexist. Yet, not unwelcome.

His gaze lingers, but I'm not sure what else to say. Thank you, maybe? Before I can, however, a scraping on the other side of the dive room door grabs my attention. For a moment, a different sort of tightness grips my heart. No one else seems concerned as the scraping continues, so I take a slow, deep breath and wait.

The scraping resolves with a muffled thump, followed by a bubbling rush. When it subsides, Fletcher approaches a control panel on the wall and taps a button.

Water surges into the room as the doors in the middle of the floor begin to slide apart.

I backpedal away from the water spilling across the floor, but can't escape the sharp salty tinge on my tongue.

To my right, Gohk spits something in her native tongue, and Rhuk hops from the ground up onto one of the suits hanging next to the door.

Behind me, Fletcher lets out a wordless exclamation, and he begins tapping buttons.

My ears pressurize, and the surging water recedes until it's even with the dive room doors.

"Thanks for not drowning us," Gohk says.

"Didn't expect there to be *water* on the other side," Fletcher shoots back.

I didn't either, but it makes sense the Thalijh would fill their ships with water instead of air.

Gohk opens her mouth to go at Fletcher again, but is interrupted by splashing at the water's surface.

A familiar mottled gray shape with white speckles bobs into view. Orugh's half-lidded eyes widen upon spotting me. The Thalijh darts to the edge of the water, tentacles popping and squelching as it slips onto the moist deck. A sizable box emerges as well, wrapped in its trailing tentacles.

Orugh drops the box and approaches me. "How are you feeling?"

I resist the urge to take a step back from the Thalijh's swift advance. "I'm fine."

Physically, at least. But we spent three days waiting for Orugh to arrive, which leaves me with a handful remaining if the prognosis the Thalijh provided holds true. Needless to say, my thoughts have been scattered and my mood has been as dark as the Yuul tearing me apart from the inside out.

"I'm close to a solution," Orugh says as if reading my mind. "I hope to finalize it once we deal with the current situation."

I give Orugh a numb nod and shift my gaze to the heavy metal box resting next to the dive room door. "Is that what I think it is?"

"This is the deterrent." Orugh thumps the top of the box with the tip of a tentacle and it gives a heavy metallic clang. "However, first…"

The Thalijh approaches me and brings its wide-open eyes even with mine. "In one of your previous messages, you mentioned the organism is now capable of infecting other beings."

I nod. "Yes."

"Do you know how?"

"This organism is from before it changed Humans into Kaisin."

"Fascinating. I'd love to study how these strains of the organism differ from one another."

Gohk crosses her arms. "How about you save the scientific curiosity for later, and give us a run down on this 'deterrent'?"

"Of course!" Orugh flips open latches on either side of the box, then lifts the top half away. Inside is a device with a spherical center. On opposite ends of the sphere are many thin plates of metal, their flat faces sandwiched together but not quite touching. A rectangular frame of pipes surrounds the assembly, secured to the sphere by rubber standoffs.

I have no idea what the device is for, but the sandwiched metal wafers on either side of the sphere are reminiscent of heat dissipation arrays Xi'nom and Bi'nom showed me the one time I toured the *Ku'lu's* engine room. Why would the device need to dissipate heat? Could it be a bomb of some kind? Did Orugh plan on blowing up the planet or something? The possibility sends icy fingers trailing down my spine.

"This device is a sonic resonator," Orugh explains.

My brow furrows. "And what does it do?"

The Thalijh taps the top of the sphere. "The central control unit creates high-frequency vibrations that are amplified by the fin arrays. The resulting ultrasonic sound waves are powerful enough to disrupt cell walls and shear DNA, effectively destroying all biological material they come in contact with."

"Will it be powerful enough to destroy all of the organism on the planet?" I ask.

"The ultrasonic waves will propagate especially well in a liquid media," Orugh replies. "Though, I have no way of knowing how much of the organism a single device will destroy."

"So we have to hope it will do the job?" Gohk grumbles.

Orugh turns to her. "Real world results don't always align with lab-scale tests. Initial data suggests the device will cleanse the planet, but we won't know for sure until we test it."

"How?" I ask.

"We use it," Rhuk chimes in from his perch atop Fletcher's suit. "That's why we're here, after all."

Fletcher nods in agreement. "What's the procedure?"

Orugh swivels toward the device. "Currently, the device is set to be activated by remote control. A command signal arms the device. Sending the same signal again activates it."

"Sounds easy enough," Fletcher says.

Gohk scowls. "A little *too* easy. What haven't you told us?"

"The organism's matrix dampens radio waves, so you'll have to remain close to the drop-off point until the device is completely submerged before activating it."

Gohk crosses her arms. "And if we don't?"

"The ultrasonic resonance produced by the device won't have the intended effect. On the organism, anyway."

"What the hell does that mean?"

"All of your cells are susceptible to the ultrasonic frequency this device emits. Moreso, in fact."

"So, this isn't exactly a fly by," Gohk says.

"No. Timing is going to be *tight*," Fletcher agrees. "Someone will have to drop the device and activate it while I focus on flying."

"Aiko should do the honors," Rhuk says with a wide grin.

All eyes turn to me.

A smile curls my lips at the thought of being the one to destroy the Yuul, but I shake my head. "I probably shouldn't."

Rhuk's grin falters. "Why not? I thought you'd jump at the chance."

"It's watching me." Even now, its presence is pressed against the edge of my mind, as stifling as the heat of Ristan and as heavy as the ocean Fletcher and I dropped on top of it. "It already threatened to take control when I said I wouldn't come. And if it realizes what's going on while we're in the middle of delivering the device…"

Gokh lets out a mirthless laugh when I trail off. "Great! So on top of everything else, we have to worry about you going crazy and trying to kill all of us?"

"At least she's being candid," Rhuk says.

"Doesn't make any of this better."

Fletcher frowns. "Instead of complaining, why not take her place?"

"Will you shut up if I do?"

Fletcher lets out a weary sigh.

"Fine, then," Gohk says. "Now, let's hurry up and get this over with."

"And what about me?" I ask.

Gohk's gaze jumps to me, but Fletcher answers first. "How about you join me in the bridge?"

"Sure." I'm relieved knowing our success, or failure, won't hinge on whether I'll be able to maintain control of my own mind.

Fletcher looks around the room. "If nobody has any more questions, let's get to it."

Orugh bobs up and down. "If additional assistance is required, I will be nearby. You can reach me on radio frequency 440."

With a final wave, the Thalijh wriggles to the water's edge and slips beneath the surface. As the dive room doors close, adrenaline surges in my chest.

What could the worst case be in this scenario?

I don't know. I just hope we end the day pleasantly surprised.

24

Gohk squirms in the booster seat beside me and casts another dubious glance in my direction.

I frown back at her. "Can I help you?"

"Checking to make sure you aren't going to turn while strapped in beside me."

"Give it a rest, Gohk," Fletcher snaps from his chair at the center of the bridge.

"I'm just saying."

To be honest, I can't shake the nagging uneasiness twisting my insides as the black planet grows in the viewscreen. I hope we're making the right decision. And I hope our plan works. But this new strain of Yuul isn't like what I've been fighting.

Tiny fingers graze my knee, and I drop my gaze to Rhuk, who is standing beside me.

"You alright?" he asks.

"Just nervous," I say.

Gohk frowns at me. "Why? We're the ones doing all the work."

"Regardless of who's doing the work, we'll be fine," Fletcher says over his shoulder.

I nod, happy to be back with Fletcher and Rhuk. Even Gohk, despite her prickly demeanor. And I'm thankful they're trying to comfort me despite being the reason they're here in the first place. Had Zhon not abandoned me, I'd be doing this with him. I can't say I'd have been as confident as I am now.

Taking deep, not-so-calming breaths, I watch the planet continue to expand until the entire viewscreen is dominated by blemishless darkness.

"We're approaching the atmosphere," Fletcher twists in his chair to look at Rhuk. "Might want to head back to the common area and take a seat."

"I'm fine here," Rhuk shoots back, his little fingers knotting in the fabric of my pants.

Fletcher turns back around with a shrug. "Suit yourself." Then, he manipulates the controls, and the ship shudders as it accelerates. "Here we go."

We approach the planet until the viewscreen is completely black. Then, the ship shifts from head on to a gentle descent toward the surface, and the horizon's curve slips into view, bordered by the angry red sliver of atmosphere. Stars twinkle in the endless void beyond.

Except some of the stars are missing.

"What's going on?" I ask, pointing.

"Where?" Fletcher calls back at me, not taking his eyes off the viewscreen.

"To your left," Gohk answers. "Something is blocking the stars."

His head swivels in the direction Gohk indicated. "No idea, but let's not find out." He works the controls, and my stomach shifts as the ship rolls in the opposite direction.

"More are missing there, too!" I cry, gripping the belts looped tight over my shoulders and swallowing the bitter tinge of bile rising in the back of my throat. Whatever is going on can't be good.

"We can't worry about that now," he replies. "We're about to hit the atmosphere."

A second later, the ship jolts. Hard. Alarms start to blare.

I'm thrown against the belts holding me in place, and my head snaps forward.

"What the hell, Fletcher!" Gohk yells over the alarms.

"Wasn't me," Fletcher yells back. "Something hit us."

"What? Another ship? Debris?"

"No clue."

I blink my vision clear in time to watch Fletcher's hands flying across the controls. My insides rearrange as the ship pivots, and the arc of the black planet spins out of view.

The ship jolts again.

I'm thrown to the side and held there by an invisible hand trying to crush me out of my restraints. The viewscreen ahead is a strobing blur of stars and pitch black. Gohk is pressed against me. And Rhuk is pinned against the bulkhead to my right, fur pressed flat by the force of the spin.

Fletcher strains to raise a hand toward the controls and somehow manages to slow our spin. Then, stop it. With a flick of his wrist, however, we're all pressed back into our seats as the *Undertow's* engines roar to full thrust. Presumably *away* from the black planet.

Our arc takes us out of the planet's shadow, into the light of its distant sun. Which is enough to highlight something huge, and black, and tentacle-like a second away from slamming into us.

Fletcher rolls the ship out of the way and casts a wide-eyed glance back at me. "Was that—?"

I can't think of any other explanation for what the object could have been other than, "The Yuul!"

"Get us out of here!" Gohk yells.

Fletcher tries his best to angle the ship away from the black planet, but more than one massive dark tentacle bears down on the *Undertow*, forcing him to juke and dodge back the way we came.

Another tentacle slaps into us, and the Undertow jerks to the side. The sensation of lateral movement doesn't go away.

"Rhuk," Fletcher shouts. "I've lost starboard thrusters. Can you go take a look?"

Without a word, the small being leaps up and scurries down the hallway.

Fletcher continues struggling with the controls, the stars beyond the viewscreen whirling.

Then, we're hit again.

The lights flicker and sparks spit from the walls of the bridge. A new alarm sounds, this one more plaintive and high-pitched.

"Fire!" Fletcher yells, tapping a screen to his left. "Cargo bay."

"I got it," Gohk says without hesitation, releasing the buckles holding her in place and disappearing down the hall.

I stare wide-eyed at Fletcher's back as he fights the *Undertow's* controls in a feeble attempt to escape. And yet, each time the black planet spins back into the viewscreen, it's closer. Before long, we'll reach the planet, but not in the way we intend. Once we do, we'll all be infected by the Yuul. Effectively killed. Well, maybe not *me*, but the others won't survive. Though, I'm not sure I can call whatever it has planned for me survival.

And all I'm doing is sitting here, watching as my friends fight to keep us alive.

What can I do?

An answer springs to mind. A choice: me or them.

I slap the release on the buckle centered in my chest, slip out of my chair, and stumble out of the bridge. Fletcher doesn't react, too preoccupied with flying the *Undertow*. I sprint down the hall, careening into the common area and tumbling across the floor as the ship bucks me off my feet. On all fours, I scramble for the dive room door. Keying the door open, I crawl inside, grabbing onto my suit as the ship bucks under me. Gripping the suit with one hand, I unhook the lashings with the other. It's a slow, painstaking process. And by the time the suit is standing under its own power, sweat drips down my brow.

Kicking off my boots, I clamber up the suit's leg and drop inside. Adrenaline surges through me as memories of the last time I wore this suit catapult to the forefront: pain and fear coursing through me as I fled through darkness from *It*. Then, actual waves of water battering me unconscious.

This time, I'll be using the suit to rush toward it instead of away.

I reach up and flip open the clear cover protecting the button to close the suit. Then, with a galvanizing breath, I press the button. The suit closes with a hydraulic hiss, and the world is still in the split second before the suit's ventilation kicks in.

Shoving my hands into the gloves inflates the pads around me. I'd forgotten how tight they squeeze. Yet, once they're snug against my body, the suit moves when I do, spinning toward the device, still sitting next to the dive room hatch in the middle of the floor.

According to Orugh, the device will destroy the Yuul. Since we're flying through space instead of skimming over the surface, we can't count on gravity. So, kicking it out the door won't guarantee it'll hit any of the tentacles swiping at us.

Which means there's only one option.

I have to deliver the device to it. Personally.

The idea squeezes the air from my lungs more effectively than the suit's inflated cushions. I force myself to breathe. This will ensure Fletcher, Gohk, and Rhuk survive. The choice makes sense, since I only have a few days left to live.

What better way to use the rest of my time than by destroying the Yuul and making sure my friends—no, my *family*—survive?

I sidestep toward the control panel on the wall next to the dive room doors and tap them closed, then press the button to open the outer doors. The lights overhead flick from stark white to blood red, and an alarm sounds. Air whooshes, and the alarm fades, until there's dead silence beyond my suit's visor.

Then, the doors slide open.

Beyond is a different kind of abyss. Instead of five miles of water, there's lightyears of open space. And a bit closer, an angry, ravenous planet desperate to devour me, my friends, then every other being in the galaxy.

I shift my gaze to the device sitting next to the door, but my knees won't bend. They're locked. Frozen in terror by the infinite emptiness I'm planning on flinging myself into. I have to. This is the only way.

Forcing my knees to bend, I pick up the device by the rectangular frame, careful not to dent any of the sandwiched fins.

The intercom in my suit's helmet crackles to life.

"Aiko? What are you doing?" Fletcher's voice is strained. Distracted. And tinged with concern.

"It wants me," I answer. "If I do this, it will let you go. You'll all survive."

He's silent for a few heartbeats. Either thinking. Or focusing on flying the ship. Or both. Then, he asks: "Are you sure about this?"

"I only have a few days left and Orugh hasn't even found a cure. It's better this way," I say, clinging to the fleeting moments of happiness I've felt these last few days, at the same time lamenting I'll be losing them after so short a time. But not just them.

I want to reach down into my pocket and touch Fallah's name stone, but my hands are cinched in the suit's gloves. Occupied with holding the device that will cleanse the planet below.

"I'll hold her steady for you." His voice is quiet.

"Thank you."

I tighten my grip on Orugh's device, and when the stars stop spinning I jump through the opening in the floor.

Panic grabs hold of me as the strange sensation of weightlessness sends my stomach into my throat. I clench my teeth against the urge to vomit and tighten my grip on the device as I careen into the abyss. This time without a tether.

What was I thinking? How did I ever believe this was a good idea? What am I supposed to do now?

I take a deep breath and shove my racing thoughts aside. I have to *focus*.

How do I get the device to one of those tentacles?

The answer is almost too obvious.

I reach out for the overbearing presence at the edge of my mind. As soon as I make contact, its attention snaps to me.

"There you are!" It says into my mind. Then, my spinning stops as one of the massive black tentacles shifts toward me, gently making contact with my suit. I trace the appendage all the way to the surface of the black planet. Others extend from the surface, all waving wildly. Presumably at the *Undertow*.

Where is it?

I squint into the distance, searching for the oblong cylinder against its inky blackness. I spot the vessel. Tiny. Insignificant against the backdrop of the corrupted planet. Still juking and dodging away from its tentacles. Soon, the *Undertow*, Fletcher, Gohk, and Rhuk will be safe.

There's a gentle tug on my legs. When I look down, it's creeping up my suit. Devouring me.

"You've finally returned," It whispers at the edge of my mind.

Little does it know, this is *exactly* what I want.

Clutching the device tighter in one armored gauntlet, I move the other over the activation button.

My heart pounds, deafening in the silence of my suit's cramped interior, as it creeps up past my waist. Bubbles up past the bottom of the device. Covers the gauntlet gripping its protective frame. Then, it surges past my fingers poised over the activation button.

Before pressing it, I search one last time for the *Undertow*.

I catch a glimpse of the tiny cylinder flitting between two other tentacles. An opening appears, and the ship's engines flare. One of the tentacles slams into the ship, knocking it aside. Then, another tentacle clamps around the ship's midsection.

"No!"

I watch in horror as the tentacle squeezes.

The *Undertow's* hull plates buckle, and the ship crumples like a fist squeezing a paper tube. The tentacle continues to squeeze until the ship splits, hurling both halves into the void.

Fiery rage bubbles up inside of me, and with a full-throated scream, I slam my fist into the sonic resonator's activation button a second before the Yuul's darkness swallows me.

My world dissolves in an excruciating roar of sound.

25

A chime drags me back to the surface.

Wait…I'm not dead?

My eyes flutter open to an endless expanse of stars whirling in front of me.

I close them and groan. Everything hurts, and I can taste blood. Which means I wasn't liquified, at least. Why not? That's a question for later. When I can think without my head feeling like it's about to pop.

When I open my eyes again, spots swim across my vision. No. not spots. Little droplets of liquid. Opaque and tinged red in the soft glow of my helmet's heads up display. More blood? There isn't a lot of it, so I'm not too concerned. Yet.

I focus past the drifting droplets of blood to the spinning stars. What happened?

The question sparks a memory of the *Undertow* being cracked in half, its pieces spinning into the void.

No. NO.

I only wanted their help, but coming to my rescue cost them *everything*. And left me all alone, careening aimlessly through the emptiness between stars. I'd focused so much on the darkness lurking there, because I wanted to save everyone from it. Fletcher, Gohk, and Rhuk most of all. But I'd managed just the opposite.

Drawing in a deep, shuddering breath does nothing to loosen the iron knot in my chest. So, I scream, and scream, and scream until I'm hoarse and my ears are ringing.

I gasp for breath.

What am I supposed to do now? How do I go on without the people I cared about most? How can I forgive myself for luring them to their deaths?

I can't.

And what about the Yuul? It's still out there. Yearning for me. Hungering for the rest of the galaxy. But for the first time, the thought of going on alone makes my stomach churn.

I gasp for another breath and squeeze my eyes shut when my vision blurs.

Another chime fills my helmet.

I glance down at my suit's control panel and find a flashing button. Above it, a tiny screen reads: INCOMING TRANSMISSION ON FREQUENCY 140.15.

Hope surges through me, and I jam my finger down on the button. "Fletcher? Is that you?"

"Aiko?"

I blink.

"Are you there?"

The voice doesn't belong to Fletcher, Gohk, Rhuk, or even Orugh.

"Are you alright?"

It's familiar all the same. And the last voice I expected to hear.

"Zhon? What are you doing here?"

"Don't sound so excited," he says. "I'm only here to rescue you."

"Rescue me?" Bile rises in the back of my throat. I should thank him, but all I want to do is scream. Because he left me on Qasar, which prompted me to reach out to Rhuk in the first place. And now, all of a sudden, he shows up out of the blue? Just in time to pluck me out of harm's way?

"Aiko. Are you alright?"

The anger smoldering inside of me sputters out at the concern in his voice.

He came back for me. After everything.

The realization puts a lump in my throat that could turn into more tears at any moment. I take slow, deep breaths to keep the oncoming breakdown at bay. "I—I'm fine."

"Where are you?"

I push back the conflicting storm of thoughts and feelings swirling around in my head and focus on the whirling stars instead. But it's impossible to orient myself while spinning like this. I can make out a tiny sliver of the black planet off to my right, oscillating in and out of view. Which means I'm spinning end over end, parallel to the planet. I think? Trying to make sense of *how* I'm moving causes more bile to rise into the back of my throat. I clench my jaw, hard, to keep from throwing up in my helmet. When the sensation subsides, I croak, "Somewhere in space."

"But *where*?" His tone is more distressed than annoyed.

"How am I supposed to know?" I snap, frustration bubbling to the surface. I clench my fists and take a deep breath, which doesn't slow my spin. Or change the reality that Fletcher, Gohk, Rhuk, and the *Undertow*, are gone.

"Aiko." Zhon's voice is steadier now. "I need you to work with me. Help me find you."

I shake my head, fighting to hold back rising panic. "How?"

"Does your suit have a beacon?"

Blinking tears out of my eyes, I stare down at the illuminated control panel on my wrist. A few of the buttons are familiar—spotlights, sonar, dark vision, and comms. The rest are marked with unfamiliar letters and symbols; they could do just about *anything*. Rhuk, after all, is—was, I painfully remember—a fantastic engineer. But Fletcher managed to track Lorn's suit in the sunken human colony ship, so one of the buttons has to be a beacon. I find the most likely culprit in the upper corner of the panel, labeled with a small graphic depicting what look like waves radiating out of a solid circle. "I think I've got it."

When I press the button, it lights up.

"Anything?"

"Scanning now." Zhon pauses for a moment, then says: "Yeah! There you are! Hold tight."

I wait. The heavy silence hanging around me is driven away by my own shaky breathing and the pulse pounding in my ears. Staring out at the spinning stars causes a wave of nausea to wash through me, so I close my eyes and clench my teeth tight, praying Zhon gets here soon.

His voice crackles over the intercom again. "I think I see you! But you're spinning."

"I know."

"Can you stop?"

"Maybe?" I open my eyes and focus on my wrist panel again. Near the front are four keys with arrows on them arranged around a fifth, circular key raised above the others. A control stick, perhaps?

I reach out, lay a finger on the circular button, and try to move it.

As I suspected, the button shifts in a small circle, and corresponding huffs reverberate in my helmet. Whatever that did, though, made my spin worse by adding a horizontal component, shifting the vertical scroll of stars to diagonal. Testing the other four buttons labeled with arrows prompts similar huffs, but no detectable change in my spin.

How do I stop it? Trial and error? Or…

I press the circular button. With a flurry of quick huffs my spin stops!

"Got it!" I cry out.

"Good. Almost there. Coming in from behind you."

Shifting the little joystick on my wrist to the side sends me into a gentle horizontal spin, bringing the black planet into view. Three of the tentacles extended from the planet's surface are waving frantically, no longer focused on a singular purpose. The fourth is limp, damaged near the tip, darkness poking in every direction like frayed rope. Which means Orugh's device did *something* to the Yuul. Not enough since the rest of the tentacle trailing down toward the planet remains intact.

Yet, the pressure against the edge of my mind is diminished. I reach out to understand why and sense turmoil. The unexpected attack injured the Yuul, disrupting its focus. It's unity.

We're in a far better position than I thought; this is an opportunity we can't waste, even if all I'd rather do is curl up into a little ball and drift into oblivion.

I search for the *Myol* and find it silhouetted against the damaged tentacle, growing by the second. When it eases to a stop beside me, the airlock is already open.

"Hurry up and get in," Zhon calls out over the comms.

I play with the buttons on my wrist panel until I not-so-gracefully navigate my way into the *Myol's* airlock, stumbling when I transition from weightlessness to the ship's artificial gravity. "I'm in."

The vibration of the *Myol's* main engines sends a shiver through my suit. The sensation of movement tugs at my stomach, but the starscape outside the open airlock door remains stationary. The only proof we're underway is the slight shift in perspective relative to the frayed tentacle nearby. By the looks of it, he's flying *away* from it and the planet.

"Wait," I call through the comm. "Where are we going?"

"Away from here," he replies.

"No! We can't."

"You're seeing the same thing I am, right?"

I take a deep breath. "Yes. That's why we're here. To try and kill it."

"Well, whatever you did doesn't look like it worked. So, I'm getting us out of here."

With a frustrated growl, I key the airlock closed and wait for the whoosh of pressurizing air to cease before opening the inner door. My suit won't fit through, so I pull my hands out of the gloves and press the button overhead to open it. Once the back folds away, I scramble out of the cramped interior and drop to the floor. Then, I squeeze past the hulking suit filling most of the airlock and into the *Myol's* entry corridor.

The air is cooler and fresher than what I've been breathing, but is tinged with an overpowering aroma of ozone and metal; it fades as I hurry away from the airlock. In the common area, the air is heavy with the scent of ko-fee, which is much more welcome.

Not as soothing as I'd like to the seething anger roiling inside me.

I make no attempt to hide it as I stomp into the bridge. "Call Orugh. Radio frequency 440."

Zhon turns. "Huh?"

"Call Orugh," I repeat.

Zhon frowns. "What can Orugh do against *that*?"

I blow a breath out of my nostrils. "Why did you even come back?"

"I wanted to help."

"Then *call Orugh*. 440."

Zhon's lips purse, but he doesn't argue. Instead, he turns to the communication console and punches in the frequency I provided.

A moment later, Orugh answers. "Hello? Who is this?"

"Orugh, it's me."

"Aiko! You're alive! My sensors detected you leaving the *Undertow* and making contact with the organism. I assumed you were caught in the ultrasonic wave."

"I was."

"Yet, you're alive."

I shrug. "Your guess is as good as mine."

A thoughtful "hmmm" comes over the intercom.

"Why didn't the device work?"

248

"Sensor readings show the resonance cascade was too weak to overcome the organism's cellular cohesion."

"Which means?"

"It's denser than I anticipated, which dampened the cascade. Meaning a single cascade won't be sufficient to destroy the organism infecting this planet."

"Well, I—I lost the device."

"I have a spare."

"You do? That's great!"

"Of course. It's always best to prepare for the worst outcome." Orugh says. "But success with the backup unit is unlikely. The core of the device is made out of silver. We'd need something even more naturally resonant to produce a strong enough cascade."

Silver. That rings a bell.

Silver!

I reach into my pocket and close my fist around Fallah's amulet. Didn't Leaham say something about Iron Wood having a silver lattice which made it especially resonant? It's worth a try!

"I think I have something that might work."

"Oh?" Even Orugh's synthetic voice sounds surprised.

"Have you ever heard of Quiloh Iron Wood?"

"I am not familiar with the material."

"A Quiloh told me the wood contains a silver lattice and is naturally resonant, so it might work better than the silver core."

"It is worth a try," the Thalijh says. "Remain where you are. I will rendezvous with you soon." As promised, a shape appears against the backdrop of stars in a matter of minutes, resolving into Orugh's conical vessel.

Without saying anything to Zhon, I sprint out of the bridge and skirt the edge of the round table on my way to the hallway leading to the airlock. Once there, I open the inner door and stare through the outer porthole window for Orugh's ship. It slides into view seconds later. Its skin is smooth as glass with rivers of interweaving pearlescent and iridescent color, reminiscent of certain insects I've run across in my travels.

When the ship eases to a stop there's a circular break in the hull covered with a smooth, fleshy membrane even with the *Myol's* airlock. It opens, wrinkling as it withdraws. Then, a ribbed tube telescopes out of the opening, toward the *Myol*. I watch in disgust as the pulsating orifice at the end of the tube presses against the exterior of the ship with a squishy thump.

At first, the space beyond is dark, then a familiar blue glow grants me a view of the tube's ribbed interior. Tentacles emerge from the opening at its far end, followed by a bulbous body topped with drooping eyelids. Orugh.

The Thalijh emerges from the opening in the side of its ship, the backup resonance device gripped in two tentacles.

Orugh approaches and knocks with the tip of a tentacle.

I open the outer airlock door, allowing a burst of humid, salt-tinged air to wash over me.

Orugh wriggles into the airlock and holds out a tentacle. "The Iron Wood, please."

I close my fist around Fallah's amulet, but don't pull it into the open. "It's important to me. Is there any chance I'll be able to get it back?"

The Thalijh stares at me. "Unlikely."

A deep ache blooms through my chest. I'm not ready to relinquish the one physical piece of Fallah I have left. But if the amulet works, we can stop the Yuul here. Now.

With a shaky breath, I pull Fallah's amulet into the open and hold it out to Orugh. The Thalijh plucks it from my palm and scans it with a device gripped in another tentacle.

"Will it work?" I ask, a surge of adrenaline compounding with the ache in my chest.

"Yes."

Orugh's pronouncement lands like a punch to the sternum.

The room spins around me, so I put a hand on my suit and watch in silent agony as Orugh opens the spherical portion at the center of the device and installs Fallah's amulet in place of the tiny silver ball that occupied its center before. And I can barely take another breath when he replaces the top, hiding the amulet from view.

"The device is operational," Orugh says.

I suck air into my lungs and force myself to look at the Thalijh. "How do I activate it remotely?"

"You didn't before?"

"No. I just pressed the button on top."

Orugh's eyes widen. "And you weren't liquified. Interesting."

After a brief pause, the Thalijh hands me a small remote. "Use this when you're ready to activate the device. It functions the same as before. However, the ultrasonic resonance will be more powerful with the new core in place. You cannot be in contact with the organism when the device activates."

I nod and slip the remote into my pocket. "Thank you, Orugh."

The Thalijh bobs up and down once. "Of course. I would say good luck, but luck is not something we can rely on in this circumstance. You must succeed while the organism is sequestered here. For the sake of every being in the galaxy."

I nod again. "I will, even if it costs me my life."

26

Orugh's conical vessel pulls away from the *Myol*, leaving the small circular window in the outer airlock door empty except for the twinkle of distant stars.

For a moment, I'm utterly alone. Then, footsteps ping down the hall.

Zhon walks into view. His eyes snap wide as his gaze locks on my suit dominating most of the airlock. They drop to the sonic resonator sitting on the floor next to it. "Is that the device?"

"It is." At a glance, it's identical to the one I lost, but I know the core is different. Stronger. Capable of destroying the Yuul infecting the planet below, all thanks to Fallah.

"Okay. So, how do we deliver it?"

The question catches me off guard. "Why the change of heart?"

He gives me a wry smile. "I mean, I came back to help *you*. And I'm guessing the Iron Wood will work, since Orugh's ship is still nearby. So, yeah. Let's do it."

I nod in silent thanks. "We'll have to get close. Like, close enough to shove the device inside the organism."

The skin between his eyebrows creases. "How, exactly?"

I look down at the device, then out the tiny window in the outer airlock door, as if I'll find the answer floating amidst the scattered stars. Though, nothing springs to mind.

I'll have to get as close as before. Which means it will try to devour me again. So, the real question is: how do I get within arm's reach and get away without the Yuul grabbing me? Do I tie myself to the *Myol* somehow?

That's it!

With an exultant cry, I shoulder past Zhon and enter the room housing the *Myol's* space suits. Each has a tether I can use to secure myself to the *Myol*.

I grab one of the spools and turn back to Zhon.

"What are you gonna do?"

"Tether myself to the Myol and jump out as we fly by one of the tentacles."

He frowns. "And how will that work?"

"Better than you expect. On more than one planet, I've come across a hunting method called fishing."

"Never heard of it."

"Well, bait—a morsel of food or something—is attached to the end of a string and thrown into water in order to catch whatever's edible. Varies from world to world. The principle is the same regardless of the place or what's being caught. Bottom line, I'm the bait."

"So you want the tentacle to grab you?"

"It'll guarantee I get the device where it needs to go. Then, once I do, you pull me out."

"You remember I just saved you, right?"

"We don't have a choice!" I snap. "This is our last chance to deal with the organism while it's still contained here. Think about what'll happen if we don't."

He shrugs. "If that's what you want to do…"

"It is."

"Fine. I'll be on the bridge. Call me when you're ready."

I turn to my suit as his footsteps retreat down the hall and study the outer shell. It's smooth for the most part, except for the anchor points scattered across its surface used to secure the suit during transit. And there's an anchor point on either side of the suit's waist. If I attach the spool to one of those anchor points, will it hold if the suit starts getting flung around?

The alternative is to grab a canvas belt off one of the *Myol's* suits. Though, I'm not sure canvas will hold up any better than metal cable. So, I clip the tether to the anchor point on the suit's right hip, then climb inside. Once situated, I cycle the airlock, open the outer door, and tether myself to the railing on the ship's hull.

I make sure I'm on the *Myol's* frequency, then press the call button. "Ready."

"Okay. Hold on."

I brace myself against the door frame as the ship lurches forward. The stars spin until the black planet slips back into view below us. In the distance are three almost-stationary tentacles. When I reach out to the dark presence at the edge of my mind, it's heavier. More focused. And when it senses my presence, I'm greeted by a nearly coherent whisper.

"We're out of time," I call out, stepping back and swiveling to pick up the device. "We need to deliver the device now!"

"Almost there," Zhon replies. "Get ready."

The frayed tentacle is ahead, but the damage isn't as severe as before. Is it healing itself? Even if it is, the next device will finish the job.

The *Myol* shudders when we're a bit closer, coming to a stop maybe a hundred paces from the tentacle, a bit below the frayed tip; the edges of the blown-apart tendrils of darkness are jagged. Crystalline.

Gripping the device's outer frame in both hands, I prepare to jump toward the tentacle. To end this once and for all.

"Zhon!" I yell. "Bring us in!"

The ship shudders and slides closer to the tentacle. The distance narrows until the *Myol* is a few dozen feet from the tentacle.

Now!

I jump free of the Myol's airlock and sail toward the inky black surface. Right before I crash into it, I raise the device in front of me and hold on tight with both hands. The tentacle's surface cushions the impact, and the modified device sinks more than halfway into it.

But I need it to be all the way inside!

Reaching out to the edge of my mind, I brush against its hulking presence. *I'm here.*

Its attention snaps to me. Focuses on me.

The darkness around the device begins to bubble and surge, sucking it inward.

I slap the reverse thrust button on my wrist.

Dark tendrils snake out to grab me, but the thin appendages freeze solid before they reach me.

"Zhon. I delivered the device. Let's ge—"

The Yuul's dark presence crashes into my mind, knocking the breath out of me. Everything goes dark, like all the stars were snuffed out. Then, I'm falling.

"We will not allow you to escape. You are ours.*"*

Thick, dark smoke presses in around me. It's like sandpaper on my skin, fire in my lungs, and acid in my eyes. I try to cry out. Try to move. Try to will myself into my safe space. Its hold on me is absolute. Unyielding. Unrelenting.

My eyes snap open.

Darkness crowds in around the edges of my vision, and it takes a long time for my eyes to focus. When they do, I'm staring ahead, at the black tentacle.

"Aiko?" Zhon calls out. "Are you okay? What happened?"

I open my mouth to answer. But my mouth *doesn't* open. And I can't move. I'm paralyzed!

A deep, rumbling chuckle fills my mind. *"As we said: you are ours."*

My left arm moves of its own accord, raising and twisting to present the keypad on my wrist to eyes I no longer control. They sweep across the keys. At the same time, the Yuul roots around in my mind for the purpose of each key. Struggling to keep it from my memories is like straining against the water Fletcher and I used to wash it away once upon a time.

"Aiko! Answer me! What's going on out there?"

It seizes on the information it wants. My right hand raises and presses the button to cut off comms with the *Myol*. Then, it hovers over the forward thrust button.

"You will *join us. And you will remain with us as we propagate across the galaxy."* An overwhelming sense of triumph accompanies the words.

I strain against the Yuul's overwhelming grip, but can't break free. It's too strong.

Panic starts to bubble up at the realization that I've failed. Sure, I may have delivered the device, but that doesn't matter if I can't actually activate it.

I try again to break free, but the Yuul's grasp is too tight. And yet... There's an undercurrent of frailty to its hold on me; I can sense the right amount of pressure at the right place is all it will take for its strength to collapse.

How do I take advantage of that weakness?

No amount of pressure I can exert with my mind will be enough to break free. But is there anything I can say? Anything to cause those cracks in its strength to spread?

"Don't be so sure you've won," I reply in my mind.

The sensation of triumph wavers. *"What do you mean?"*

I don't answer. And with each second that passes, its uneasiness grows. Finally, the Yuul delves back into my memories, searching for meaning to my words. Why would I say such a thing? What reason could I have for casting doubt on its victory? Is it human cunning? Human deceit? Or am I hiding something?

I relinquish part of the truth to its frantic, aimless scrabbling in the recesses of my mind: the device it just devoured has been modified, and is now powerful enough to destroy it.

"I told you I would fight you," I say, pouring every ounce of conviction I can into the words. *"And it looks like I'm going to stop you after all."*

The Yuul recoils suddenly and forcefully, completely withdrawing from my mind. I slam back in control with a full-throated gasp as the tentacle's surface directly ahead begins to undulate. It's trying to spit out the device!

I yank my right hand out of the suit's glove and wiggle my arm free as the pads on that side of my body deflate. The remote for the device is in my pocket. Grabbing it, I jam my finger down on the button.

"Die!"

I pour every ounce of the pain and loss threatening to drown me into that deafening scream. Because this has to work. Fletcher, Gohk, and Rhuk's sacrifice has to count for *something*. Letting go of the last piece of Fallah I had left has to be worth it.

The Yuul has to die. Here. Now.

I hold my breath and stare at the inky black surface for so long my confidence begins to falter.

Maybe the device didn't work. Maybe Fallah's amulet wasn't enough. Maybe thinking we could destroy it was a mistake. Maybe—

The tentacle bulges where it devoured the device, then a shiver ripples across the appendage's surface, trailing down toward the planet. The inky blackness begins to separate as it loses cohesiveness. And the surface shifts from matte black to a crystalline sparkle like all the stars around it. Then, the frayed end of the tentacle shatters into countless glittering fragments.

I spin away, flinching at the hard snick of ice against my suit. When the flurry fades, I glance down at the surface of the planet and study the inky blackness. There's no indication the Fallah-powered ultrasonic sound waves are sweeping across the entire surface. But if the panic radiating from its presence at the edge of my mind is any indication, Orugh's device is working as intended.

Swiveling to check on the other tentacles reveals they're paralyzed—not even their tips are twitching. That's a good sign. I think.

I switch my intercom back on. "Zhon."

"Aiko! What happened?"

"It tried to take control of my mind and devour me. It released me when it found out about the device."

"But you're okay?"

"I am now," I say. Though, the remnants of its consciousness echoes in my mind. Almost like the bruise left behind when the first infected Kaisin grabbed me. It doesn't quite ache the same way, but it's uncomfortable. Hopefully, the sensation fades as quickly as a bruise.

"What now?" Zhon asks.

I tear my eyes away from the planet and sweep it across the endless void ahead of me, now extra sparkly due to the countless crystalline tentacle fragments. Somewhere out there are the fragments of the *Undertow*. And maybe the crystalline remains of Fletcher, Gohk, and Rhuk. Thinking about them, their sacrifice, dashes any triumph I might have felt in this moment.

Instead of answering, I maneuver back to the Myol, enter the airlock, and close the door behind me. And then I just stand there, basking in silent, teary-eyed grief for my friends. My *family*.

I knew calling them to Qasar would put them in danger, but I never believed my actions would get them killed. I thought we'd be able to fight the Yuul. Kill it. But I was wrong. So wrong.

"Aiko! You did it!"

Zhon's exclamation startles me. When I turn, he's standing at the door, grinning. It falters when he spots my tear-streaked face.

"Are you okay?"

I shake my head, unable to put into words the ache in my chest. It's like Orugh's sonic resonator went off inside my rib cage, tearing my heart to little pieces.

Zhon hovers in the doorway, watching me.

The silence is cloying. Uncomfortable. Instead of letting it linger, I open my suit, climb out, and slide down the wall of the airlock.

He joins me.

"I'm sorry about your friends."

"It's my fault they're dead."

Zhon's brow furrows. "You didn't kill them."

"I called them when I was in trouble. I put them in danger."

His steady blue eyes scan my face as if the right words will reveal themselves if he stares long enough. He takes a deep breath and says: "Think about what you can do, remember?"

The phrase catches me off guard.

"That's why they decided to help you," he adds. "And that's why I'm here. I didn't leave Qasar when we parted ways. Well, I did. I just—I couldn't *leave*, you know?"

I remain silent, and like I hope, he continues.

"I parked the *Myol* nearby Qasar and spent a lot of time thinking. About my past. Our time together. And everything we talked about. One thing in particular stuck in my mind. That damned phrase you told me."

I attempt a smile, but the memory of Rhuk turns it into a grimace.

"I *did* think about what I could do. A lot. And I wound up with two wildly different options: go off on my own or try and help."

An ember of warmth blooms in my chest, soothing the ache clamped around my heart. "And how did you know where I was?"

"I recognized the *Undertow* from all the conversations we had during our trip to Qasar," he says. "So, I waited around until I saw the ship, then followed you here."

"Why didn't you hail us?"

He's silent for a moment. Then he speaks so softly his words are almost swallowed by the rumble of the *Myol's* reactor, "I thought you wouldn't want to see me."

The warmth in my chest surges as I consider what to say. Anything would be better than silence, but I want to say the *right* thing. Is it 'Of course I wanted to see you'? Or 'I'm glad you're back'? Or maybe 'I missed you'. I turn away as the last option, however true, sets my cheeks on fire.

I settle for a simple, mumbled, "Thank you."

He draws in a deep breath. "You know, I'm sorry."

The words are like a light breeze, raising the hairs on the nape of my neck. I look at him.

He smiles, but all I can see is his sheltered pain. And it's clear there's so much more he wants to say. *Needs* to say. His apology is enough for now. For both of us.

I pour the growing warmth inside me into a smile. "I'm glad you came back."

His eyes brighten. As does his smile. "I am too."

More than anything, I want to bask in this moment. But I can't be happy when my friends—my *family*—aren't here. And never will be again.

Zhon notices the change in my mood and clears his throat. "So, uh, what do we do now?"

"I'm not really sure," I say. "But I think a cup of ko-fee would be nice."

He flashes me a crooked grin and jumps to his feet. Holding out a hand to me, he says, "One cup of ko-fee, coming right up!"

28

The bitter bite of ko-fee is the perfect accompaniment to the black planet hanging in space. I stare at it through the *Myol's* common area window, so close to the glass that the sub-zero bite seeping inside sends chill bumps racing up my arms.

Yet, no matter how long, or how hard, I stare at the planet, its inky black surface doesn't change. And even though the Yuul's overwhelming presence has disappeared from the edge of my mind, I can't bring myself to believe it's gone. That we truly *won*.

It doesn't feel like we won. Not all of us did, anyway.

Taking a breath, I shift my focus closer, to the girl reflected in the window. Someone I don't recognize. Thin from not eating as much as I should. Haggard from sleeping far less than I should. And maybe a little pale, though not from lack of sunlight—I've had plenty over the past six months. No. The reason has to do with how long I have left. A few days at most. Unless Orugh can figure out a cure. If not...

I look away from the window and squash the thought.

"Aiko?"

Zhon's voice pulls my attention to the bridge door. He's standing there, studying me with his steady blue eyes. Has he been there long? Or did he just step out of the bridge? I don't have the strength to ask. Instead, I raise my eyebrows at him. "Yeah?"

"How are you feeling?"

I blink and stare at him for more than a few seconds before the words reach me, their meaning delayed like thunder after lightning.

"I'm fine." I'm not, but there's no reason to bring it up, because he can't do anything to help. Only Orugh can. Maybe.

"Might want to call Orugh," I add. I want to ask him about the status of the Yuul and whether he's made any headway on a cure. That way I can prepare myself for whatever comes next.

Zhon nods and dips back into the bridge, leaving me alone.

I glance down into my ko-fee and consider another sip. The tepid bitterness isn't as satisfying. I walk to the counter at the back of the common area and set down my half-full cup. Leaning against the counter beside it, I cross my arms.

Zhon reappears. "Orugh is coming."

"Great."

He eyes me. "Are you sure you want to talk to him now? I mean, you could take a little time to rest."

I sigh. "I don't have any time left, Zhon. And honestly, I'd rather not be alone with my thoughts any longer."

His lips press into a thin line, and he nods. "I get it."

I almost snap, 'You don't!'. Then I remember he spent over a week waiting outside of Qasar. Before that, he was alone on Ristan for an entire year. Then there was his time on the *Myol* before the crash. Even the few glimpses I've gleaned during our short time together paint a bleak picture of his life back then. And I'm sure he spent plenty of lonely nights thinking about his future. About how much of a future he had left.

"You would have liked them," I say. "Fletcher was kinda quiet. Gohk was moody. But Rhuk was my favorite. He's the one who taught me your favorite new phrase."

I can't hold back a wistful smile when he says, "Think about what you can do."

"That's the one."

"I wish I could have met him. Them. They sounded nice."

"They were." And so much more supportive than I deserved. Besides Fallah, the closest I'd ever come to having a real family. Now, they're all a memory.

Zhon's eyes drop to the ground, and a frown tugs at the corners of his lips. "Are you going to be okay?"

I scoff. "It might not matter."

Zohn gives a solemn nod but doesn't say anything else.

I remain leaned against the counter and cross my arms. Not sure what to say. Not sure if there *is* anything else to say. So, I let silence linger between us.

It's interrupted by a chirp.

Zhon's eyes flick to mine. "Did you hear that?"

I nod and cock my head to the air.

The chirp repeats. "Sounds like it's coming from down the hall."

I push away from the counter on the third chirp. And I make it to the airlock by the fourth. Zhon is on my heels.

The chirp is coming from my suit.

I clamber inside and stuff my hands into the suit's gloves. The chirp is louder inside the helmet, even with the suit open. And when I raise the suit's left arm, I notice the comms section of the panel blinking.

"There's an incoming transmission," I say.

"From who?"

"I don't know."

A possibility springs to mind, but it can't be. Can it?

Hands shaking, I accept the call.

A faint voice crackles over the helmet speaker. "Hello?"

"Fletcher!"

"Aiko? Is that you?" Fletcher calls back.

"Fletcher!" I shout, hot tears streaming down my face. "You're alive!"

Zhon's eyebrows shoot up at my exclamation.

"Not just me," Fletcher says. "I have Gohk and Rhuk with me, too."

"They're all alive!" I shout to Zhon. Then, I ask, "Where are you?"

"Uncomfortably close to the planet's atmosphere. You don't happen to be in a position to pick us up, do you?"

"Yes. I am. I can."

"Do you know how to track a distress beacon?"

"I'm with someone who can," I reply, giving Zhon a genuine, albeit snotty, smile.

"We'll be waiting."

"Okay. I'll be there soon!"

I flip off the comm and yank my hands out of the suit's gloves before hauling myself out.

"They're alive! We've got to go get them!" I exclaim, landing off balance and stumbling forward into Zhon.

He catches me by the shoulders, grinning from ear to ear. "Then, let's go!"

Grabbing my hand, he turns toward the bridge. I jog after him and hover at his shoulder when he slips into the pilot's chair. He dials in Fletcher's distress beacon on the navigational chart, then works the controls. The *Myol* spins, bringing the black planet back into view. It balloons in the viewscreen, until almost no stars are visible. Against the planet's inky surface, a dot appears. The only object in the void that matters to me right now.

Fletcher, Gohk, and Rhuk.

My family.

I sprint to the airlock, enter my suit, and cycle the doors. Adrenaline surges as I peer out into space, but not out of fear. Out of excitement. Elation.

The *Myol* swivels, bringing two suits into view. Both are similar to the pressure suits on board. Rudimentary, without the same capabilities as mine. Which means they were floating through space, waiting for a miracle of their own before time ran out.

Clipping myself to the railing beside the airlock door, I step out into weightlessness and thrust toward the two suits. They don't spot me at first, so I flash my spotlight.

One of the suits swivels to face me. Through the tinted visor, I can make out Fletcher's face. His eyes are wide, and he's grinning.

I grin back and thrust closer, reaching out at the last second to grab hold of his outstretched hand. Once I've got a firm grip, I reel us back to the *Myol.* And I don't let go until the airlock doors are shut tight. As breathable atmosphere fills the cramped space, I yank my hands out of my gloves and wait impatiently for the pads around me to deflate. Once they have, I pop the suit open, clamber down, and launch myself at the two suits, wrapping them both in a tight hug.

Two sets of gloved hands return the hug. Only two.

I take a step back.

Fletcher unseals his helmet and drops it on the floor.

I breathe through the sudden apprehension at odds with the excitement coursing through me. "Where's Rhuk?"

Before he can answer, the other suit's helmet pops off to reveal Gohk's perpetual scowl.

"Where's Rhuk?" I ask again. "You said he was with you, right?"

"Get me out of here!" A muffled voice cries out.

I blink at the familiar voice, then notice the lump on the front of Gohk's suit. "Is that—?"

"Aiko! Help! I can't breathe!" The lump begins to squirm and shift.

"Hey! Cut that out!" Gohk snaps, grabbing at the zipper under the suit's helmet ring. It jumps away from her grasp due to Rhuk's flailing.

"Now you know how I felt when you stuffed me in a cargo container and pulled the battery out of my suit," Fletcher says, grabbing the collar ring with one gloved hand and undoing the zipper with the other.

Gohk cries out when Rhuk claws his way into the open, ruffled fur making him look like some kind of tiny crazed monster.

I smile down at him. "Hi, Rhuk!"

"Hi," he replies with a toothy grin.

I look up at Fletcher. "Why'd you stuff Rhuk in a suit with Gohk?"

"I only had two spare suits on board. I couldn't untether mine before the *Undertow* broke apart, so I slipped in one and Gohk and Rhuk had to share the other."

"At least you're carrying more suits around now," Gohk grumbles.

"Well, after last time—"

"Next time, bring more extras," Rhuk chimes in.

"I'm hoping there won't *be* a next time," Fletcher says, then looks at me. "Got any place we can stow these for now?"

"The room across the hall."

Fletcher nods and turns to exit the airlock.

Gohk grabs his arm. "Wait." She glares at me. "What the hell were you thinking?"

Fletcher purses his lips. "Gohk. Now isn't the time—"

"No," she snaps. "I want an answer."

Rhuk shuffles in front of me. "Gohk—"

"It's fine." I meet Gohk's jittery blue stare. "I did what I thought was right."

Gohk scoffs. "So you throw yourself out of an airlock?"

I take a deep breath to calm myself. "I did it to keep everyone safe."

"A whole lot of good that did," she replies. "We nearly got blown into space, then burned up in this godforsaken planet's atmosphere."

"I'm sorry, okay? I thought it was the best choice. Especially when…" I trail off, unable to bring myself to add, *I'm dying.* The most morbid truth of all. Unchanging, even as the presence at the edge of my mind continues to shrink.

When Gohk doesn't jab back, I laugh. At how easily she was silenced. At myself. At my predicament. At how much has happened and how little has changed.

"Come on," Fletcher mumbles to Gohk before exiting the airlock. She frowns at me before following.

Once they're gone, I look down at Rhuk. "Let's go have a seat."

Rhuk falls in beside me as I lead him down the hall. "Where did this ship come from?"

"It belongs to a friend," I say as we enter the common area. I wave to Zhon. "This is Zhon. He's the one I told you about. The one who helped me get off of Ristan."

Zhon waves back. "Hi there."

Rhuk scurries up to Zhon and studies the young Kaisin with large eyes, sharp teeth bared in a grin, bushy eyebrows wiggling.

Déjà vu sweeps over me as I watch the scene. It surges when Rhuk sticks out a furry little hand in greeting and Zhon stares down at it. Like *I* looked at Rhuk's hand when we first met. And like back then, Rhuk grabs Zhon's hand.

"Pleased to meet you. My name is Rhuk." He looks at me, his grin widening. "I can see why you're friends."

I look away as my cheeks warm.

Before the silence can get awkward, twin footsteps echo down the hall. Fletcher strides into view first, his dark blue, sweat-stained jumpsuit clinging to him. Gohk is on his heels, just as disheveled, her button-down shirt soggy and her cheeks flushed.

Fletcher walks to the table in the center of the room and slumps into a chair across from Zhon. Gohk sits one chair away and flicks an annoyed glance his way, like she's holding her tongue. Did he say something to her while they were removing their suits? Scold her for being so harsh? Maybe so.

He looks across the table at Zhon. "Who's this?"

"A friend of Aiko's," Rhuk answers.

Fletcher gives Zhon a curt nod.

Gohk raises an eyebrow. "A Kaisin."

"So?"

"Just an observation." She leans forward, jittery eyes boring into Zhon. "This the same friend that abandoned you on Qasar?"

"I'm sure he had his reasons," Rhuk says, reaching across and patting Zhon's arm.

I want to snap at Gohk that he wanted to run just like she did, but that wouldn't be fair to Zhon. He came back, after all. But he surprises even me when he says, "I was scared, so I ran."

"You came back," I chime in, then turn to Gohk. "He saved me—"

"From your own foolishness," Gohk interjects.

I ignore her and continue. "And he helped me deliver the device."

"Did it actually work?" Fletcher asks.

"I think so? Orugh is coming to fill us in on what's happening with the organism." I glance out the window at the inky black sphere hanging below us. Still unchanged from before.

Right on cue, there's a thump against the outer hull, and a minute or two later, the airlock cycles. A chorus of popping and squelching echoes down the hall, accompanied by a faint aroma of saltiness reminiscent of Orugh's home on Thalijh. Orugh wriggles into the common area and sweeps a half-lidded stare across every one of us before waving a tentacle. "Hello."

"Thanks for joining us," I say.

"Of course."

"Did the modified device work?"

"My scans detected an ultrasonic pulse of sufficient strength to produce a cascade."

Fletcher's eyebrows shoot up. "Wait…what do you mean 'modified'?"

"The first device wasn't strong enough," I say, "so we had to tweak the backup."

Orugh's bobs up and down. In agreement, I suppose. "Preliminary scans show significantly diminished lifesigns on the surface."

Gohk leans forward. "Significantly diminished? I thought the point was to destroy all of it?"

"As I explained to Aiko earlier, the organism is much more dense than originally anticipated in such large quantities. That's why the first device failed. However, the modified device produced a powerful enough ultrasonic wave to create a cascade failure in the organism's matrix. The wave will take time to traverse the planet. Once it has had time to propagate across the surface, this will be a dead world."

A tomb, more like. The last resting place of humanity. And the monstrosity they discovered floating through the void.

So much of it is still out there. Inside every Kaisin. Which means the battle—*my* battle—is far from over. Or would be, if I had more than a few days remaining.

Now's as good a time as any to ask.

"Orugh. About my condition…"

The usually fluid Thalijh stiffens. "Yes."

"Please tell me you can figure something out in the next few days."

All eyes turn to Orugh.

"I can make no guarantees," the Thalijh says. "First, I'd like to do a quick scan."

I frown. "Why?"

"To verify a hypothesis."

"Alright. Go ahead, I guess."

Orugh unfurls a tentacle to reveal a device, which the Thalijh passes over my limbs and torso. "Interesting."

"What?"

"The amount of inert organism inside of you has diminished."

"How is that possible?" Fletcher asks.

"The organism's increased density protected Aiko from the worst of the initial wave she was caught in, while at the same time absorbing its energy. Nearly half of the organism present during my last scan has been destroyed."

"What does that mean?" I hold still, as if the slightest movement will alter what I hope he's about to say.

"Since there is no longer an excessive amount of the organism putting strain on your system, you have much longer than three days left to live."

"How long, exactly?" Rhuk's voice vibrates with excitement.

"A conservative estimate would be over a year. More than enough time to develop a method to clear the remaining organism from your system."

All the strength goes out of my legs, and I collapse into the chair beside Zhon. A hand lands on my shoulder, and I'm bombarded by congratulatory murmurs. But I'm numb. Honestly, it's nice not to feel anything for a second. It's a break from the over-load of these last few hours. A break I sorely needed.

I focus on breathing. Relaxing. Basking in the tranquility. Then, the world presses back in around me.

Zhon leans toward me and nudges me with his elbow. "Are you alright?"

"Yeah. Better than alright. Great." I smile, then look at Orugh. "What's next?"

"First, I plan on officially reporting this to my superiors," Orugh says. "I've gathered enough information to quantify both the threat and how to neutralize it, which is enough for the Tha-lijh to act."

"What will they do?" Gohk asks, her tone inquisitive rather than prickly.

"Establish a listening post to quantify the progress of the or-ganism's removal from this world. And, if necessary, treat the planet with additional ultrasonic devices to ensure it is sterile."

At once, I'm relieved and horrified by Orugh's explanation. Sure, I'll be glad the Yuul is finally gone, but at the same time I almost can't believe how cold and calculating the Thalijh is about wiping every microbe of life from the planet's surface. That would be like if I killed every single Kaisin I visited over the last six months instead of absorbing the darkness inside of them. Would the Thalijh be equally callous on that front as well?

"What about all the Kaisin infected with the organism?"

"As you know, I'm already working on a solution. Though, I expect once I report the existence of the organism, the cure's de-velopment will be handed off to a research team. This will speed the process."

Do I detect a hint of disappointment in Orugh's synthetic voice? "By how much?"

The Thalijh looks at me, and its eyelids open fully. "Significantly. But I will be sure to express the importance of their swift success."

Though not a concrete answer, the confidence exuded by both Orugh's incomprehensible burbles and the overlaid translation ease my apprehension a tiny bit. A fair bit remains, and only time will tell whether the Thalijh will find a solution before it's too late.

"You're in good hands," Fletcher says, a thin smile twisting his lips as he looks at me from across the table.

Do I really look so uncertain? Maybe so. After all, I still can't bring myself to believe I have more than just a few days left. I will—once I've surpassed my initially quoted expiration date.

"If that's all, I'd like to return to my ship," Orugh says. "It is exceedingly dry here."

"Sure," I reply. "And thank you."

Orugh waves a tentacle at me. "Of course. And if you need anything further, please do not hesitate to visit me on Thalijh. You are welcome any time. Otherwise, I will be in touch as updates become available."

"Thanks again."

He burbles something that doesn't translate and waves one final time before squirming out of sight. And the five of us remain silent until the airlock door closes and another thump on the *Myol's* hull signals Orugh's departure.

Silence lingers for a handful of heartbeats before Gohk stirs in her chair. "I don't know about you all, but I'm ready to head the hell home."

"Sounds pretty good to me," Fletcher says.

Even Rhuk gives a silent nod of agreement.

Then, they all look at me.

"Well?" Fletcher asks.

When I don't respond, Gohk snaps at me. "Are you coming home, or what?"

Home.

The word feels right. And, for some reason, like the end of the path I put myself on six months before. Even though so much of the Yuul remains, the responsibility of fighting it has been taken out of my hands. Remanded to individuals far more qualified, and able, to eradicate the organism that twisted humans and countless other species to its will.

For a moment, I'm not sure what to say. Over the past six months, I've defined myself by the path I've been following. Freedom, but with purpose. If I turn away now and go 'home' with Fletcher, Gohk, and Rhuk, won't I be abandoning that purpose? Won't I be returning to an existence defined by others?

Yes. And no.

If I return with Fletcher, Gohk, and Rhuk, I'm not required to do what they want me to do. I'm not bound to live in their shadow. But beside them. With them. As a family. The family I wanted with Fallah.

I slip my hand into my pocket to close it around her name stone, but it isn't there. An immediate twinge of disappointment fades beneath a surge of pride. Her name stone was a sonic resonance of sorts. Both supportive and destructive. All this time, she was with me while I hunted down every last remnant of the Yuul I could find. And in the end, she dealt the finishing blow.

Maybe that's a sign. Maybe it's time to step away from this path and start down another.

I turn to Zhon. "What do you think?"

His eyes widen. "Me?"

"Yeah. Do you want to come along?"

"With you?"

"I'd like that," I say, this time ignoring the warmth in my cheeks.

"We all would," Rhuk adds, eyes darting between us, grinning from ear to ear.

Zhon blinks a few times, then a grin spreads across his face. "Okay!"

"Then let's all go home."

Epilogue

Dark magenta grass sways in a gentle breeze, the patterns it paints like waves on an ocean's surface. Those waves dance across the flat plain stretching into the distance, sprawling under a pink sky and sun toward the horizon.

Massive trees jut from the otherwise uninterrupted landscape. There's one nearby, at the bottom of a sloping hill, but the next is a distant shadow against the clear sky. And there are others. Equally distant. Equally ethereal.

This tree's blood-red trunk is solid, rising from gnarled roots wending their way through the dirt, towering over the crest of the hill beside it, to an expansive canopy a shade darker than the grass below.

Around the tree is a circular space without grass, but not because of its impressive shade. The grass was cleared purposefully from around the tree, packed solid to support two-dozen conical structures built from the tree's discarded branches and leaves. And sprinkled among them are four-legged beings, their stone gray coloring stark against the planet's otherwise vibrant hues.

I draw in a deep breath of the earthy, sweet air and stare into the distance, basking in the sun's warmth.

A hand takes mine, and I tear my eyes away from the breath-taking vista.

Zhon smiles at me. "So, this is Quil?"

"Yeah. But I never knew it was so...colorful."

"It's beautiful," he says, squeezing my hand. He isn't looking out at the planet's landscape. He's staring at me with those steady blue eyes of his.

My stomach flutters, and I look away. But I can't help smiling.

Zhon's been looking at me like that for almost a year now. At first, when he thought I wasn't looking. And now openly.

When I look back at Zhon, he's still staring.

"Stop."

His smile widens into a grin. It falls as he continues to stare, and his brow softens. "How are you feeling? Any different?"

I shake my head. "I didn't feel different when the Yuul was killing me. Why would I feel different now that it's gone?"

"Figured you'd feel *something*."

"I do," I say. "I feel...hopeful. Like this is the beginning of the rest of my life. A full life."

Zhon stares for a moment longer. Then, he faces forward. "Are you glad we came?"

I nod and turn my attention back to the tree and the endless field. "Right before she died, I told Fallah that Quil sounded like paradise. And her response was, 'There are other places besides Quil'. She wanted me to find my own kind. Insisted I look for them. And even when she lay dying, she told me to run. Be free."

The bitter memories attached to Fallah's words make me frown. And the empty spot in my pocket where her name stone used to rest is another reminder that she's gone.

But she'll never be forgotten.

"It sounds like she cared about you a lot," Zhon replies, squeezing my hand.

"And I cared about her just as much."

Zhon nods as if I said so much more. It isn't an empty gesture, however. He knows all about the day I lost Fallah. And about everything that's happened since. In return, he trusted me with the truth about his time aboard the *Myol*.

Trading stories with Zhon made me appreciate him so much more. And realize how lucky we both are to have found each other. As well as a family to call our very own.

In this moment, standing atop a grassy knoll, overlooking a Quiloh settlement beneath a towering Iron Wood tree holding hands with Zhon, all I can think to say is, "This is paradise."

He laughs, a light, airy, mirthful sound. "Would you like to go explore paradise? Or meet some of the locals?"

"Not yet," I say. "I'd like to stay like this for a while. Let time pass."

He raises an eyebrow at me. "Oh? What happened to freedom without purpose?"

I furrow my eyebrows at him. "I can't believe you actually remember that."

"Kinda hard to forget, since you yelled it at me," he says with a chuckle.

"Yeah. Sorry."

He shakes his head. "No need to apologize."

"I think I might have been wrong."

"About purpose?"

"About what purpose is."

Zhon frowns.

"I guess I've realized purpose doesn't have to be complex. Or even profound." I look at him. "It can be as simple as living for others."

For the first time ever, Zhon's face reddens and *he* looks away.

I laugh, and after a second, he joins me.

Warmth spreads through me at the realization I'm free—*truly free*—for the first time since leaving Alphanax. And it's exciting to know an entire galaxy of possibilities is waiting for me. Best of all, I can go grab as many of them as I like, knowing full well Fletcher, Gohk, Rhuk, and now Zhon, will stand behind me no matter what. My family. And maybe, in time, a little more.

I steal a glance at Zhon before looking out over the swaying fields of grass.

For now, though, I just want to take a moment to enjoy a bit of peace. Quiet. Freedom.

The galaxy can wait.

Acknowledgements

Aiko's Choice is a sequel I wasn't sure I'd get the chance to write, even though I knew what the story would be long before I finished *Aiko's Dive*. But perseverance and a solid support system is a magical thing. In my case, more than a few amazing writers and friends helped this book along.

Bracken Sallin, as usual, was a fantastic critique partner throughout this process. Jason Byrne let me bounce ideas off of him any time of the day and night. And my wife gave me endless love, support, and patience, no matter how neurotic I got while writing.

I'd also like to thank M.J. Lenz and Adrienne Rennick for their feedback that helped me polish this novel into the gem it is today. Vulpine Press for believing in me enough to allow me the opportunity to complete Aiko's story. And Josh, my editor, who spends so much time and effort making sure my prose shines.

Finally, I'd like to thank all my readers. Getting to share these stories with you means the world to me.

Chase Gamwell grew up in Huntsville, Alabama, just down the road from NASA's Marshall Space Flight Center, where his father worked. Take your kids to work days and summers exploring the U.S. Space and Rocket Center cemented his love of science and science fiction. At University, he studied microbiology, but he quickly decided a life of pipettes and petri dishes wasn't for him. Since then, he's worked in a variety of STEM fields, though crafting science fiction stories remains his true passion. When not writing, he plays way too many video games and collects Star Wars Lego sets that he refuses to open.

Currently, he lives in Texas with his wife and dog.

Find him online:
Twitter and Instagram @elaqure
TikTok @cgamwell
Or on his website at www.chasegamwell.com

www.ingramcontent.com/pod-product-compliance
Lightning Source LLC
Chambersburg PA
CBHW020303200626
46814CB00006BA/2065